PRAISE FOR ~~CLARISSA KAE~~

A hauntingly romantic debut

— ESTHER HATCH

Eerie. Inspiring. Masterful.

— ADAM BERG

Clarissa Kae entraps readers with her exquisite writing and master storytelling. I couldn't stop reading.

— JESS HEILEMAN

Congrats

TAMING CHRISTMAS

CLARISSA KAE

CARPE VITAM
·PRESS LLC·

ACKNOWLEDGMENTS

This story would have stayed on a shelf if not for my writing tribe. Esther Hatch and Jess Heileman, thank you for holding my hand while I jumped without looking.

Ranee and Kaylee—you are the Book Godmothers of all time. Thank you for answering my panicked pleas.

To my writing family, the unsung heroes of any literary world, Adam Berg, Connie Williams, Loretta Porter and my ARC readers, Sarah Reynolds, Jill Warner, Chantell Farley, Shelley Strong and Evelyn Hornbarger.

Most of all, to my family.

When I feel unworthy and exhausted, they push me forward, refusing to believe that I am anything but good.

—Clarissa

I

ELISHEBA BEVUE

The wind turned with a snap, raking the countryside with twists and turns toward the sea. Perched on the dark mountain, Elsie slowed her mare to a walk, taking in the lush valley on her right and the swirling sea to her left. She had heard whispers of a cold holiday season, but like most coastal towns, snow wouldn't touch them. The mare fidgeted, eager to stretch its legs once more. With a sigh, Elsie circled back, urging the horse onward. Neither horse nor lady wanted to return to the estate, but both relished the freedom of the Welsh countryside.

Elsie hesitated, wishing this moment would never end. The view and relative solitude were too tempting to leave. She should rush home but her mind refused. She had only a few hours to tidy her sanctuary of the last two years. Her mother's note still sat on her late father's desk in a study as disheveled as Elsie's hair.

Wisps of smoke appeared just around the bend, the small enclave where an abandoned estate lay. Elsie had covered every inch of the county—every inch without a roof. She'd not been brave enough to converse with the town or neighbors. Even now, with the chimney smoke growing to a steady steam, she turned her back and headed toward the barn, the threat of her family arriving more menacing than the possibility of a new neighbor.

Leaning forward on her modified saddle, Elsie gave the mare her head, allowing the horse to devour the crisp ground in hungry strides. Rich shades of emerald and chocolate rushed past her. Approaching the barn, she slowed the eager horse and dismounted before the old stableman could arrive. The estate kept only the minimum number of servants—part of her penance, according to her mother. It was hardly punishment; fewer people suited Elsie quite nicely, and the estate had been her late father's childhood home. She felt closer to him in the forgotten hills of Wales than in the busy London home where she was raised.

Griffiths walked toward her, his wrinkled brow furrowed in worry. In a voice rough with age, the stableman asked, "What would you have me do?"

Elsie stopped short; he'd lost the jovial expression from a few hours earlier. "With what?"

He gestured to her saddle. "Your saddle?"

And there, in that little phrase, Elsie's world shriveled to nothing. She gripped the reins in her hand, feeling small and trivial—she'd not felt this way in years. Just a moment ago, Elsie had felt the rush of freedom and witnessed again the untamed beauty of Wales. She'd had two glorious years to ride as she pleased, tinkering with her sidesaddle until tossing the entire contraption, opting to ride like a man, her legs astride on her custom saddle. But now, with her family arriving, her freedom would be gone. As would the relaxed relationships Elsie had enjoyed with her small band of servants. Elsie retreated a few steps, her pulse racing. She should have stayed on the ridge. The countryside was safer than the lovely home before her.

Griffiths gently pulled the soft reins from her hands, his voice tender. "I didn't mean to upset—"

"I hadn't thought about saddles," Elsie admitted, running a hand along the saddle she'd help modify. She hadn't thought about anything of import in ages. Her family had never bothered to come for holidays, not since her skirmish with the earl. "I can't ask you to hide it. Not with my brother arriving." The estate was his even if he abhorred all things Welsh.

"I'll not hide it." Griffiths waited for her to meet his gaze, a mischievous glint in his eye. "But it won't be found. Not anytime soon."

"Thank you." Elsie threw her arms around the stableman. He, along with every other servant, had become her family, consoling her through the dark, lonely years. Michaelmas had been particularly lonely, the days gloomy and the few letters from her mother even darker.

"Ah, 'tis nothing, child." Shrugging, he pulled her arms from around his neck.

She cocked her head to the side. "It's everything."

A wide, crinkled smile brightened Griffiths's face. "That's the look you should give your mother. That'll melt her heart in a moment."

The little warmth Elsie had begun to feel faded in an instant. She wasn't ready to face her family. Not today. Not tomorrow. Their weapon of choice was silence—and scripture.

"They'll want an apology." And the appearance of a contrite lady, something Elsie could not—*would* not give. She'd done the unthinkable; she'd raised her hand against a gentleman.

"I suppose." Griffiths guided the mare toward the barn, patting her neck. The animal had appeared months ago, without a hint of who the giver was. "Have you given her a name yet?"

"Other than *Direidus*?" Elsie brightened at the old man's chuckle. She'd learned a phrase or two from her newfound Welsh friends.

"Ay, she is mischievous, isn't she?" He beamed at the mare, the affection palpable.

Elsie swallowed the lump in her throat, wishing her family would find her faults endearing. Whoever had given her the mare had taken pains to conceal himself. But now Elsie suspected it was a peace offering from her family. Either that or a hopeful bribe, her submission the cost. Every joy carried a price.

"She's a beauty." Griffiths switched the bridle for a halter, murmuring, "You'll come around, now won't you, *Direidus*?"

Elsie grabbed a brush, but Griffiths pulled it from her hand. With a nod to the house, he offered, "Avoiding that storm won't keep it from coming."

"I'd rather stay dry as long as possible." Her family was discipline perfected. Their veiled barbs and polite insults were cloaked in proper decorum. Elsie was everything they were not, her feelings raw and words unchecked. She'd not seen them in years, and the timing of their visit was too suspicious. Her mother loved Christmas in London, not Wales.

"No one stays dry in a storm." Griffiths lifted the saddle from the mare's back. "But you could learn to dance in the rain."

"It's never just rain." Elsie could feel the chill of her mother's frown —a feat, considering she'd not see her mother's face recently.

"Never pegged you as a coward." The stableman bit back a grin.

"No, only *improper* and *uncouth*." The words fell from her lips, each one cutting her to the core like they had two years before.

"Oh, child." Griffiths froze in place, the saddle pad in hand. "I didn't mean to harm you."

"It's true all the same." Elsie stroked the mare's forehead. Only Griffiths could make *child* sound loving.

"No, I'll not have that kind of talk in here." He shook his head, his voice firm. "You're a fine lady, Elsie."

"Don't let my family hear you."

"Ay, you're right." Griffiths's eyes widened. "You'll need to be called Miss Bevue. That'll be a tough change for us."

Elsie grimaced at her given name. "I meant the part where I'm a *fine lady*."

He shot her a conspirator's grin. "You'll be Elsie 'til the day I die."

The sound of an approaching horse echoed into the barn. Elsie's heart sank; she'd hoped for more time before everyone arrived. She shrank to the shadows, her hands trembling at her sides. She wasn't ready. The stack of unanswered letters from her family underlined that fact. They were convinced—according to their own words—that her silence was a confession of an irreverent, unrepentant heart.

Griffiths shot her a silent apology and guided her mare into the nearest stall. Sliding the stall door shut, Griffiths mumbled a greeting to the rider, allowing Elsie to escape through the barn's side door. This

Christmas would have been her third in isolation. Just a month ago, the prospect felt lonely. Perhaps Elsie had been too hasty in wishing for company. There was safety in being alone—in answering to only one person's expectations.

Her mind crowded with all the little tasks she should have done instead of indulging in a morning ride with the mare. Her late father's library was a disaster, to put it mildly, as was the dilapidated glasshouse. Elsie had no talent in keeping the collections of plants alive. She'd tried—oh, had she tried. But just as she wasn't able to draw or play the pianoforte, no matter how long she practiced, she'd failed at yet another talent needing delicacy. And patience.

Her thoughts raced with dozens of failings, from the way she spoke with the servants, to her refusal to visit the neighbors, and even the simple task of replacing her wardrobe. She'd been anything but the proper lady. Her face flushed. She'd loved her time in Wales. The joy had grown with the arrival of her mare.

Elsie entered the house through the servants' doors and slipped into her father's study. She froze—gone were the stacks of novels on the desk and chairs. The pen and papers strewn across the neglected desk were tidied, her father's journals tucked back into their snug positions on the bookshelf. A lump formed in her throat as she ran her hand along the edge of the desk, overwhelmed with competing emotions. She was grateful for Doris, the housekeeper, and even a touch guilty at adding to the woman's full day of work, but there was a suffocating element to the tidiness. When Elsie's father was alive, he'd been a walking, benevolent hurricane; mess and disarray followed and gathered around him, herself included.

She caught her reflection in the window, her hair spilling out of its plait and a smudge of either grass or mud on the shoulder of her riding habit. She was her father's daughter, through and through. The door opened behind her—she inhaled sharply, praying for courage.

"He'll be here shortly," her butler said softly behind her.

Elsie spun around in time to see the butler shut the door—and the back of a tall man. "Oh."

The stranger turned, surprise in his pale blue eyes. His plain face had a smattering of freckles, and his coat was modest but well made. He dipped his head of ordinary brown hair but said nothing.

There was a familiar quality about him, but Elsie couldn't place how she knew him. "Have we met?"

His eyes softened. "We have."

Two words weren't enough to dissect his background, and that was the least of her worries. She shouldn't have asked, and she shouldn't be in the study alone with him. And yet she stayed. Her family was due any moment. She'd paid dearly for her unruly tongue. Being alone with this stranger was far worse.

Recognition lit his face, and without a word, he opened the door. Being alone with a woman wasn't on his priority list either. Elsie stepped forward, too curious to let him leave. A burst of loneliness pricked her heart. Until that moment, she hadn't realized how long it'd been since she last spoke to someone her age.

The man extended a hand, his smile inviting. "Fitzburgh Smith."

"Elisheba Bevue." Elsie slipped her hand in his. A warmth, a feeling of both safety and adventure, hummed beneath his touch.

He arched an eyebrow. "Did you mean Miss Bevue, as in the sister of—"

"I'd prefer if you forgot that part." She felt the flush of her cheeks. She'd not meant to speak the words. She didn't want to be reminded of her brother just yet. Or any other family member.

"Done." Mr. Smith cracked a wide smile, transforming his face from plain to merry—a joy Elsie didn't think she could forget. There was kindness instead of judgment. "So long as you call me Fitz."

"Elsie, if you please." Again, the words came without permission. She should have waited for a proper introduction, but she felt a strange thrill in his presence. She'd gone far too long without a proper conversation. There was a trace, just a hint, of a Welsh accent, the same singsong way her father had spoken. Mr. Smith, a complete stranger, had somehow become a balm. She shook the thought. Grief pricked her heart—and yet, it didn't stay. The feeling was a gentle wave, like the lapping of a pond instead of powerful waves crashing against rocks.

Dumbly, she stood before Mr. Smith. Her emotions—and her tongue—were sharp and severe, but there was something different with this stranger. She stepped back, confused by the onslaught of feelings. Her grieving was already healed. She had no need of Mr. Smith. Or anyone.

"Elsie." He gestured to her, encouraging her to say his name.

"Fitz." The word felt odd in her mouth, but his answering grin warmed her. Elsie slipped her hand from his and circled him, heading toward the door. "I should go."

"The door is open." His brow furrowed, concern etched in the lines of his face. "Is that not enough?"

"To be honest, I'm not sure." She shrugged. He was a simple man with an air of authority. He more than likely had delivered something and needed to be paid. "Shall I call the steward in?"

"No, why—" Mr. Smith stopped himself, the realization on his face. "I didn't come to settle affairs with your steward. I came to speak with your brother."

Your brother. The words came heavy, shrinking the room and stealing the joy. Of course the man was here to see her brother. Disappointment hung in the air. Mr. Smith wasn't here to sooth her grief—not that she was still mourning. No, Elsie was fine. She straightened her back. She prayed her worry didn't show on her face.

Family was supposed to be a sanctuary, yet she'd only felt peace when they were far away. *Your brother.* Her family was here—or would be any moment—and everything would change. Her solitude would now be snuffed out, like a candle in a darkened room.

"Are you alright?" Mr. Smith held her arm.

She glanced at his hand, surprised she'd not flinched. Warmth flowed once more from him, willing her heart to a gentle rhythm. She blushed. It'd been years since her family had embraced her or given any tender affection. And yet here she was, soaking up his gentle touch like a starved child. Without meeting his gaze, she whispered, "I'm fine."

"It's been awhile, hasn't it?" he whispered back.

The room went cold. *It's been awhile.* He knew of her isolation. That was the only thing he could have meant. If he knew of the isolation, then he knew of her humiliation. Blinking, she retreated, backing up against her father's desk. Her brother had told him. That was the only

7

explanation. She shouldn't be surprised. Matthew reveled in her frustration.

Mr. Smith's face fell. "I've said something wrong. I meant no offense." He mirrored her steps, keeping the distance even. His words jumbled together. "I live up the road. I'm sorry. I didn't know it was—"

Elsie held up her hand, the pieces fitting together. Fitzburgh Smith. The modest estate up the hill, just after the fork in the road. That must have been where the smoke was coming from, a warm fire in a cozy home.

"Truly, I meant no harm." His voice was smooth, sincere—how her brother could sound just before a cutting remark. Alarm rang in Elsie's head. Mr. Smith had already confessed he'd come to speak with Matthew. Her brother pivoted from riotous to righteous depending on the day. If this stranger did business with Matthew, there was little doubt they were the same.

She pasted a smile and gave a polite curtsey. "It was good to meet you."

He cut off her escape, his eyes pleading. "Elsie, truly—you are the last—"

"Fitzburgh?" Matthew's deep voice cut across the room, piercing Elsie. With a chuckle and pat on the back, he greeted Mr. Smith, not sparing a glance to his worried sister.

Staring at her brother, Elsie hesitated, her mouth hanging open in yet another unladylike position. Matthew had grown a mustache, while his hair was short about the ears. His coat appeared grand, although the edges were threadbare. He must not have been greeted by the butler, his top hat still donning his head. It appeared to be a size too big, falling forward on Matthew's small brow. He looked nothing like Elsie's father, appearing less like a baron and more like a boy playing dress up.

Elsie slid from behind the men, hoping to disappear to her room. Her brother ignored her presence completely. *A blessing,* she tried to tell herself, but the shock, the pain of the dismissal, fell heavy on her heart. She'd anticipated a reckoning of some sort, not the removal of all affection.

"Els—Miss Bevue?" Mr. Smith turned from Matthew, concern

written in his pale eyes. He ran a hand through his hair. His dress and manner were plain, so unlike her brother.

"You've met?" The suspicion in Matthew's voice was unmistakable. He'd been in her presence less than a second, the accusations already forming.

Facing her brother, Mr. Smith straightened his posture. His face hardened. His entire frame transformed from mousey to masculine. He appeared to tower over Matthew, despite being the same height. Matthew, with his golden hair and handsome face, didn't seem to notice the change, his focus on Elsie.

"I believe we've all met before, sir." Mr. Smith soured at *sir*.

"Right." Matthew didn't take his eyes off Elsie, despite speaking to Mr. Smith. He waited a beat, his eyes flicking to the neighbor. With a softened voice, Matthew said, "It is good to see you, Elsie."

Elsie narrowed her gaze. Matthew Bevue was the son of a Welsh baron and clung to the bottom rung of nobility. Their father had been the third son and, only after tragedy, had hesitantly inherited the title. Matthew was the only son and wore the title with pride—except in front of plain Mr. Fitzburgh Smith. The sudden appearance of a forgotten acquaintance had bridled her brother.

"Good to meet you, Mr. Smith." Elsie didn't fight the smile. Hope blossomed in her chest. Perhaps the impromptu family gathering was something to be celebrated, especially with such a friendly ally.

"You've forgotten." Mr. Smith grinned. "I'd asked you to call me Fitz."

Elsie ignored the shocked look from her brother and left the room with an answering smirk.

𝕊 2 𝕊

FITZBURGH SMITH

With her dark eyes dancing with mischief, Elsie left the late Lord Bevue's study. Fitz was tempted to follow, but the clearing of a throat paused his pursuit.

"So it's Fitz, is it?" Matthew circled the desk before sitting in his father's chair. He made a gallant show of keeping his hands up and his chin lifted as if he were the queen, not a destitute baron. He'd always been the performer, taking credit for someone else's work.

Standing in the middle of the room, Fitzburgh Smith was torn between elation and worry. He'd waited years to speak with Miss Bevue again—or *Elsie,* as she'd generously offered—but didn't understand the sudden turn of events. Her brother had barged into the study. Fitz had come seeking Matthew, the newest Lord Bevue, but was surprised that Elsie was in her father's study.

He'd only recently found out where her family had stashed her. He didn't know how or why, nor did he really care. He wasn't a believer in miracles, but this Christmas seemed much more promising than before. The years melted away as she stood before him. She'd not yet changed from her riding habit. Her dark, unruly hair had escaped her plait, framing her face.

But Matthew had inserted himself into the room, completely

ignoring his sister. Elsie's brow had furrowed and her shoulders sank, the light in her eyes dimming. Not seeing Elsie was impossible for Matthew—or any man. It was an intentional cut by her brother. A decade later, nothing had changed. Matthew still echoed his mother's hollow niceties, barely concealing the arrogance beneath. A feat, considering Lady Bevue was the daughter of a vicar. And Elsie ... the thought of her made Fitz pause. She'd changed, not just the physical manifestation of a woman, but she'd been muted, filtered somehow. Her spirit wasn't nearly as bright as it once was, and Fitz wondered if he was too late.

He clenched his teeth, arguing to himself that it was better than clenching his fists. It'd been ages since his temper had bested him, but Matthew Bevue had a knack for provoking him. They'd known each other far too long, or more specifically, their fists.

Elsie seemed to have forgotten the once ginger-haired neighbor, but Matthew knew quite well who Fitz was—and why he'd come. Fitz glared at him, remembering Elsie's spark in her gaze. Her fire, which had saved him in more ways than one, warmed him, just like it had years before.

Matthew leaned back in the chair, settling in for a game of chess, except the pieces were people, not figures. "And just how long were the two of you alone?"

"With the door open." Folding his arms across his chest, Fitz stood front and center in the study. There'd been a hidden part of his heart that belonged to Elsie, a secret he'd told no one. But Fitz navigated the treacherous waters of finance; a family was not on his horizon. He was a determined bachelor, and nothing—save a true miracle—would change that. "Forcing a marriage wouldn't help your finances."

"I could make you pay for damages to her reputation." Matthew's eyes were eager. "It'd be quite a sum."

"Would you like the name of my solicitor?" Fitz would never give a penny to Elsie's brother.

Matthew paused for a moment before clearing his throat. "Yes, I believe I do."

"Can you even afford a solicitor?" Fitz ran a hand down his face. "Before you answer, keep in mind, my visit is a gentleman's warning."

"A warning?" Matthew scoffed, but his unsteady voice belied the concern. Matthew was in debt up to his neck. "For what?"

"That I've purchased Glamorgan Bank." Fitz rubbed his jaw, glad that he'd kept the Bevue family last on the long list of visits. "During the purchase, I was made aware of all accounts in default."

"What are you suggesting?" Matthew stood slowly, his voice low.

"Fact, Matthew. There is no suggesting. I'm here to give you the facts and work out a new payment plan." Fitz had spent his youth alongside his father, collecting debts and building businesses. He could smell a lie before the thought was hatched. Matthew was no different than the hundreds of other debtors Fitz had dealt with. "If, of course, that's possible."

Matthew tapped a finger on the desk. "You accost my sister in my late father's study and now you accuse—"

"You can repay the loan, or I can seize your assets. Your debt is too high to qualify for bankruptcy, assuming you could have afforded the filing fee." A wave of guilt washed over Fitz. The man before him was Elsie's brother. The roof over his head was the same shelter that kept Elsie warm at night. If Matthew had a less deserving sister, Fitz could revel in the sweet justice of Matthew's predicament.

Matthew held out his arms. "I was unaware my father had left us in such a disaster."

"Your father didn't." A better man than Fitz would have left the comment unchallenged, but the late Lord Bevue was honest, a bit scatterbrained, and disorganized, but unfailingly truthful.

"So, you've come to enact revenge? Was it too much to handle, all those times I bested you?" Matthew straightened his back and threw his hands in his pockets, the muscles on his neck taut.

Fitz worked his jaw. He was still the son of James Smith, a steady man who chose his wife over an inheritance. Fitz was still the baby born too early and bloomed a decade after his peers. He held no title but had made his own way in the world, thanks to the same education his father—and Matthew—had received. He was bested by no one.

"Tell me, Fitz, does Elsie know how soundly I beat you time and time again?"

"Does she know you've spent her dowry?"

Matthew's face darkened. "Her actions negated her dowry."

"A dowry is for marriage, not—"

"She punched the Earl of Tyndeth." Matthew folded his arms, mimicking Fitz's earlier stance. "Tell me she's marriageable after that."

"How is she *not* marriageable after that?" Fitz couldn't stop the smile. He'd wanted to punch the wretched man a dozen times before. The earl was a miserable, nasty bag of bones who was nearing his expiration far too slowly. But hearing of Elsie's courage made Fitz wish he'd known sooner.

"You cannot be serious." Matthew's mouth fell open. "He's the Earl of Tyndeth."

"I heard you the first time." Fitz remembered the moment he'd heard of Elsie's scandal, although he'd assumed it had to do with her mother, not an earl. Lady Bevue was perpetually short on patience with Elsie and could twist her daughter in knots tight enough to burst.

"You'd marry her?"

Fitz didn't like the calculating glint in Matthew's eye. "You're in no position to negotiate a marriage, Matthew."

"She's from a respectable family—"

"That's debatable." Fitz shook his head. He'd admired Miss Bevue for years and, admittedly, wished for a chance to earn her heart. He even owed her a great debt, but he would not be bound to the likes of Lady Bevue and her son. "Your ledger says otherwise."

"Many titled families are struggling." Matthew shrugged. The hem of his collar was worn and his lips were chapped. His fall from grace was subtle, a slow descent.

"Your competency in math hasn't changed." Fitz had been here too long. This was to be a quick visit. Elsie had always been his hidden weakness, and had she been the one offering marriage, the conversation would be drastically different. If Matthew knew the depth of his affection, he would twist it to his advantage, finding a way to hurt both Elsie and Fitz. Once a bully, always a bully. "I've come to give you a gentleman's warning, Matthew. That is the beginning and end of it."

"And yet you were alone with my sister." Matthew rubbed his chin, a greedy smile creeping across his face.

"With the door open."

"I heard you the first time." Circling the desk, Matthew came to Fitz, extending a hand. "I think we can make an arrangement. Trade an asset for an asset."

"You do realize you already told me your sister was unmarriageable."

"And you quickly told me otherwise." Matthew let his hand fall back to his side. "To be honest, I'd hoped she'd catch the eye of Lord Armonde, but you'll do nicely."

"Jonathon Parr?" Cold tea had more warmth than the marquess. He was as boring and uninteresting as the day was long. Fitz could no sooner picture Lord Armonde with Elsie than fire with ice.

"So, you do remember university days." Matthew sniffed cheekily.

Fitz wouldn't give him the pleasure. He kept his face neutral and lied, "They would make a fine match."

"You are not jealous?"

"I've spoken to Elsie a handful of times. I'll not be promising eternity anytime soon." His heart twisted in rebellion. Fitz knew she'd marry one day and that he wouldn't be her husband, but Jonathon Parr seemed particularly cruel.

Matthew smiled a touch too wide. "And yet you call her Elsie."

"I will not trade a marriage for your debt. You have until Lady Day to pay, or I begin seizing your assets." Fitz tipped his head.

"Aren't you full of Christmas cheer." Matthew sniffed.

"I'll take my leave, Matthew."

"Stay for dinner."

"Thank you, but no." There was little *thanks* in his tone. Fitz was not a pawn in Matthew's game, neither was Elsie. He would find a way to keep Elsie unscathed from her family's horrid spending habits. "Good day, Matthew." He turned to the door, grateful to be rid of the new baron.

"I'll sell the mare."

Fitz froze. He'd been careful to conceal the gift, not wanting Elsie to know who'd given it to her. Gifting a horse, especially one of such impeccable bloodlines, insinuated more than Fitz could agree to. Marriage was not in his future. Fitz turned his head, allowing only his profile to show. "What mare?"

"The one you had delivered." There was a whisper of doubt in Matthew's voice.

"I'm more talented than I realized. I've been in Glamorgan less than a day but have somehow delivered a mare and accosted your sister. Is there anything else I can help you with?"

"Yes."

At that, Fitz faced him fully, shocked at the gall Matthew still had. "And what more can I possibly do?"

Matthew's smile faltered. "Elsie doesn't know the dowry's gone."

"Considering she's been isolated, I doubt she'll ask." Fitz hated that he'd let that little tidbit slip. He shouldn't admit how much he truly knew. The piercing look from Matthew made it clear he'd not missed it either.

"You obviously have some regard for her." Matthew held up a hand when Fitz opened his mouth. "Hear me out. I'll have to sell the mare, no matter who gave it to her. Although, knowing you, I have no doubt that if you didn't give it to her, you know who did."

Drat. He'd not counted on the fact her family couldn't house the animal. "If I did know, that would not be divulged."

"The house in London will be up for sale. We hope to have it sold before Christmas but not before I can tie up loose ends."

"Such as an engagement to Lord Armonde's sister."

Matthew had the mind to at least appear sheepish. Lady Alice's dowry would cure a third of his debt. "She is but one possible solution. She's a delightful girl, if she'll have me."

"If she's as dull witted as her brother, I have no doubt."

Matthew gave a wry grin. "Heavens, Fitz. Are you sure you're not Elsie's match? Both your tongues are wicked."

Fitz couldn't help but smile. "She is my favorite Bevue."

"Who could use a friend at the moment." Matthew's voice was smooth.

This was a trap even if Fitz didn't understand the whole of it. Matthew was cooking a game. Fitz should leave, wash his hands of the Bevue family. He'd seen Elsie with his own eyes and given the debt warning to Matthew. But the image of Elsie when Matthew entered the room, defeat in her shoulders, made Fitz pause. Matthew was right on one account. Elsie needed a friend.

"At least stay until dinner."

"Matthew, I—" Fitz cut himself off, an image catching his eye. A framed picture of a woman's profile sat on the bookshelf near the desk. Long, wild locks of dark hair cascaded down her back. Without thinking, he picked up the frame. The woman looked similar, almost identical, to Elsie but the portrait was too aged to be a likeness of her. His thumb caressed the frame, his resolve crashing to the floor.

❧ 3 ❧

ELISHEBA BEVUE

Elsie escaped to her room, hoping for a moment alone before the inevitable onslaught of family. She'd changed from her riding habit, throwing on her only decent dress. She hadn't done the buttons in the back and rang the bell for help. The image of Mr. Smith—no, *Fitz,* she corrected herself. His preference for the informal nickname in front of Matthew was a moment Elsie wouldn't forget. For the first time, she'd not felt alone in the presence of a family member. A quick knock on the door was followed by Doris and a girl on the cusp of womanhood.

"Elsie—Miss Bevue." Doris's face was flushed red, either from frustration or embarrassment, Elsie didn't know and couldn't ask the reason in front of the girl. It was bad enough Elsie referred to Doris by her first name. "We are expecting guests, and the baron has thoughtfully allowed for extra hands."

Elsie nodded, understanding now that this was no simple family gathering for the upcoming holiday. "And how many guests?"

"The Earl of Tyndeth, the Marquess of Armonde, and his sister, Lady Alice." Doris's eyes flicked from the young maid and back to Elsie. "And your mother of course."

"Of course." Elsie barely registered her voice. The Earl of Tyndeth had courted her mother two years before, dropping his affection because of Elsie's behavior. And here, without warning, Tyndeth had returned. Elsie set her jaw. She had not cowered to the man before. She would not cower today. Another thought crept in. The earl could be the reason for her family's sudden gathering. *Gathering.* There would be strangers and family in the home. Elsie swallowed the rising panic. She hadn't seen them in years; she hadn't a clue what was expected of her or the true reason behind their arrival. Her family had missed other holidays. Why arrive now?

Doris waved the girl forward and gave an apologetic nod to both the young maid and Elsie. "Mary will be helping you."

Doris's daughter would no longer be Elsie's maid. She had become a dear friend to Elsie but bore the stain of an unwed mother. The sin was too great for Matthew or Elsie's mother to overlook—Elsie would have one less friend to depend on. And a new maid to welcome.

Mary dipped her chin and shuffled her feet, her discomfort obvious. She was either too young to be attending Elsie or too inexperienced. Elsie needed the support more than Matthew needed a proper household—Elsie shook the thought. Her attitude wouldn't change her situation; that was something she'd learned in her seclusion.

Doris gave a tentative smile. "I'm under the impression your family and guests will stay for a fortnight. And then celebrate Christmas in London."

"Am I to leave with them?" Elsie didn't know if this was what she wanted or feared. Wales had been kind to her while London held memories better left forgotten—holiday or not.

"I do not know, love." Doris pursed her lips as if she wished to say more. She gave a curt shake of her head and left.

Elsie didn't miss Mary's wide-eyed look of surprise. She hoped the maid could keep a secret. Her mother wouldn't appreciate the close relationship between Elsie and Doris—or any of the servants.

Elsie motioned to her back. "I couldn't reach the buttons."

The young maid brightened and in a thick Welsh accent offered, "And your hair? Would you like me to do that as well?"

Elsie touched her head, realizing how horrid her hair probably looked. "Oh, I'd forgotten."

"Ay." Mary wasted no time in tackling Elsie's hair, not bothering to sit in front of the mirror or utilize the brush on the vanity. With quick, slender fingers, she combed Elsie's dark hair down her back. "Fine ladies like their hair in an updo but there's so much of yours. Your hair won't keep. It won't stay well at all."

"I'm used to having my hair redone throughout the day." Elsie's father had loved her hair and the way it came loose during the day's adventures. When her mother finally insisted Elsie become a lady and have her hair in the modern fashions, her father had sulked in his study for days. Elsie hadn't understood why until she'd moved to his childhood home and saw an old picture of her mother in his study. Her hair was undone, waving unkempt in the wind.

"I could do a pipe braid, circling your head like a crown. It's not as fancy as the other braids, but it'd keep your hair in place. Although, it might give you a terrific headache by the end of the night."

Elsie nodded, grateful that at least her hair would be tamed. She couldn't promise anything more. Not with the earl coming.

Mary finished and made quick work of the buttons on the back of Elsie's dress. There was nothing left to keep Elsie in the room and yet she stayed. The sound of busy arrivals echoed through the home, announcing the arrival of either family or guests. But Elsie didn't move.

"Is there something else I can help you with?" Mary gently asked, her hands wringing together. The Bevue estate must be her first job.

Elsie shook her head, remembering the stableman's words. "Not unless you can teach me to dance in the rain."

"I beg your pardon—"

"Nothing, Mary." Elsie stood, the stableman's voice in her head. *Never pegged you as a coward.*

She descended the stairs, her heart pounding in her chest. She held her breath—the foyer was empty. She exhaled in relief, leaning into the staircase. The sound of lively conversation came from the sitting room.

"Miss Bevue?" a warm tenor asked.

Elsie started. She was just as surprised at finding a man speaking to her as she was to hear *Miss Bevue*. A tall, slender blond stood at attention by the sitting room door. He wore a tailored coat that Elsie assumed was cut in the latest fashions. The hems were stiff and likely made not a week or so before. The man had kept his face freshly shaved, aside from generous sideburns. Doris had said the earl was coming, along with a marquess and his sister, but Elsie couldn't remember the names, her worry consumed with the arrival of the obnoxious earl.

"You are the marquess?" Elsie fidgeted. She wasn't supposed to bring attention to his title. She'd been in the company of her so-called peers before, but was now horribly out of practice—if she'd ever been *in* practice.

"That I am." He smiled, a twinkle in his eye. His accent was drenched in wealth and title. With a bit of flair, he extended an arm. "May I escort you in?"

She laid her hand on his arm, alarms ringing in her head. He was calm and smooth, a decorum that he no doubt learned as a boy. The rules of the peerage were dictated since infancy, to both ladies and gentlemen. Elsie hated it, never knowing what truly lay beneath the surface.

"That color compliments you." The marquess gave a practiced wink.

"Thank you," Elsie murmured. The slender conversations consisting of nothing but niceties would be waiting for her in London. She felt suddenly homesick for Wales, and she'd not even left.

Elsie and the marquess entered the sitting room—noise vanishing in an instant. She tipped her chin, hoping she could hide the beginning of a blush. She fought the urge to hike her skirt and run to the barn. Peeking through her lashes, she counted five people, excluding herself and her golden-haired marquess. She took a fortifying breath and lifted her head. Her mother approached, her dark hair and face not an hour aged since the day she'd sent Elsie away.

Elsie fidgeted once more. There had to be a way to hide. Her mother, ever the lady, looked deceptively like Elsie with lush dark hair and large eyes as dark as chocolate. That was where their similarities began and ended. Beneath the surface, Matthew and Lady Bevue were the same ilk—just like Elsie and her father had been.

"Mother." Elsie dipped a curtsey. Her word broke the spell of silence.

Lady Bevue reached for her daughter's hand. "Welcome home, Elisheba."

"I am home." Elsie winced, regretting her words.

Her mother arched an eyebrow and tension filled the room. In one sentence, Elsie had invited erosion, chasing peace from those who loved her most.

❧ 4 ❧

FITZBURGH SMITH

F itz paced at the end of the blasted sitting room, wishing for the tenth time he'd given Matthew the warning and left. The butler helped an elderly man to a chair, supplying a blanket and a nod. The ancient man groaned and shoved the butler's hands aside. There was something familiar about the grumpy gentleman, but Fitz couldn't place him. Fitz had avoided London for the last few years, keeping his business and person firmly in Wales or America. Anywhere was better than London and its filth.

"Are you going to stare or pay your respects, boy?" The man grunted, his spindly hand gripping the blanket.

"I'm not sure the time has come to pay respects. You're too alive for that, sir." Despite himself, Fitz walked to the chair and froze—the man was Tyndeth. The years had not been kind to the earl. He was nearing seventy but looked twice as old.

Tyndeth scoffed. "I'm waiting for God."

"Aren't we all?" Fitz leaned forward. The earl had become immensely more interesting since learning of Elsie's scandal. Fitz smiled, wishing he'd witnessed the argument. He'd give anything to applaud her performance.

"You laugh at my condition?" Tyndeth snarled but it looked more like a toddler teething. His giant frame had shrunk to a shadow of skin and bones, along with the authority he'd inherited from his imposing lineage.

"Not at all." Fitz placed a hand on the armchair—the earl pulled away like a pouting child. Fitz whispered to the old man, "I think we're all waiting for God."

"Not like me," Tyndeth snapped. "Look at me. I've been shoved to the back of the room. It's disgraceful."

Before Fitz could answer, Lady Bevue and a blonde girl—who was undoubtedly Jonathon Parr's sister, the family resemblance was uncanny—entered the room. Both ladies were donned in London's latest trends with Lady Bevue pretending to hang on every word the chit said. Elsie's mother was clearly trying to win the young girl's affection. Fitz's stomach twisted. This was an old script, one that the *ton* never tired of writing. The peerage chased money and title, selling their dignity and daughters. Lady Bevue gave a hollow laugh. Perhaps sons were sold as well.

"You and I aren't very different." A smirk crossed the earl's face, his eyes searching Fitz. He grunted again. "You condemn weakness. As do I."

Fitz winced. His own mother called him a cynic but Fitz dismissed it, thinking she was far too gentle to know the difference between reality and romance. But the earl was an entirely different sort. Never had Fitz thought he'd sunk to Tyndeth's way of thinking. Fitz tugged on his collar, feeling suddenly warm. And suddenly wrong.

"Have you met my old friend Fitzburgh Smith?" Matthew asked a touch too loud. He swaggered, his speech slow.

Fitz needed to leave before Matthew became completely drunk. This was not how Fitz had anticipated his first night home. Tyndeth's observation had sent him reeling. There wasn't a humble bone in Fitz's body, but he'd always considered himself fair. Honest, even. But if he was like Tyndeth, that meant Fitz was cruel. And heartless.

"Mother. Lady Alice." Matthew was now at Fitz's side. "One of my oldest friends, Fitzburgh Smith."

Fitz hadn't noticed their approach. He smiled and gave a curt nod. "How do you do?"

Lady Bevue dipped her head. She looked so much like Elsie that Fitz had to force himself to look away. The woman had aged well; it was a wonder she'd not remarried. "And where are you from Mr. Smith?" There was an emphasis on *Mr*. She was asking if he was indeed a lowly mister or perhaps a titled gentleman.

"Down the road, milady." Fitz kept his voice even, the earl's words still echoing in his mind. He'd been pricked but didn't fully understand why.

Lady Bevue's eyes lit with recognition. "Ah, James Smith's son?"

"Yes, I've recently returned from America." Fitz couldn't help the pride in each word.

"That's right." Lady Bevue pivoted, turning her full attention on Fitz. She mirrored the calculating look her own son had given Fitz just an hour before. "You aided the Americans, did you not?"

Drat. How the woman knew about Fitz's arms trading was beyond him. Selling rifles to both sides of what appeared to be an impending civil war was something Fitz would rather not announce to the world.

"For a time, yes. I dabbled in trading."

The earl cleared his throat. "How do you *dabble* in trading?"

For being ancient, the man had the hearing of a lion. Fitz pulled again at his collar; it was deucedly hot in the room.

"Trading, eh?" Matthew chuckled. "I had no idea you'd gone rogue."

"There's money in trading." The earl grunted. "Not that you'd have a clue what money is."

Lady Bevue's smile tightened, her gaze flicking to her son before settling back on Fitz. "Did you travel to America often?"

"As needed." It wasn't the whole truth, but he didn't want to divulge anything. Not here, not with the Bevue family.

"Did you like it there?" Lady Bevue guided their small company to sit on the couches, her arm looped in Lady Alice's.

"Of course he did. He's made a bloody fortune." Tyndeth nodded to Fitz and straightened his back. "While most of the *ton* swindled theirs."

Ignoring the look of shock from the women, Fitz left them in Matthew's care and kneeled before the earl. "You seem to know an awful lot of tradesmen for being a gentleman."

"Of course, I do." Tyndeth sniffed. "I keep a pulse on this country and its merchants."

Lady Bevue struck up a conversation with Lady Alice regarding the cut of their dresses. Both women were on the cusp of the most modern fabrics—the contrast from Elsie's riding habit was striking.

"I thought the *ton* abhorred trading. Or work of any kind," Fitz whispered.

The earl smirked. "We are the backbone of this great nation and must oversee all aspects. Everyone has his place. You've done well with yours."

Tyndeth's approval shouldn't bother him but it did. Fitz had somehow snared the old man's good opinion. He had spent his life determined to be the very opposite of the *ton* and all that it represented.

"Fitz is the best of men," Matthew bellowed, gathering the women, one on each side of him. His smile was lopsided and his eyes took on a pink hue.

Fitz wouldn't take the bait; he would reveal nothing. The family was skipping toward poverty with abandon, and Fitz would not be their salvation.

"How is it that you're such a good friend to the newest Lord Bevue?" the earl said, lifting his chin. "You're not of the same ilk. He's of high birth and low wits. You're the very opposite."

Fitz chuckled despite himself. Noise scurried from the room as Elsie and Jonathon Parr entered. Elsie had changed from her riding habit to a smart dress a few years past its prime. Her dark hair was held in an updo, exposing a delicate neck. Her skirt wasn't tight at the waist with a gradual, fashionable billow like Lady Alice but rather wide, like the outdated, crinoline circled skirts. Elsie's dark hair was in a simple updo, unlike her mother and Lady Alice's decorated strands.

Jonathon Parr looked entirely too pleased with himself. Fitz frowned. She shouldn't be anywhere near the marquess. Jonathon was dull, a simple white next to Elsie's mixture of vibrant colors competing for their chance in the sun.

"Careful, Smith," the earl warned. "I'd not saddle yourself to that one. You'll be black and blue before the month ends."

Fitz wished once more for the impossible, the ability to see Elsie plant a fist on Tyndeth's cheek. Taking in the room, Fitz watched Elsie's eyes widen, her stance shrink. She appeared to be aware of the stark contrast between herself and the two women. A rush of protectiveness surged in Fitz. She rubbed her hands together. Instinctively, he remembered the feel of her small callouses, evidence of hours on horseback. She didn't belong in here. She belonged on her mare with the wind caressing her face.

5

ELISHEBA BEVUE

Elsie's mother stood next to Matthew, his attention pulled from a blonde woman to his left. Jewels glittered in the woman's golden hair. Under her family's scrutiny, Elsie was instantly aware of her threadbare clothes. Her worn hem revealed long walks through the garden, her riding habit held even more wear. Outside beckoned to her now more than ever. She felt more herself with the grass and horses than with her own kind.

Lady Bevue pasted a smile, not too bright and not too wide. She squeezed Elsie's hand in hers, saying, "It's good to see you."

Elsie searched her mother's face for a hint of sincerity, for genuine affection. "It's good to be seen."

Lady Bevue's smile faded at the comment. A blush crept across Elsie's cheeks. She'd not meant to embarrass nor bring attention to her isolation. This wasn't the reunion Elsie had hoped for.

The fashionable blonde woman approached them, her delicate face framed by blonde curls. "You've met my brother, Jonathon."

"The Marquess of Armonde," her mother quickly injected. She released Elsie's hands, replacing them with the young woman's. "And this is Lady Alice Parr."

As if on cue, Lady Alice beamed at Elsie's mother. "So good to be here."

Elsie nodded, wondering how many times she'd heard *good*. It wasn't quite dinnertime and she'd heard it three times too many. She'd not seen her family in years. There was so much to say, so many questions, but with the two blonde siblings, Elsie had to pretend all was well. She couldn't ask why her family had ignored her for every holiday, sending sermons instead of affection. Nor could she ask about the Christmas timing of their visit—or even more disturbing, she couldn't inquire about the earl.

Fidgeting, she caught her mother's attention. She straightened her posture and followed her mother to the sofa, wishing she'd stayed in her room for another hour. Or ten.

"How was your travel?" It seemed the safest question of the hundreds bouncing around in Elsie's head.

"Good," Lady Alice answered.

I wasn't asking you. Elsie swallowed the retort. "Mother ..." She waited for Lady Bevue to look at her. "Did you travel well?"

"I did." Lady Bevue gave a half smile but turned to Lady Alice. "How are you faring?"

Lady Alice blushed—quite prettily to Elsie's annoyance—and touched her porcelain forehead with the back of her petite hand. "Much better, thank you."

Matthew fawned over Lady Alice. "We can't have you feeling unwell."

Elsie faded from the little circle, trying her best to not *tsk* or shake her head. She'd never been the delicate flower like Alice Parr. Or her mother.

Movement in the corner of the room caught Elsie's eye. Fitz, the man from her father's study, was nodding along to a grey haired man in a chair. Elsie took a step toward them. Fitz caught her gaze. He smiled —not the practiced, measured expression of the marquess or his sister, but a true, honest smile. A hesitant warmth filled Elsie. She felt like she was coming up for much-needed air but didn't trust the feeling. Nor did she trust any man in contact with her brother, Fitz, or Lord Armonde.

"... that's why nobody ever listens anymore." The older man's voice shook.

Fitz squeezed the man's shoulders. "I'm sorry to hear that." He didn't look sorry. He didn't look anywhere but Elsie's face. He was at her side in an instant.

"Are you staying for dinner?" She was curious, nothing more.

"Would you like me to?" Fitz asked quietly. He didn't reprimand her. He leaned in, his scent of hay and grass swirling around her. He raised his eyebrows and scanned the room. "I've been invited, but I think only to even the numbers."

Without thinking, Elsie glanced back at her family and the siblings. "Nope. Looks like you were truly invited. There's four of them and three of us." She motioned to the ancient man. His head snapped up. She froze. The Earl of Tyndeth stared at her, his black eyes as piercing as the day she'd slapped him. He'd shriveled into himself in the few years since she'd left him, standing in horror, a hand on his face.

"Miss Bevue." His voice dripped with fury. "How is the prodigal child?"

The world shrank. Elsie struggled to breathe. She turned from Fitz's worried glance.

"Elsie?" Fitz whispered.

"I'm fine." She pulled away. The last think she needed was her mother to see her. She said, in the same false tone as the other women, "I'm *good*."

The Earl of Tyndeth folded his spiny hands under the blanket on his lap. His body had weakened. Elsie fought the vindication. Perhaps there was justice after all.

Sniffing with disdain, he turned his head. "Lady Bevue, you darling woman, I feel such sympathy for your plight."

Elsie's mother scurried to the earl's chairs. "Oh, you're too kind."

Clenching her hands into tight fists, Elsie felt the rising anger. Her mother had never come running to her father like this, nor had she kneeled next to his chair like a long lost puppy. This wasn't her mother. And the earl would never be her father.

"I wouldn't do what you're thinking. He's not long for this world."

His voice was low and soothing, reminding Elsie of her father. Fitz guided her a few paces from the others.

"And how would you know what I'm thinking?" She should've softened her retort with a smile. But she didn't. Elsie wanted out of the room and out of the house. This surprise holiday gathering of her family was the largest group she'd endured in years. Her isolation was supposed to be a reprimand—she dearly wished for another punishment.

"You don't hide much." Fitz cocked his head to the side, his pale, light blue eyes were filled with quiet curiosity.

"I'm aware." With tremendous force, she tore her gaze from his. The room had become a touch too small. For days on end, she'd been alone in this home, aside from her servants. She'd taken her meals at the end of the dinner table and spent hours on horseback, riding. Words were kept to a minimum with calm silence filling the walls. No judgement. No arguments. And no mistakes. "I've spent two years in purgatory for a wicked tongue."

"Funny, I heard it was another appendage." Fitz's face was blank. Not a twitch of a smile or a darkening look of judgment.

"He deserved it. I will not apologize." Elsie's soft voice sounded more like a petulant child than a grown woman. She straightened her back and waited for the reprimand. She'd slapped the earl—oh, he'd wailed like a stuck pig. Elsie'd do it again if need be.

"I have no doubt." Fitz tugged at the collar of his shirt. "If I wasn't such a lowly mister, he'd have kissed my fist as well."

Elsie's mouth hung open in shock. Words abandoned her—all thoughts ceased. She was catapulted back to her first—and only—dinner party a week before the season officially began. One moment of anger and she was in a carriage and deposited in Wales. But Fitz didn't seem to care. Rather, he approved. Was he teasing her? Was this an elaborate scheme?

"Oh, you're not alone Elsie, dear." Fitz chuckled softly. A flock of brown hair fell across his forehead. He was simple. And endearing. "You're just the only one brave enough to put the Earl of Tantrums in his place."

She covered her mouth, a giggle escaping. The sound was of laughter, but Elsie felt much more than that. She felt understood—a somewhat foreign notion. Her mother sent a questioning look, softening only when her gaze turned to Fitz.

"Earl of Tantrums. Oh my, he isn't nearly as awful when I think of him like that." Tension fell from Elsie, her heart filling with gratitude. "That nickname is a gift I won't soon forget."

"Funny how that happens." Fitz's voice turned heavy, all playfulness gone. "I wonder if he'd change, or if he'd even care what we think of him?"

"He's aware of my opinion." Elsie fidgeted, the walls closing in. She tugged at the sleeves of her dress. She felt a sudden shyness—an odd sensation. Fitz made her feel confident and unsure. She needed to clear her head.

"People become what's expected." His pale eyes searched hers, as if begging for understanding. "Some of us need that."

"Perhaps I can help?" Matthew's voice burst through. With an arched eyebrow to his sister, he clapped Fitz on the shoulder, pretending all was well. "That's how we work. Elisheba creates the problem, and I give the solution."

Elsie bristled and turned from both Fitz and her brother. It was only a matter of time before Fitz looked at her the same way her family did. Matthew could fill Fitz's mind with plenty of memories of Elsie's behavior.

"Are you sure about that, Matty?" Fitz's low voice carried as Matthew tried to pull him away.

No one had called her brother Matty in ages, not since Elsie was a child. Back when her father insisted on their pet names, Elsie and Matty. An image appeared in her mind, a memory from when she was a child. She tossed a glance over her shoulder, hoping Matthew could help, but her brother's clenched jaw was at war with his hunched shoulders. Fitz had the upper hand in whatever scheme they'd hatched. She felt torn, wishing she could trust this stranger.

In a soft tenor, Lord Armonde asked, "Are you going to miss it here?"

Elsie matched the marquess's warm smile. She'd been so focused on

Fitz that she'd not heard a word Lord Armonde had said. "Are you enjoying yourself, sir?"

He raised his eyebrows. "I am. I've only just arrived but yes, Wales is delightful."

Elsie hoped she didn't flinch at *Wales is delightful*. Wales was more than delightful. It was grass so lush and green, emeralds were mad with envy. Wales was wild as the wind and as powerful as the ocean currents. It was freedom—it was home.

"You'll miss it then?" the marquess asked, his eyes gentle.

"I've no intention of leaving." Elsie hadn't realized the truth of her words until she'd spoken them. She didn't really have a choice; the land belonged to her brother. He determined who resided and who didn't. Her father had kept a pension for her, but she'd not receive access for another year—unless she married, then the account would be used as a dowry. She didn't know if the amount was significant, Matthew relished keeping information from her.

"You've a faraway look in your eye."

Elsie glanced up, wishing the marquess had not witnessed the moment.

"Lord Armonde." Fitz nodded to the marquess and cupped Elsie's elbow. "Miss Bevue, might I steal you for a ride tomorrow?"

"Fitz, you can't possibly leave already." Elsie didn't miss the disappointment in Lord Armonde's face. She was a lady and shouldn't ask the comings and goings of a neighbor, but she felt strangely encouraged instead of caged—a complete and utterly ridiculous notion.

A knowing grin crept across Fitz's face. "I've stayed longer than I planned."

"Oh, I'd thought you'd stay for dinner." Elsie blushed like a schoolgirl and made an awkward curtsey—to whom or why, she didn't know. Fitz stifled a laugh while Lord Armonde arched an eyebrow. Elsie's face burned with embarrassment, unsure if she should flee the room or pretend to faint on the spot. She'd never fainted and hated the idea.

"I dare say you should put the woman out of her misery and stay." Lord Armonde smiled, an even, perfect expression. There wasn't a note of jealousy or any other emotion.

"No, I'm sorry." Elsie retreated, the blush creeping down her neck and chest. She was burning from her own stupidity. She was better with horses. Animals didn't require words. "I shouldn't keep you, sir. It's been awhile—I just didn't—"

"Is there a problem, child?" Lady Bevue's smooth voice cut through the room. She glided to Elsie just as the housekeeper appeared at the door. Lady Bevue nodded to Doris. "Ah, Mrs. Thelm. Just in time."

The housekeeper gave a formal nod to Elsie's mother, signaling dinner was ready. Instead of disappearing back to the dining room, she stood, her eyes searching Elsie's.

"Is there anything else, Mrs. Thelm?" Lady Bevue asked, a warning in her tone. She'd caught the concern in the housekeeper's expression.

"No, milady." Doris tucked her head and left.

Elsie felt her blush deepen even more, wondering if her body could ignite from the sheer heat of embarrassment. The butler helped Tyndeth to a stand, but instead of directing him toward the dining room, the butler guided him to the only guest room on the main floor. Relief flooded through Elsie. Tyndeth wouldn't be at dinner. Heaven help her, Elsie clenched her hands to keep from clapping. She would behave. She had to.

"There you have it, Elsie," Fitz whispered. "I'm to even the numbers."

"What are the chances he'll stay in the room for the rest of their visit?" Elsie covered her mouth. Her mother narrowed her eyes. "She heard me."

Fitz coughed, failing to cover a chuckle. "I think everyone heard you."

She grabbed his arm. "Please, stay."

Fitz covered her hand with his. "Only if you promise to ride with me tomorrow."

"Save me from this evening, and I'll do anything you want." Elsie winced. Her brother's mouth fell open. She groaned and briefly closed her eyes. "Why can't I just stop?"

Fitz squeezed her hand, his skin warm. "I hope you never do."

Elsie opened her eyes with a snap. Her heart lifted. With his hand on hers, she felt strong. Capable. The bumbling mess of emotions and words was gone. Before she could speak, Matthew beckoned everyone forward. He held out an arm for Lady Alice. Elsie waited for Lord Armonde to accompany her mother—if her family was anything, they were proper and would follow procedure.

Smiling, her mother squeezed the marquess's extended hand. "Oh, dear boy. You don't want to accompany me. Take Elisheba in. Indulge an old woman. I haven't spoken to Mr. Smith in ages. He's an old family friend, and I'm dying to hear from him."

Elsie raised her eyebrows in surprise. Her mother never—as in *never*—broke protocol. Lord Armonde was the highest ranked man in the home, her mother being the highest ranked woman. They should walk in together. Elsie was the lowest, as was Fitz. She waited, wondering if this was a trap. Her mother had lied. Fitz wasn't a family friend, and her mother wasn't a gossip wishing for news of any kind, especially not of an old Welsh town.

"You might want to close your mouth, or she'll know she's got the best of you." Fitz fidgeted next to Elsie. "If she has her way, I might not speak to you the remainder of the evening. I'll be at the stables at ten tomorrow morning. Promise me you'll be there."

"I promise." The words came before Elsie could stop them. She hadn't a clue how she was going to survive the dinner ahead, let alone escape to the barn tomorrow.

34

❧ 6 ❧

FITZBURGH SMITH

Confined to the dinner table, Fitz couldn't hide his annoyance for another moment. He cursed under his breath. He shouldn't have stayed for the meal. He'd hoped he would sit next to Elsie, as rank demanded, instead of her mother, Lady Bevue. Every clink of silverware or forced pleasantry made him cringe. Lady Bevue had dominated the conversation, keeping his attention on her and away from her daughter. Elsie was placed directly across from him, but with Lady Bevue on his left and Lady Alice on his right, there was little respite. He was sandwiched between conniving and ridiculous. Lady Alice had as much substance as the tea in his cup.

Matthew tapped a spoon to his glass. "I've an announcement."

"Oh, do wait, Matthew." Lady Bevue dabbed the corners of her mouth with her napkin. "Our guests haven't finished yet."

"Deepest apologies, Mother." He beamed at her.

The expression appeared genuine, softening Fitz's heart. Perhaps Fitz was just as heartless as the earl, too consumed with his own judgement to see the love between mother and son. Matthew winked dramatically at his mother, shattering the feeling. They were playing at something, and Fitz wouldn't stand for it.

"Please, do tell." Lord Armonde set his napkin on the table. His petition fell flat, his bored frown underlining his lack of enthusiasm.

"Oh, yes, do tell." Lady Alice did exactly as her brother, the napkin to the side of her plate. She blushed like the debutante she was, complete with a fluttering of lashes.

Elsie scoffed and rolled her eyes. Fitz's gaze snapped to hers. She blushed, realizing Fitz had caught her. She tucked her chin and nibbled her lip. Her cheeks flamed, the flush creeping down her neck. Her genuine embarrassment was captivating—her dark hair contrasting the crimson hue on her skin.

"Mr. Smith, I believe you're quite taken with my daughter." Lady Bevue's voice was so low, it took a moment for Fitz to realize she'd spoken. She placed a hand on his forearm. "How long have you been in town?"

"I arrived yesterday." He pulled his arm from under hers.

Matthew waited for complete silence before waving his hand dramatically in the air. "I've secured an outing for us. We'll be visiting every site of the Prince of Wales tour, starting tomorrow." Lady Alice clapped excitedly—the only eager audience.

Lady Bevue turned to Fitz, her son's announcement completely forgotten. "Matthew tells me you delivered a horse."

Fitz scanned the table, grateful the Parr siblings were in an animated conversation with Matthew about the Prince of Wales visit. The blasted prince had come the summer before, and the country had placed markers at each of the sites. Fitz hated the idea. The Prince of Wales was the queen's son, the heir to the English throne. Wales had been the ignored relative of England long enough. Fitz didn't give a fig about the prince or his ceremonial visit.

"Mr. Smith?" There was a soft chastisement in her question.

"Excuse me, your son's announcement was diverting." The lie came easy. Perhaps he was no better than his present company.

Lady Bevue tried again. "I am not one to think gifting a horse is scandalous."

"Neither am I." Fitz would admit nothing. If Elsie was born to a different family and Fitz didn't travel abroad for business, he would have been married fresh out of university. He would have clasped Elsie to him and never looked back.

"Is horse flesh something you dabble in as well?" With delicate hands, Lady Bevue placed her napkin on the table, keeping a hand on the linen.

Fitz shrugged. "I'm not sure it's possible to *dabble* in horses. You either ride or you don't."

"Is that how the friendship began?"

"My friendship with whom?" Fitz innocently asked.

"My daughter, Mr. Smith." Lady Bevue didn't raise her voice, nor did she give anything away in her smooth expression. "Is that how you formed your attachment? Through the mutual adoration of horses?"

"I was unaware of any attachment." Fitz would not be cornered. He was not bound with the moral obligation of the *ton*. He would not be muzzled by politeness.

"Gifting a horse seems to suggest a deep attachment."

"Then it might bode well to find the giver." Fitz sipped from his cup, the tea weak. The leaves must have been twice used, a little trick Fitz had used in his leaner years to make the tea stretch between meals.

"I believe I have." Lady Bevue grinned, her eyes lit with mischief—looking very much like her daughter.

"I wouldn't play false, Lady Bevue. It doesn't suit you." Fitz gave a wink, hoping it softened the accusation.

"I'm the daughter of a vicar, my dear, Mr. Smith."

"I'm sure you're the picture of daughterly affection and obedience." He sat back in the chair. "But you'll not get the information about the mare from me."

"I wasn't aware it was a mare."

"You should have become a magistrate, Lady Bevue. Your interrogation skills are astounding," Fitz said wryly. "But my answer's the same. I was not here when the horse was delivered."

"But you knew when it was."

Fitz shifted in the chair. The conversation growing more tedious. "Every stableman in the county knows about that mare. Your daughter has ridden all over Glamorgan."

Lady Bevue's confidence slipped for a moment. "She has loved the outdoors all her life."

"As do many fine ladies." Fitz caught Elsie's gaze. He hesitated, wondering how much of the conversation she'd heard, if any at all.

"You admit it, then?" Lady Bevue demurred. "She has captured your interest."

"I'm afraid the earl is just as interested." Fitz winced, noticing the wide-eyed look from Elsie across the table. She ducked her chin. She'd heard him. The earl was a thorn in Elsie's side, that much he knew. Fitz hadn't meant to dig up the pain. He'd only meant to stop the onslaught from Lady Bevue, who'd become suspiciously quiet. Fitz wasn't meant for the delicate dance of polite conversation. His strength was negotiating profits and planning acquisitions, not feelings or attachments.

Matthew offered a joke and the invitation to move to the sitting room—at least, that's what Fitz assumed. He'd not heard the words, his focus still on the disheartened woman across the table.

The ladies stood—except for Elsie—followed by Matthew and Lord Armonde. Fitz pushed his chair back but couldn't fully stand, his gaze on Elsie's hunched shoulders. In less than a day, he'd brought both a smile and frown to her lips. His plan to visit Wales was to remind Matthew of his debts, but truly, Fitz hoped to lift her spirits not add to her sorrow.

The conversation became muffled as the party left the dining room, Fitz and Elsie still at the table. The door closed with a muted thud—Elsie shot to a stand.

"I'm sorry," Fitz blurted.

Her eyes flicked to his. "I'm fine."

"You're not." Fitz gripped the top of the chair next to him. "And it's my fault."

Elsie forced a smile, looking less like herself and more like her mother. "I promise, it's fine."

"I shouldn't have mentioned the earl." He rubbed his neck, wishing again he'd not stayed for dinner. "I just wanted your mother—"

"You don't have to explain yourself to me." She gave an awkward curtsy and made her way to the other end of the room where the servants had shuffled plates to and from the kitchen.

Fitz scurried after her. "Yes, I do."

"And why is that?" She pierced him with the fire in her eyes, becoming wickedly beautiful. "Would you be apologizing if I'd not overheard you? Because that's how it works, isn't it? Gossip is whispered and secrets are hushed. The only sin is actually hearing it."

"Elsie, please."

"Please? Truth is often hidden except when spoken in anger. Don't pretend otherwise." Her arms stiffened at her sides. "Just don't, Mr. Smith."

"Fitz." His pulse was racing. The rise and fall of her temper was dizzying, but her lack of trust was crystal clear. With a brother like Matthew, Fitz could hardly blame her, but the defeat in her posture was caused by him. Fitz shouldn't care but he did. He'd always cared what she thought of him. "Please, at least call me Fitz."

"Any other requests?" She folded her arms, anger growing with every moment.

"That's not what I meant."

"Enlighten me." Elsie narrowed her gaze.

"I'm trying to apologize." Fitz was wrong, that he knew—but how he'd made things worse was the question.

"I gathered that." She raised an eyebrow.

"Am I not supposed to?" He rubbed the back of his neck. "I have no idea what I'm doing."

Elsie's face softened at his admission. "Neither do I."

"I am sorry." He motioned to the door to the sitting room. "Will you please go with me in there?"

Elsie hung her head. "I'm not sure that's a good idea."

"Because of what I said?"

She straightened. "No."

"Then what?" He stepped closer, feeling a sudden urgency to protect her.

Elsie ran a hand over her skirt. "I don't belong in there."

"Neither do I." He held out his hand. "We can *not belong* together."

"Don't." She shook her head and looked away.

"Don't what?" Fitz came closer, wondering why he couldn't leave her.

"Don't pretend. It doesn't suit you."

"Pretend?" Fitz balked. He pointed toward the sitting room. "I'm not like them."

She lifted her chin and folded her arms around her waist, looking both proud and vulnerable at the same time. "Did you not just apologize for saying something you didn't mean? All you wanted was for my mother to leave you alone. That, dear Mr. Smith, is pretending. And here, just now—" She swallowed hard. "You pretend to care. You offer your company, but at dinner you made your interest, or lack thereof, very clear."

Elsie grabbed the handle of the door to the kitchen. Fitz slid in between her and the door, surprised at his brash behavior. The scent of rosewater tickled his nose. They were inches from each other. Fitz's pulse raced. There were four little freckles dusted on her cheeks—he counted them twice to make sure. She was infuriatingly captivating, just like she was as a young girl. Her eyes dark as chocolate.

She backed away. "Mr. Smith—"

"Blast it, woman. I've asked you to call me Fitz. Mr. Smith is my father." He groaned. Only he would curse at Elisheba Bevue. He risked a glance and froze.

Her wide-eyed expression faded to a smirk. Her lip curled to a perfected look of mischief. "Well look who decided to become the Earl of Tantrums."

7

ELISHEBA BEVUE

Lady Alice batted her lashes at Matthew before inviting him to turn her pages at the pianoforte. Watching them soured Elsie's stomach. She should be happy for her brother, not wanting to run from the room screaming. Or better yet, shake a fist at the ancient man her mother pretended to dote on. Elsie could feel the earl's fury from across the room. Even without Tyndeth, her family's presence had sent her nerves on edge. They'd not given a reason for their sudden arrival and hadn't given an explanation for inviting the Parr siblings.

Elsie had no doubt her brother was up to something, despite his innocent smile. And Fitz, the man who shifted uncomfortably for the tenth time on the sofa, had ignited a curious intrigue. She hadn't yet decided if he was to be trusted. Her suspicion grew as her mother spoke with him during dinner. He had arrived minutes before her family. Admittedly, he'd come to speak with Matthew. There was a scheme between them, and Fitz had the upper hand—for now. Matthew tolerated those he could use or control. Not the other way around.

"Do you play, Miss Bevue?" Lord Armonde asked, circling a finger toward the pianoforte his sister played with gusto. He sat, extending his arm to invite Elsie to do the same.

"I do not." Elsie hesitated before sitting and wondered if he'd caught her watching Fitz. "I'm not as accomplished as Lady Alice."

Lord Armonde nodded, turning his attention back to the pianoforte. Matthew stood next to Lady Alice, offering another piece for her to play. With Matthew's dark features and Lady Alice's golden hair, they'd make a handsome couple, even if Lady Alice was well above the rank of a mere baron.

"They are quite a pair, aren't they?" Lord Armonde asked flatly.

"Are they? I mean, is there an understanding?" Elsie hated asking a virtual stranger the status of her brother's love, but she'd never been close to Matthew. Or her mother.

"I believe her interest is genuine." Lord Armonde set his cup on the end table. He'd taken only one sip of the amber liquid while Matthew had downed two cups before assisting Lady Alice at the instrument. Fitz had declined the offer of brandy and sat in the farthest corner of the room, his gaze drifting to Elsie's every few minutes.

She blushed, realizing she'd ignored Lord Armonde again. "Do you approve?"

He raised his eyebrows. "Approve?"

"Do you approve of the match?" Elsie tucked her chin. Asking personal questions wasn't ladylike, and if her mother wasn't fawning over the earl, Elsie would have been chastised for her behavior.

"It's not up to me." For a brief moment, the facade slipped and worry showed in the lines surrounding Lord Armonde's eyes and mouth. And then it was gone. He smiled warmly and offered, "Thankfully that is a concern for my parents, not me."

"But you are concerned. Aren't you?" Elsie's opinion of Lord Armonde thawed. Perhaps he wasn't as shallow as Matthew.

"Your brother is a fine fellow." Lord Armonde shifted on the couch next to her. There was a hesitation in his words.

"But is he worthy of your sister?" Elsie touched his forearm. "I think it honorable to worry about her. Or any family member."

Lord Armonde searched her face, the mask slipping once more. He held her gaze and covered her hand on his arm. "Thank you, Elsie."

A memory pulled at the back of her mind, murky from years of neglect. She was young, older than a child but still young. A boy spoke to her, his skin pale. *Thank you, Elsie.*

"Have we met before?" she asked, immediately regretting the question—Lord Armonde was in the middle of speaking.

Lord Armonde quirked an eyebrow. "As in earlier today?"

"No, I meant when we were younger." Elsie shook her head. "The way you said my name ..."

Lord Armonde took her hand in his, squeezing it affectionately. "I should have asked permission to call you Elsie."

"How did you know that was my nickname?"

He hesitated and gave a sheepish look. "I heard you and Fitzburgh speaking."

"Oh." Elsie was deflated. The brief memory had given her warmth and the absence of it gave her a chill. There were many memories tucked in the corners of this home. She'd spent her childhood summers exploring the estate and spying on her brother and his friends.

Releasing her hand, Lord Armonde asked, "May I call you Elsie?"

"Of course." There was no feeling in the permission. So unlike the moment Elsie had shared with Fitz in her father's study. There had been a tingling on her skin and a thrilling sensation in her head. She had been curious, her interest more than piqued. Nothing like Lord Armonde. The exchange with Fitz had felt natural.

"Please, call me Jonathon." There was a twinkle in Lord Armonde's eye as he spoke.

Fitz shot her a questioning look. Elsie straightened, all too aware of how close her head was to Lord Armonde's. "I wouldn't say that too loud."

"Why is that?" Lord Armonde chuckled.

"My mother will see that as an opportunity to pry." Elsie quickly placed a finger to her lips.

Lord Armonde shrugged. "Most mothers do."

Elsie held up both hands. "You've been warned, Lord Armonde."

"Jonathon."

She rolled her eyes. "Fine. You've been warned, Jonathon."

"That I have." Lord Armonde relaxed in the sofa, the facade appearing to be permanently abandoned.

Elsie folded her hands in her lap, unsure of how she felt. Not a day before, she was alone in the house, aside from the few servants, but now she was surrounded by family and their friends. She didn't know which she preferred. She'd thought giving permission for Christian names was something to be treasured. But she'd only been to one dinner party—and that had ended rather abruptly, with a slap to be more precise.

Lady Alice finished with a flourish and curtseyed to the small audience. Matthew beamed at her side, clapping with enthusiasm. The earl scoffed, a fist holding the blanket covering his lap tightly. Lady Bevue patted the earl's shoulder affectionately—much to Elsie's horror. Her mother couldn't accept the earl's courtship, not after all that happened. The betrayal cut, twisting Elsie's stomach. This couldn't be the reason for her family's sudden gathering. *Please, no.*

"You don't approve," Lord Armonde whispered, following her gaze to the earl and Lady Bevue.

Mimicking his earlier comment, Elsie said, "It's not up to me."

"He's of impeccable lineage." He shifted next to her, his fingers playing with the seam of his pant leg.

"If I was in the business of horse breeding, that would matter." Elsie's mouth went dry as she watched her mother reposition the blanket on the earl's lap. "But I'm not."

"Temperament matters in breeding." Lord Armonde clucked to himself. "Although, I confess I am not an expert."

"Temperament matters in people." Elsie's shoulders fell. She had nothing to recommend herself. Her breeding—as Lord Armonde called it—was on the lowest rung of nobility, and her temperament was found wanting, especially to Tyndeth.

"Will Miss Bevue be playing for us?" the earl asked, his voice gravelly.

Elsie straightened her back. "I'm afraid not."

"Perhaps you could play something simple?" Lady Bevue prodded. There was pleading in her words.

"I have not played in years." Not that Elsie had ever played well. Her cheeks warmed as everyone's attention turned to her. She was horribly out of practice in hosting—and conversing. She couldn't sing. Or draw. Her stomach dropped. This was her penance for her troublesome temper—utter humiliation.

"Humility is a virtue," Lord Armonde murmured.

"So is honesty." Elsie wasn't humble. She had pride for days—her refusal to apologize to the earl had earned her family's ire and her seclusion in Wales.

"So what have you been doing?" Tyndeth smacked the arm rest. "You've had two years of repentance and have nothing to show for it. You've not spent the time in retrospect, that is apparent in your prideful manner. What have you done? What has my monthly stipend bought?"

The air left Elsie's lungs. She struggled to breathe. *Monthly stipend.* She'd assumed her family had sent her to Wales, keeping her with minimal staff and away from the *ton's* watchful eye. Her family hadn't provided for her sentence—no, they'd let the one man who hated her most send her away.

"I will have an answer." Tyndeth scowled. "I have tolerated enough from this family. I will have answers or there will be consequences."

The room dimmed. The faces blurred. Elsie's mother, knowing exactly how Tyndeth regarded Elsie, still chose him over her own daughter. The Bevues had gathered because Tyndeth wanted them to, not for a family Christmas. And not to check on Elsie. No one cared for Elsie—not since her father died.

Lady Bevue's eyes flicked from her son to Elsie, then back to Matthew. She swallowed hard—an expression Elsie rarely saw on her mother.

Elsie struggled to breathe, reeling from the earl's revelation. Her mother had allowed the seclusion, hiding her improper daughter from sight. This so-called family gathering was a test, a review on Elsie's supposed repentance progress.

"Elsie," Fitz's low voice carried across the room.

She couldn't look at him. He was a stranger, but Elsie couldn't handle another witness to her embarrassment. Lord Armonde's gaze narrowed, his head turning from Matthew to the earl. Elsie tucked her chin, wishing she'd never known the truth of her stay in Wales. The beautiful countryside now seemed dirty. And cold.

"Elsie, love." Fitz kneeled before her. Lord Armonde cleared his throat, clearly uncomfortable with Fitz's presence. Fitz laid a warm hand on hers. "Look at me."

Lady Bevue gasped and Tyndeth growled. "Do not pander to her, Smith. Do not let a pretty face twist reason. She knows—"

"My mother would have my head if she knew I saw a lady in a distress and did nothing." Fitz squeezed her hand, and Lord Armonde softened his posture.

"You're alright, aren't you, Elsie?" Matthew inserted a hefty chuckle, nothing short of playacting.

Elsie stood, her hand slipping from under Fitz's. She curtseyed to the group, never raising her head. "Forgive me, I am tired and am in need of rest."

"Tired?" Tyndeth balked. "Tired of running your mouth. Tired of being deceitful. Just like your father. Never an apology." His voice shook. Lady Bevue cooed in his ear. He recoiled, saying, "I'll have none of it. This was an agreement, and she has failed."

Without a word, Elsie fled the room, her heart pounding in her chest. Fitz caught her arm just as she reached the stairs.

"Elsie."

She stopped, a hand on the rail. "Please don't. You'll only make things worse."

"Is there anything I can do?" His voice caressed the hurt, but his presence reminded her of a glaring fact—no one else had left the room. Not her mother. Not her brother. Fitz circled her, standing between her and the first step. "Earl or not, he was wrong to say those things."

"Do you believe him?" She still could not meet his gaze.

"Do I think you're deceitful?" Fitz chuckled, his ordinary face turning merry—a peek of sunshine in a dreary room. "I think he's got the wrong Bevue for that one."

"Truly?"

Shrugging, he added, "I've not seen you run your mouth so I can't attest to that." She dipped her head. He lifted her chin with his finger. "But I would love to be a witness. It would be glorious to behold."

He stared at her, his gaze unwavering. A warmth spread in her chest. Her face flushed.

"Thank you, Fitz." At least one person thought her worthy.

His lips quirked to a smile. "Until tomorrow, Elsie."

She nodded and climbed the stairs. She glanced back, and there he stood, waiting for her to ascend to safety. She slipped to her room, exhausted. The day had been filled with dizzying emotions and new gentlemen, from Lord Armonde to Fitz.

Everything felt wrong and tainted by the earl's words; the house, her family, the mare. Elsie paused. Had Tyndeth given her the horse? Only the cruelest of men would give something so exquisite, so personal—only to take it away.

Her maid entered the bedroom. Elsie ignored the pity in the girl's face and allowed herself to be undressed. She wrapped her robe around her and sat by the window, the moon giving more chill than light. Mary left without a word.

The murmurs of tense conversation waxed and waned below but Elsie didn't move. Her door opened but Elsie refused to greet the intruder.

"I believe this conversation is overdue," her mother spoke softly. There was a hint of sadness in her words.

Elsie didn't face her, scared her mother's sudden softness would fade, replaced with harsher tones. Elsie placed a palm on the cold glass of the window, wishing for freedom. And affection.

"The earl is upset—"

"The earl's upset?" Elsie swung around. "What a revelation."

"That's not what—"

"There is no conversation. Overdue or otherwise." Elsie willed herself to stop, to listen, but her mother's defense of Tyndeth instead of Elsie was too much. Fitz had been the only one concerned about her welfare.

"Elsie ..." Her mother held out her hand, only to let it fall to her side. She wrung her hands together. "We need him."

"We do not need him." Elsie hated that her voice caught.

Lady Bevue sat on the edge of Elsie's bed, her shoulders drooping. "All that you see is because of the earl."

"This is my father's house."

"That is paid for by Tyndeth." Lady Bevue straightened her back. "He's saved us from ruin, Elsie."

"He was my ruin."

"Your temper was your ruin, child." Lady Bevue stood and folded her arms. Her hair appeared dark as ink in the candlelit room, sharpening her features. "You did not have to strike him."

"Did you even hear what he said that night?" Elsie had never forgotten. The earl hated her father and thought him weak-willed and careless. She mirrored her mother, standing with folded arms. "Did you hear the lies he told?"

"They were not lies." Lady Bevue stepped closer, her jaw tight. "Your father was not the man you thought he was."

"You believe it?" Elsie felt dizzy, the world shifting around her. Her family had abandoned both Elsie and her father with one swallow of Tyndeth's truth. His price was too steep for Elsie. She would never cave. "You cannot possibly believe it." Her father had been kind and loving. He'd valued Elsie's honesty, even at the expense of her wicked tongue. He would not have left his family destitute. Not the man who'd lovingly cared for her.

Lady Bevue nodded toward the door. "Your brother has shouldered the burden, protecting you from the harsh reality."

"Protecting me?" A fire burned in Elsie's chest, growing hotter with each passing moment. Matthew didn't think of her. He'd only written to admonish her. He'd not bothered to visit her. Not once. "Protecting me or protecting his own precious name?"

"It is one and the same."

"It is not!" Elsie flinched, her shouting echoing in the room—and more than likely down the hall.

Lady Bevue arched an eyebrow. "You will apologize to Tyndeth."

"I will do no such thing."

Lady Bevue walked to the door, asking, "You would let your family starve?"

8

FITZBURGH SMITH

Standing next to his horse in the early morning light, Fitz slipped the end of his reins under his elbow and rubbed his hands together. His hands had never fully recovered from the severe winter in America's New York City. Wales might be farther north than New York but the warm Atlantic winds staved off the harsher temperatures.

Fitz mounted the horse and urged the gelding toward the low mountain separating his lands from the late baron's. Fitz questioned his errand, wondering if Elsie would remember her promise to meet in the stables. Or if she still cared. He'd thought he'd check on her and make sure she loved the horse, but being in Elsie's presence had tugged at his heart. He hadn't planned on spending time with her. Or her family.

He clicked to his horse, the reins back in his hand. Horse and man crested the ridge, just like Elsie had done the day before. It was a sight to behold even now in Fitz's memory. He'd watched her, loving the look on her face as she raced to the top, her mare devouring the ground in graceful, fluid movements. The horse was a beauty—like its mistress—both craving the countryside instead of shelter. Like a fool,

Fitz had thought yesterday was the perfect time to head toward her home.

That was his first mistake.

The second was his botched apology for bringing up the earl at dinner. Fitz shook his head. His apology had somehow made things worse. His penance? Watching the decidedly dull Jonathon Parr sit next to Elsie. Fitz forced himself to stay silent for the rest of the night —his third mistake. He'd sat dumbly as the earl berated Elsie in front her family. He should have taken the earl to task but like a coward, he'd only comforted her *after* Tyndeth had attacked her character.

Fitz guided the horse down the mountain, wishing for inspiration on how to mend things. He had ignored the letter from his American partner, his mind unable to focus on anyone but Elsie. When Tyndeth had announced his generosity, Elsie's wide-eyed look had pierced Fitz. She hadn't known of her family's dire situation. She more than likely didn't know it was her brother's doing.

He neared the Bevue lands. His gelding offered a greeting to the morning fog. An answering neigh came from the direction of the Bevue stables. Fitz smiled, grateful that at least Elsie had the mare, a way to escape the confines of her family. At least, for now. Fitz had wondered how the family had kept both their London and Welsh homes despite their deep debt; the answer lay with the earl. Tyndeth was paying for a wife—and Fitz dearly hoped it was Lady Bevue and not Elsie. Fitz had no right to claim Elsie, but he wanted to at least see her happy.

Fitz dismounted in front of the barn while his gelding offered another greeting. He patted the neck of his horse, whispering, "Shall we see to it, then?"

"See to what?" Elsie's voice came from behind Fitz.

He turned, feeling both sheepish and hopeful. Clad in a navy day dress, she stood with her hands clasped in front of her. She was deucedly beautiful, striking a fetching image he'd never forget.

"You don't have your riding habit on." Hope sank. Fitz wouldn't be riding with her today. He'd watched her ride from afar but wanted to be near, as if her joy could pass to him. He'd envied her obvious contentment as a young girl. Fitz had never felt settled. Not here, not in America. There was a busy ambition inside of him. And yet, when he saw Elsie ride, he yearned to feel what she did. But if Tyndeth had his way, she never would. The earl would go to great lengths to steal her joy.

Elsie glanced down as if realizing the same. "No, I suppose I'm not riding today."

"I am sorry. I truly am—"

She held up her hand, her lips turned down. "Can I ask a favor?"

"Anything." Fitz meant it. She'd captured him a decade before with her wild eyes and clever tongue. Even now, bathed in the morning light, her hair appearing more dark and her skin more white—otherworldly in the most captivating way.

"I was given a mare …" She hugged herself and nibbled her lip. "And we are leaving. I don't want her to be neglected while I'm gone. Will you … will you take care of her for me?"

"Why me?"

She glanced back at the house. "You might be a stranger, but you're the only one I trust."

Questions filled him. Fitz walked a thin line, unsure what Elsie had been told. He'd given her the mare to enjoy, not worry over. "Where are you going?"

She frowned. "London."

"Why?" Elsie didn't belong in England; she was needed here in Wales. Fitz knew it, her late father had known it—any idiot could take one look at her long, dark hair and curious eyes and know she was Welsh through and through.

"I think two homes is a bit much to ask of the earl." Elsie rubbed her upper arms.

Fitz fought the urge to pull her to him—for warmth. Only warmth. Not for affection. Fitz's stomach twisted in protest. She hardly knew him. Nor did she know he'd watched her every summer. She'd think he was mad if Elsie knew. Her temperature should not be his concern.

"When everyone arrived yesterday, I thought I'd have a few weeks. Apparently the earl is tired and wishes to return to London."

"When?" Fitz barked. He cursed under his breath when Elsie flinched.

"Day after tomorrow."

"Then ride with me today." He sighed at his tone. "I meant, *please.*"

Her lips quirked. "Is that a yes, then?"

"Out of the question." Fitz stared at her, wishing to memorize her features. If she went to London, she would be married off just as quickly. He'd not courted her, nor any other woman, but there was an urgency now. He didn't want her shackled to an old man like the earl —or someone as dull as Lord Armonde. "You are not going to London."

Elsie covered her mouth, a smile peaking from her fingers. "Is that so?"

"Yes."

"And where am I going?"

"To Scotland." He held out his hand. "We'll marry. You'll have your freedom and your mare." He felt the color drain from his face; it made the most sense—at least, until he'd said it out loud. Fitz solved problems. That's all this was. His racing pulse said otherwise. His parents had rushed to Scotland's Gretna Green to avoid opinionated parents, neither being of age.

Elsie's eyes widened. "That ... was unexpected."

"Is that a yes?" Fitz's pulse pounded in his head, his chest heavy. He didn't know what he was doing, only that she'd saved him once and this was him repaying his debt. He knew it was more—he wasn't so daft that he couldn't recognize his own lie. He'd wanted Elsie since he was a boy, but he wanted her happiness even more. If that meant marriage to him, so be it.

Elsie blinked and looked away.

"We could reach the border in two, maybe three days' time. It'll be a rough go but—"

She faced him and stepped forward. Placing a hand on his chest, she stood on her tip toes and kissed his cheek. "Thank you for that."

Fitz held his breath, not able to move. The world stopped spinning, his skin ablaze from her soft kiss. She swiped at her cheek with the back of her hand and turned, walking back to the house. It took a moment for Fitz to regain control of his body. He touched his cheek, capturing the kiss to memory.

He tied his horse to the barn's outpost and raced after Elsie. He circled her, placing both hands on her shoulders. "Shall we leave, then?"

Elsie didn't meet his gaze, only shook her head.

Fitz gently lifted her chin with his finger. "Look at me."

Eyes filling with tears, she obeyed.

"I promise I'll not mistreat you." The words fell flat. He'd never proposed to anyone before and hadn't the slightest idea how it was supposed to go. He'd helped his friends write marriage contracts but that was hardly enticing to a woman in tears. She'd kissed him. He blinked. He hadn't the foggiest idea what to do or how to proceed.

Elsie smiled, her cheeks flushed. "You would be civil, I'm sure. But that's not fair to you. Or really, to me."

"Of course it's fair."

She lifted her chin from his finger. "You'd resent me when you finally found *the one*. And my brother would never allow it."

Matthew had all but given her away yesterday in the study. Not that her brother had the slightest hint of Fitz's feelings toward her. If Matthew knew, he'd twist Fitz to do his bidding—erasing Matthew's ridiculous debt. "*The one* is rubbish, and I have it on good authority your brother would be happy to give his consent."

Elsie arched an eyebrow. "Do I want to know how you know that?"

"I would guess no." Fitz felt foolish. The conversation with Matthew in the study felt suddenly crass. They'd discussed Elsie's future like a business transaction.

"Lord Armonde has asked my brother for permission to court me."

"He what? He just met you." Fitz recoiled. The spineless Jonathon Parr was courting Elsie? Parr was more concerned with being proper than being a man. "Your family's destitute."

Elsie's mouth fell open.

"That came out wrong."

Her eyes darkened. "Is that why you proposed? Because you thought I was desperate? Because my family is destitute? I couldn't refuse you because of how dire the situation is?"

"No, no, no." Fitz waved his hands in the air as if he could erase the words. "That's not what I meant."

"By all means, enlighten poor, little, destitute me." She narrowed her eyes and, blast it all, the woman was beautiful, eyes full of fury and a hand on her hip.

Fitz felt the anger rolling off her frame. "The Parr family cares more about titles, bank accounts, and decorum than anything else. I can't imagine his parents would welcome your family. I'm still shocked Jonathon allows your brother to pay Alice any attention."

"Decorum? How can you propose in one breath and then call out my behavior in the next?" Elsie snapped.

"It's not your behavior I'm calling out, Elsie," Fitz roared, towering over her. The dratted woman was twisting his words. "Your brother is a scoundrel and a gambler. How anyone would let that man court his sister is criminal. That is what I meant."

Elsie's face paled, her eyes taking on a faraway look. "Oh."

"Blazes, I shouldn't have yelled." Fitz closed his eyes briefly. He'd said more curses in front Elsie than ever in his life. She had a way of pulling the worst from his tongue.

"I'm going to miss Wales," she whispered, the tension gone from her shoulders.

"Don't go."

She held up her hand. "Please take care of my mare. She means the world to me—it's hard to explain but I—I—just need to know she's going to be taken care of. I don't know when I'll return. Or if I will at all."

Fitz took her hand between his, ignoring her wide-eyed expression. Touching her was natural. Despite their tempers, he felt more at home with her near than anywhere in the world. "I will take care of her on one condition."

"I can't elope with you, Fitz," she said softly. "It isn't right."

"Promise me you won't marry him." Her hand shook in his. He held it tight. "Promise me."

"I can't let my family starve."

"Your family will not starve." Fitz would make sure of it.

"That's not something you can control." Elsie smiled sadly.

"What if I could?" Fitz had lost his mind. The cool, collected man of business was nowhere to be found.

She forced a laugh. "Then I'd run away to Scotland."

"I'd settle for a ride."

9

ELISHEBA BEVUE

Donning her worn riding habit, Elsie ran to the barn, feeling both vulnerable and confident. Fitz had waited for her to change after his impromptu proposal. He promised to take care of her mare, so long as she didn't marry Lord Armonde. She had no intention of marrying—but neither did she want her family's complete ruin. One thing she did know, there was a price for every kindness. Even with Fitz, someone she dared call a friend.

Elsie was grateful they were alone when Fitz had offered his hand. If her mother had heard—Elsie paused, wondering what her mother would actually do. Lord Armonde had asked Matthew for permission to court her yet her mother seemed curious about Fitz at dinner. Her family kept their motives from Elsie, dictating the next move rather than discussing.

"Griffiths?" Elsie passed her horse's empty stall. She had debated on using her modified saddle or the side-saddle ladies were supposed to use. It was deucedly difficult to ride side-saddle and horribly uncomfortable with her hip leading the way. When Elsie complained as a young girl, her mother would admonish her, telling her the pain would help curb her time on horseback. It hadn't.

In the tack area, Griffiths stood smiling, holding Fitz's gray gelding while Fitz finished adjusting Elsie's modified saddle. Elsie's heart warmed. No one—other than Griffiths—had encouraged Elsie's peculiar riding. Her father had looked the other way, pleading ignorance. Fitz was physically helping Elsie ride astride. He was several feet away from her and yet his simple act felt intimate. Most men barely tolerated women riding, fewer encouraged. And no one—no one—openly approved of women riding like a man.

Fitz rubbed the mare's neck, ending with a pat. She turned to nip at him. Fitz chuckled good-naturedly. "Ah, so this is how you've earned your name, *Direidus?*"

"She's both beauty and beast, that one." Griffiths beamed.

"That she is." Fitz took a step back, admiring the mare.

Elsie felt her face flush, feeling oddly exposed at the scrutiny of her animal. *Direidus* neighed and bobbed her head, throwing the attention forward onto Elsie. Fitz straightened, his face softening. Just a day before, Fitz was a stranger. Today, he'd crept into Elsie's heart. Blushing, Elsie focused on her mare, running her fingers through the horse's forelock.

"Look at that." Fitz's voice came soft and low. "She knows who's boss, doesn't she?"

Pride tugged Elsie's lips to a smile. "I don't think she'd ever admit that."

"I think she just did." Fitz nodded at the mare. "She's lowered her head."

Outside the barn, Fitz mounted his gelding and gave a nod to Griffiths holding *Direidus's* reins. "Don't give her a head start."

"Are we racing?"

"The thought never occurred to me." Fitz shot Elsie a mischievous grin.

"I never race," Elsie lied. Every day, she raced her emotions to the mountain—every day, she won.

Fitz's eyes glinted in humor. "Because you are the picture of ladylike riding?"

"Exactly."

Fitz spurred his gelding onward. "Ha!"

Jumping out of the way, Griffiths dropped the reins. *Direidus* sprang into action, pounding the grass with greedy hooves. Elsie leaned forward, allowing the powerful haunches freedom. The wind whispered in her ear, singing promises of better days and lifting her spirits. The grass greeted her, beauty in the jewel-colored countryside. Fitz and his horse grew closer. Elsie relaxed her grip on the reins, giving the mare her head. *Direidus* pounded the ground, closing the gap. She neighed, the sound rippling through her body. Fitz's gelding answered.

Grinning, Fitz turned his head in greeting. "Shall I slow him down?"

Elsie pulled up beside them, both horses slowing to a trot. "Admit it. You're impressed."

His face sobered. "I am always impressed."

She knew she was blushing, her face was on fire. She'd not ridden with anyone, not since her father passed. He had believed horses and quiet countrysides fed the soul. She eyed Fitz, wondering how a stranger inspired such trust from her. They trotted along the ridge, the same route she took as a young girl. A pang of homesickness pierced her. She'd not yet left Wales but felt the loss. Her childhood summers were spent in the lush Welsh landscape. She could spend hours alone, the wind an accommodating chaperone. Her brother's friends would rotate. They'd become either bored or arrogant, always annoyed by her very presence. Her escape was on horseback.

In a silent agreement, the horses perched on the same flat surface Elsie had stopped the day before. It'd only been a day, but her world had unraveled since she'd left this spot. "I'm going to miss this."

"She's going to miss it more," Fitz added softly. He shook his head, rubbing the neck of his horse. "She's a fine horse and needs a fine rider."

"Your gelding should be nervous." She needed to lighten the mood but couldn't look Fitz in the eye. Sharing the ridge with Fitz felt intimate. A piece of her heart would always belong to Wales. "Once you ride *Direidus*, you may never ride yours again."

"Is that so?"

Elsie took a palm to her chest and batted her eyes. "I never lie."

"And never race."

"Never."

Fitz guided his horse around to face Elsie straight on. "Promise me you'll still ride."

"I cannot take her with me."

"That's not what I asked."

Elsie ran a thumb along the seam of her custom saddle, feeling homesick all over again. "I will not have access to a horse in London."

"You could—"

"My mother has never approved of my riding, and if her peers see me with this ..." Elsie motioned to the saddle. "I'll never ride again."

Fitz's brow furrowed. "Society's rules are ridiculous."

Elsie stifled a laugh at the ferocity of his frown. He looked more like a toddler than a grown man. Her heart lifted at the expression. She felt seen. Understood. "I completely agree."

His face softened and he tugged at his collar. "There're rules for everything. What you can say, what you can't. Even if you can work or not. Wealth and title is everything but don't you dare earn the money." Scoffing, he rolled his eyes. "It's enough to make a saint swear."

"You are no saint."

"But I can swear." Fitz laughed, the sound deep and true. His eyes sparkled, turning his ordinary features into remarkable.

"You do have a foul mouth."

He cocked his head to the side, appearing playful like a puppy. "Too many years as a bachelor I suppose."

"Do you like it?" A pang of jealousy hit Elsie. She would never have his freedom. "Being able to come and go as you please."

"I do. I shouldn't admit it, but I do." Fitz sobered and ran a hand through his hair. "I'm driving my mother to an early grave, but I do love the autonomy. I've no family to care for or tie me down. I've only my business and my own needs to keep pushing me forward. I love the thrill of a hunt, the growing of a business. Or solving a problem."

Elsie forced herself to look away, emotions swirling inside her. Jealousy gave way to loneliness—and then grief. Fitz hadn't proposed earlier because he cared. It was just another solution to a problem he happened upon. He didn't want a wife any more than Elsie wanted to leave Wales, but the truth stung all the same.

"You'll marry." Elsie forced the words. "In time, you'll marry."

She watched the wind tease and pull at the emerald grass, her heart sinking. Fitz was a fine catch, despite his apparent lack of marital ambition. His heart was kind and his mind solid. He'd be fair and tender to his wife, whoever that might be.

Fitz shrugged. "Marriage is supposed to be this huge sacrifice, a dedication to one person. I'd be the worst sort of husband. I can't imagine where I'm going to be next month, let alone next year. A woman couldn't depend on me."

"And yet you still proposed."

Fitz flinched, his face sheepish once more. "I did."

"It's all right." Elsie's voice was stronger than her heart. "I'll not hold you to it."

"Why not?" There was a hardness in his eye.

"I know what it's like to be trapped." She twisted the ends of the reins in her hand. Fitz craved freedom. It shone in the faraway look in his eye. In the way he set-down talk of attachment—aside from his cavalier proposal earlier. "I'd never do that to you. Or anyone."

His shoulders relaxed. "It's not a trap if I'm offering."

"Do you listen to your own words?" Elsie rubbed the bridge of her nose. "One minute you're extolling the virtues of your eternal bachelorhood, and the next you're insisting I marry you."

A sheepish grin crept along his face. "It does sound a bit mad."

Fitz dismounted and reached for the mare's reins.

"I don't need help." Elsie used her modified saddle for this very reason. She could jump, or dismount or, thank the heavens, ride for hours.

"I never said you did." And yet he tied both reins from each horse to the nearby tree and held out an arm. "You might not need help, but what if I need to help you?"

"You are absolutely addled."

"Maddeningly so." Fitz smiled, the gesture unabashed and honest.

Elsie felt the same thrill she'd felt at the staircase after Tyndeth had criticized her. She placed her hands on his forearms, her pulse racing. Her hands felt the strength of his arms. Her gaze crept up his arms to his broad chest. He eased her to the ground but didn't release her, his hands at her waist. He pulled her closer, his face inches from hers. She gripped his forearms, drinking in the feeling of safety, the warmth of Fitzburgh Smith.

"Is it so bad?" he whispered, his eyes searching hers.

"What?"

He lifted her chin with his finger. "To be helped."

"To be helped," Elsie repeated, her heart sinking once more. He didn't want her, he only wanted to save her. She sighed. She shouldn't care.

"I've said something wrong." Fitz stepped back, his brow furrowed.

"No. You've been honest." Elsie hugged herself. She was a silly girl. For a moment she'd thought ... she swallowed. "And to be fair, I'm out of practice. I've spoken more in the last day to my family, or really anyone, than I have in years."

"London will be worse." He frowned, concern washing over his features.

"I'm sure I'll manage."

"It's okay if you don't."

Elsie lifted her chin. "I'm perfectly fine, Fitz."

He held out his hands. "I meant it's okay if you dislike London. Heaven knows, I do."

"I've spent more time in London than in Wales. I know what I'm getting into." She winced, hating the sharpness of her words. The tone had soured between them, and she didn't know why.

"The marriage mart is like nothing else." Fitz chuckled, further irritating Elsie. "If you think Lord Armonde is tedious, wait until there's dozens of empty-headed men vying for your time."

"I don't think he's tedious."

He stopped laughing. "You don't?"

"He's kind." Elsie's voice wasn't.

"And his conversation is captivating?" There was an edge to Fitz's question.

"Riveting."

"You're lying." Fitz narrowed his gaze.

Elsie marched to her horse, her neck and face flushing. She had no idea why she was angry or how the beautiful morning had suddenly become an enormous disappointment.

"Elsie, wait," Fitz said softly, his hand on her arm. He slid between Elsie and her horse. And then closer. Her resolve wavered. Tenderly, he whispered, "I'm saying everything wrong."

Her arm burned from his touch. She couldn't move. She couldn't speak.

"Elsie, please." He gently turned her around and wrapped her against his chest. "I'm sorry."

She stiffened. She'd never been comforted like this, not since her father died. Alarms rang in her head. This was wrong. They shouldn't be alone. Her maid didn't ride and Lady Alice didn't have a horse to ride—not that Elsie wanted to be anywhere near them.

Elsie's pulse raced. She shouldn't be in Fitz's arms.

"I'm sorry," he whispered.

Elsie melted, her heart limping toward him. She closed her eyes and breathed in his woodsy scent—her head against his chest. She relaxed in his embrace, wrapping her arms around him. She nestled against him. He kissed her forehead. She stifled a whimper, memorizing the feel of him—and the feeling of safety. Wrong felt right. Fear crept in. Elsie had lost her father and was on the verge of losing Fitz, a stranger who'd quickly gained her confidence. Truth be told, Fitz had settled into the void her father had left. Elsie wasn't ready for the impending heartbreak.

❧ 10 ☙

FITZBURGH SMITH

itz left Elsie's barn and took the long way home, back and around on the lonely road instead of the countryside. Not an hour ago, he'd held Elsie in his arms. Fitz had never pulled a woman to him. The gesture still confused him. But it had felt natural, her body against him. When Elsie had pulled away, he'd felt cold. The chill lay with him still. They'd gone from tender to torment in a matter of seconds. This was why Fitz should stay a bachelor. A woman's mind would always be a mystery. And yet there'd been a pang the moment he'd left her side. Elsie had etched her mark on his heart years ago— only to now claim it fully with one simple embrace.

His house came into view, as did the Parr carriage. Fitz groaned as the horses slowed to a halt beside him in front of the house. Matthew exited with a buoyant step. Jonathon followed suit, his expression unreadable. Elsie's words rang in Fitz's ears. She hadn't thought Jonathon was tedious. The idea bothered Fitz more than it should.

"How can I help you, gentlemen?" Fitz hoped he sounded as forced as he felt. He dismounted with a heavy sigh.

"We've come from town and saw you." Matthew eyed the gelding and with a sly look, murmured, "I see you've learned to ride."

"And you haven't." Fitz clenched the reins in his hands. Instantly, he was transported back in time—he was the helpless boy and Matthew the incessant bully. "There's quite a few things you haven't mastered."

"Oh, come, now." Matthew laughed loudly. The caution in his eyes belied the feigned humor. "We've come to invite you to dinner."

Jonathon's stoic expression slipped, revealing frustration. It came and left so quickly that Fitz thought he'd imagined it. Perhaps Jonathon was not as empty-headed as Fitz thought.

"Aren't you leaving for London?" Fitz asked but kept his focus on Jonathon.

"There's always time for friends." Matthew threw an arm around the marquess. "Why not repeat the success of our last dinner. Besides, you'll even out the numbers."

"I wouldn't use math as your excuse." Fitz couldn't help himself. Matthew's joy was obnoxious—especially when Elsie was hurting.

"That's why I have you around." Matthew wasn't giving up—pricking Fitz's suspicions. "One more dinner, that's all I ask."

Fitz gripped the reins, eying his horse. "I'm not sure that's a good idea."

Jonathon stepped forward, his expression still neutral. "Why?"

Fitz's gaze flicked between the two men. Before his visit to Bevue, Fitz had thought he was a fair man, but now he'd love nothing more than to divulge the Bevue's financial concerns to one and all. "Yesterday was just an errand. Not a social call."

"So call it an errand." Matthew elbowed Jonathon. "Besides, this gentleman is dying to go for a bruising ride."

"I've just come from a ride." Fitz folded his arms. Matthew was up to something, and Fitz would have no part in it. "I think it's time to say whatever it is you're wanting."

Jonathon smirked, earning a nod from Fitz.

"Nothing, nothing." Matthew waved his hand in the air. "Just inviting an old friend to dinner."

A memory prodded Fitz. He smiled mischievously. "Instead of dinner, shall all of us go ride?"

Matthew blanched, recovering quickly. "No, no."

Jonathon must have caught the hesitation, his eyebrow arched. "We couldn't deprive you of the fun."

"The mare is the only horse fit for riding." Matthew scoffed as if this were the obvious excuse. He motioned to the carriage horses. "These are trained for driving, not riding."

"I've plenty of riding horses." Fitz patted the gelding's neck. He'd never felt more smug. "They're exercised regularly."

"There you have it." Jonathon's smirk reappeared. "When should we go?"

"Are you mad?" Matthew rolled his eyes. "There is a very real reason I need the two of you gone. I have a certain lady I would like to monopolize."

Fitz didn't buy it. Something else was going on. Matthew was forever at play.

"Ah, right." Jonathon sobered, the mask slipping back in place. He apparently wasn't keen on speaking about his sister. "That you do."

"You two would have plenty to talk about in my absence." Matthew motioned to both of them. "Elsie, for one."

Fitz stiffened. The delicate camaraderie with Lord Armonde was shattered. "And why would Jonathon and I speak of your sister?"

Matthew gave a sly grin. He'd won this round in their battle of wits. "What else do you have in common?"

Jonathon shrugged. "We both like to ride."

Matthew's confidence slipped. "And so you shall."

"Maybe Lord Armonde likes to bare his knuckles too." Fitz relished the fear sliding across Matthew's face. Although Fitz would have preferred both men to be taken aback.

"I never took you for a pugilist." Jonathon's mask vanished, a warm smile in place.

Matthew shrank, his gaze flitting about.

"Only occasionally." Fitz's gelding pawed at the ground, mirroring what Fitz felt inside.

"What are the occasions?" Jonathon asked.

Fitz paused, gauging Jonathon's interest. "Dishonesty. I've been known to pummel a dratted lickfinger or two."

Jonathon's eyes widened—he slapped his knee and burst into laughter.

"Fitz is one of a kind," Matthew said cautiously. He waited a beat before playfully elbowing Fitz, taking credit for a friendship that didn't exist. "Always has been."

"I'll take my leave, gentlemen." Fitz gave a nod to the stableman waiting a few feet from where they stood. He felt a twinge of guilt, realizing the man must have stood waiting for some time. Fitz hated being waited upon but found himself relying heavily on servants in recent years, his business requiring more travel and attention than Fitz could handle on his own. He'd once criticized the titled as too lazy to help themselves. And here he was, drowning in his own hypocrisy, waiting for someone else to take care of his gelding. Fitz handed over the reins just as Matthew climbed into the carriage, his expression bored.

"You seem to know the Bevue family well." Jonathon's face was smooth, almost glass-like. No hint of emotion.

"Despite what Matthew says, I do not."

Jonathan glanced back at the carriage. "Does Tyndeth speak the truth? Are they destitute?"

Fitz hesitated. Matthew deserved a shredded reputation but Elsie did not. "Tyndeth is cruel."

"But is he honest?"

"Is there a reason you've taken an interest in their dealings?" Fitz swallowed hard, knowing the answer he was about to receive.

Jonathon blinked twice. "Yes."

"Is that reason Elsie?" Fitz nearly choked on the words. She would drown in the Parr family, every word and dress scrutinized. She needed to be cherished not criticized.

Jonathon tossed another glance over his shoulder to the carriage. "I don't trust Matthew."

"So that's a yes, then." Fitz hated the confirmation in Jonathon's eyes. Elsie's words echoed in his mind. She'd not thought him tedious. Fitz swallowed his pride. He cared for her. He always would. "Elsie deserves more than what her family has done."

"She is a mystery."

Fitz chuckled despite himself. "That she is."

"My family won't tolerate scandal." Jonathon sighed and shook his head.

"If your family is allowing Matthew to court your sister, they must tolerate gossip to some degree." Fitz was an idiot. He was encouraging Jonathon to court Elsie. He stifled a groan. Jonathon was the better match, according to the peerage, but did the marquess understand who Elsie was? Did he know she needed freedom?

"They don't know."

Fitz stared at him. "What do you mean, they don't know?"

"My parents don't know about Matthew."

The Parr family knew everything—*every*thing. Jonathon's grandparents gossiped about Fitz's parents' elopement along with the rest of the *ton*. The entire peerage was drunk with juicy tidbits of the forbidden marriage. Fitz's mother could try and rewrite history with a romantic view, but Fitz would always be disgusted with each and every one of them.

Jonathon kicked at a pebble in the road. "My family thinks we are visiting a friend from university."

"They know who the Bevues are."

"And they know who Tyndeth is."

Realization dawned on Fitz. "Tyndeth is playing chaperone."

"My parents think I'm courting Elsie." Jonathon threw his hands into his pockets. "They haven't a clue about Alice and Matthew."

"Are you?" Fitz shouldn't ask. But he did—and he always would.

Jonathon shrugged but his mask was back in place. "According to Matthew, yes."

"Does she know?"

Jonathon met his gaze. "Even if she did, she doesn't prefer me."

Fitz took a step back. "You think *I'm* courting her?"

"Are you?" Jonathon's eyes went cold, emotionless.

"No, why?" Fitz lied.

"You might want to tell her that." Jonathon's stance didn't relax, his eyes boring into Fitz.

"Why would I tell her that?" He wasn't in a position to marry—not yet. Elsie's family would make a marriage to her either impossible or tortuous. Fitz would not be saddled to the Bevues.

Jonathon sighed and rubbed his temples. "You are either the greatest liar or the dumbest man I've ever known."

"I've no regard for title, Jonathon," Fitz snapped. He'd had enough of Jonathon's arrogance. "I'll throttle you just as I did Matthew."

Jonathon's eyebrow arched. "No wonder she's enamored. What's not to love about someone pounding Matthew?"

"She's not enamored, Jonathon." Fitz waved at him. "Go off and sing your sonnets. Woo your lady."

"You'll not stand in my way?"

"Did Matthew put you up to this?" Fitz would have a word with Matthew. Blast it all, Fitz could not stand idly by.

Jonathon shook his head, smirking. "You truly do not like him."

"Give me a reason I should."

"Elsie," Jonathon whispered, his eyes again on the carriage.

Fitz glanced down at his arms. He'd held her just a moment ago. It'd felt natural—easy. But that's not what love was. He would know. His mother spoke of nothing else. Love went both ways, without conditions. Fitz would never accept Matthew or Lady Bevue. Those were glaring conditions that even Elsie couldn't hurdle.

"I do not think I will ever marry, Jonathon," Fitz said softly. His heart sank. Just as holding Elsie felt right, his words felt wrong. "But I will not stop looking after Elsie."

Jonathon's brow furrowed.

Fitz pointed toward the carriage. "I will not stand idle while her brother has influence over her future."

Jonathan straightened his stance. "And if she marries?"

"Depends on the man."

Jonathon narrowed his gaze. They stood there, both staring at the other until Jonathon gave a curt nod. "I hope I am that man."

"Only time will tell." Fitz watched the carriage leave, jealousy and worry jockeying for the lead in his head. He was a bloody liar. He wouldn't stand aside for a coward like Jonathon. Elsie was more than a mystery to be solved. Jonathon didn't know her long enough or well enough to stake his claim. He didn't know Elsie's need for freedom.

His family would try to bridle her, tame her into another pretty face, vacant and shallow. Elsie was a force of emotions. She needed a safe harbor, not a muzzle.

Fitz glanced once more at his hands and wished he'd held Elsie for a moment longer.

❧ 11 ❧

ELISHEBA BEVUE

The housekeeper's arms were filled with sheets while Elsie's heart was overflowing with regret. The sheets would don the furniture until a family member would return, but nothing could cover the grief Elsie had begun to feel. She stood in the center of her father's study, the rest of the house still asleep. Mary had helped Elsie dress before running off to join the rest of the servants shuttering the house.

Elsie ran a finger along the edge of the desk, remembering her mother's words. *You would let your family starve?* Lord Armonde had asked for permission to court her. She smiled at Fitz's sudden proposal outside the barn. And then his embrace. She blushed like she had yesterday, the memory as warm as the moment.

Fitz was kind, a little too rash, but thoughtful in his offering. He was a puzzle if there ever was one, both gentle and rough. His tongue could use some bridling—she winced at her hypocrisy. She might not curse like Fitz, but her tongue had delivered enough blows for one life-time. Fitz's accusations on Matthew's character had echoed in her mind.

She grabbed her father's journals from the bookshelf and then searched the drawers for the estate's ledger. Elsie scanned the room, wondering what else she could take to London. The journals reminded her of tender, fatherly moments. She could still feel her father's hand over hers as he helped her form letters into words. Quickly, Elsie slid the ledger between two of the journals and hugged them to her chest.

Movement from the window caught her eye. A man on horseback, a dappled grey like the gelding Fitz had ridden yesterday, trotted along the mountain ridge. There was a measure of comfort in his impromptu proposal, but the facts remained the same—her family needed to marry well, each and every one of them. Matthew seemed to think he could sweep the beguiled Lady Alice Parr off her feet, while her mother welcomed the earl's attention. Elsie's stomach twisted at the thought of Lord Armonde, Fitz's warning not forgotten. The Parr family might care about titles and wealth but so did Elsie's family. Although, the Bevue's motivation had more to do with avoiding financial ruin than improving their social standing.

Elsie paused in front of the old portrait of her mother, the dark hair flowing wild and unkempt in the likeness. She traced the hair with a finger, wishing she'd known the woman who once cared less about society and more about love. Elsie took one last look around, hugging the journals and ledger even tighter to her chest. Aside from the last few years, the entire ledger was scribbled in her father's handwriting. She would no longer be in his childhood home, but she could keep a piece of him with her.

She ran up the stairs and placed the books in the bottom of her case. Her maid paused in packing but said nothing. With the earl paying the bills of the estate, there was no reason to keep the ledger in the house. At least, that was what comforted Elsie. She'd never stolen before, but she didn't feel the smallest bit guilty. A knock on the door made her start. Maybe she felt a *touch* guilty.

"Miss Bevue?" The door muffled Lady Alice's voice.

Elsie quickly threw a dress on top of the books just as the door opened. "Lady Alice, what can I do for you?"

"My brother and I were wondering if you'd like a quick walk before we depart." Lady Alice leaned up on her toes, her hands clasped together as if the fate of world rested on Elsie's answer.

Elsie stifled the groan, opting to smile instead. "That would be lovely."

"Splendid." Lady Alice beamed. "I'll wait at the foot of the stairs while you grab your bonnet."

Grab your bonnet. Elsie bristled at the comment. Her mother made similar comments growing up. Her maid offered the bonnet, but Elsie just stood there, not wanting to be childish but not wanting to appease Lady Alice. Or anyone else.

A smile curved Mary's lips. "Your mother would love this color."

Elsie rankled at the suggestion. Her maid was hired by her brother —she was serving her family but not Elsie. She folded her arms. "Perhaps my bonnet was already packed?"

Mary's smile fell. "I cannot lose my position, milady."

Elsie took the offered bonnet and tossed it to the case. "*I* packed the bonnet."

"Thank you." Mary relaxed and nodded her head. "It'll be alright, milady."

Elsie could only smile, not trusting her tongue. Part of her didn't want things to be *alright*. She wanted things to crash or burn—she shook the thought as she raced down the stairs. The earl was right. She'd not grown or repented at all. She was still as juvenile as the day she'd slapped his face.

Lord Parr and Lady Alice were smiling in the sitting room, just off from the stairs. The late morning light filled the area, softening Elsie. She would miss this house, but more than anything, she would miss the freedom. The thought tugged at her heart. The earl might have thought he had punished her but it had been a wonderful, unforgettable gift.

"You've forgotten your bonnet, Elsie." Lady Alice looped an arm through Elsie's. "We'll keep to the trees so you won't freckle."

Elsie stiffened, uncomfortable with Lady Alice's use of her nickname. "My bonnets are packed."

Lady Alice squeezed Elsie's hand. "Oh, say no more. You can borrow one of mine." She turned toward Doris whose arms were bursting with furniture sheets. "Excuse me—"

"No, Lady Alice." Elsie shook her head toward Doris, mouthing, *sorry.* "I'm perfectly fine, and to be honest, I love the warmth of the sun on my face."

"You *are* a rare one." Lady Alice arched an eyebrow. "But please, call me Alice."

Elsie extracted her arm from Lady Alice's, pretending to straighten her gloves. "We should probably start our walk. My brother wishes to leave this afternoon."

"Right you are." Lord Armonde's eyes narrowed for a moment, as if trying to read her.

Elsie felt a blush creep up her neck. She'd not blushed like this in years—granted, she'd not been surrounded by gentlemen in years either. Every step, every word, seemed to be a mistake.

The butler opened the door to the outside gardens. As Elsie filed through the door, she felt a wave of nostalgia. She'd not been close to her grandparents, those memories foggy at best, but her father had visited the estate twice a year, his family in tow. There was warmth held in the portraits and in the corners of the estate. She'd had moments of joy here. The London home had once held the same bliss, but recent years had chased them away.

"It's a beautiful morning, is it not?" Lady Alice adjusted her bonnet, her focus on the barn instead of the landscape in front of her.

"I don't know, is it?" Lord Armonde eyed Elsie once more. There was a test in his question, and Elsie felt self-conscious—again.

"Oh, brother, do not tease me." Lady Alice clasped her hands like she'd done outside Elsie's bedroom door. She was apparently limited in both her vocabulary as well as gestures. "Let's start our walk by the barn."

Elsie hesitated. "Is there a specific reason you'd like to start there?"

Lady Alice's delicate mouth formed an O. She covered her mouth, shock and guilt covering her porcelain features. "Why, no!"

Elsie rolled her eyes, wishing the woman would abandon propriety and declare her undying love for Matthew. They could ride off into the sunset singing sonnets. "I'm sure Matthew would be pleased to see you."

The shock melted from Lady Alice's face. "Do you think so?"

"Go ahead, Lady Alice." Elsie waved her onward. "Your brother and

I will walk slow enough to provide both privacy and propriety." She'd hardly finished her sentence before Lady Alice dashed off.

"That was kind of you." Lord Armonde's facade had reappeared.

Elsie shrugged, cautious of this version of the marquess. "I'm not sure if I was kind or selfish."

Lord Armonde gave a curt nod. "A match would benefit you as well."

She misstepped, nearly falling. Lord Armonde offered a hand. She retreated from his reach. "You think I sent her to the barn for my benefit?"

He raised his eyebrows. "That is almost exactly what you said."

Elsie groaned. "I do not care about matches, Lord Armonde."

Lord Armonde straightened. "Then how does my sister going to your brother benefit you?"

She turned her head, pursing her lips. "I really should learn to lie."

"My dear, you are the most confounded woman I know."

Elsie let her head fall back and closed her eyes against the sun. "I am leaving my father's home and am not sure if I will ever see it again. Forgive me for not wanting to be proper." She lowered her chin and opened her eyes. "I didn't want to comment on how beautiful the day is or how fine the weather is. I just wanted to *be*."

She'd not realized she had any of those thoughts until they left her lips. This was how Elsie had always been, not knowing her feelings until she'd spoken. As a girl, her father would tease her. But here, on the edge of her father's childhood gardens, no one laughed.

"You loved your father." Lord Armonde furrowed his brow.

"Is that what makes me *confounded?*"

The facade slipped, and a brief shrug and look of sheepishness washed over him. "I admit, I am often confused by you." He offered his arm. "But I am also intrigued."

Elsie felt a growing dread. She should welcome his attentions but there was a part of her that refused the idea. Perhaps marriage was not meant for ladies like herself. Fitz had mentioned freedom, and she felt the pang of envy once more. Marriage was a cage. Even Fitz acknowledged that. Her throat tightened. Elsie had tried other avenues. She'd sent inquiries to governess positions and been refused. She needed a recommendation. Her family would never approve, let alone recommend her.

Lady Alice and Matthew were walking toward them, their arms looped together. Both their smiles were strained. Elsie picked up her skirts and rushed toward them. "What is it?"

Lady Alice dipped a curtsey to Matthew, murmuring something indiscernible before leaving Matthew's side. He grasped her arm. "Alice."

Lady Alice shook her head and pulled from his reach. Dread grew inside of Elsie as she passed Matthew. He grabbed Elsie, a hand on her forearm. "No, Elsie."

Elsie narrowed her eyes, suspicion circling them. She twisted from Matthew. "What is it?"

"We need to leave for London." An apology filled his eyes, a frown pulling his lips.

Elsie raced toward the barn, ignoring her brother's pleas to stop. She threw open the side door of the barn and saw the pale face of her stableman, Griffiths, his hands covered in blood. Elsie ran to his side and screamed—the stall's door was open, revealing her mare on the floor. Blood stained the straw, the door, and both front legs of the horse.

"I can't find the source." There was panic in Griffiths's words.

Matthew's voice came from behind Elsie. "He needs to be put down."

She spun around to her brother, ignoring his mistake of calling her mare a *he*. "Get Fitz."

Matthew held out his hand. "He's not a veterinarian."

"He'll know what to do." She pushed Matthew toward the door.

"You don't know that." Her brother balked. "He didn't even know who brought the animal."

"For once in your life, Matthew, do what is right and get him. *Now*." She spun around to Griffiths. "Did you give her chloral hydrate?"

He nodded. "Just."

Relief flooded Elsie. Her mare was on the floor because of the sedative, not from lack of blood. She patted the legs, the mare flinching with each touch.

"Be careful, Elsie," he warned, his voice catching. "She battled me hard. It'll take some time for her to settle."

"We don't have time." She continued her search. Her hands became too bloody to tell what was old and what was fresh. She started at the knee, working down along the cannon bone, using the skirt of her dress as a rag. She went the entire length of the mare's left front, inch by inch.

"She needs medicine." Griffiths adjusted his grip on the lead rope and pulled the bottle from his coat jacket.

"No, not yet." Elsie needed Fitz. He knew horses. That was apparent from the way he handled his gelding the day before. His seat and manner was from practiced ease. *Please come, Fitz. Please.*

❧ 12 ❧

FITZBURGH SMITH

T he early morning fog had lifted, revealing the green view of Fitz's country estate. There was a growing list of things for him to attend to, all of which should have propelled him away from the Bevue estate, not toward it. Fitz had no idea why he'd asked for his carriage to be brought to the Bevue estate. Ever since Fitz saw Elsie in her father's study, his brain had become addled. And then he'd hugged her. Like a fool, he was setting himself up nicely to be humiliated—or worse, to hurt Elsie.

Both the Bevue and Parr families were leaving for London soon. Fitz hated the idea, but disliking their decision wasn't reason enough to call on them. He certainly couldn't collect on any debts. He'd specifically given Matthew until Lady Day. He could visit Elsie's mare, but that would ignite a round of rumors he'd rather not start. Her mother had witnessed enough to fuel her suspicions. The fact remained, an unmarried man gifting a horse to an unmarried woman would signify a courtship—or more likely, an engagement. He would not force Elsie into any agreement. Besides, Fitz had promised to take the horse *after* Elsie had left. Not before.

Taking his head in his hands, he groaned. The butler opened the door. Fitz felt the scrutiny but walked inside, still unsure of what to do or say. The thoughts swirled about in his head. He was Mr. Fitzburgh Smith, a man who'd turned his father's tidy investments into a healthy collection of financial institutions, here and abroad.

The butler ushered him in the sitting room.

"You're here?" Matthew burst through the adjacent doors, eyes wide. "She needs you."

Without a word, Fitz followed Matthew, his pulse racing. *She needs you.* Matthew ran toward the barn. Tension filled the air. Elsie must have fallen. The mare was spirited; that was one of the reasons Fitz had chosen the animal. Guilt tugged at him.

Just outside the barn, Fitz asked, "What happened?"

"The horse is bleeding." Matthew clenched his jaw.

Fitz grabbed his elbow. "What aren't you telling me?"

"See for yourself." Matthew pushed open the door.

Fitz shouldered through, rushing toward the sound of Elsie's voice. He stood at the door of the stall—blood. Everywhere. Blood covered the straw, the floor—all Fitz could see was the color red.

Elsie's back faced him, her hands stained crimson. Using his weight, the stableman lay across the mare. His hand clenched the lead rope, holding down the horse in case it kicked.

Fitz stared; Elsie's voice pierced him, refocusing him. He hadn't heard the words—only her voice. Elsie whimpered, her hands frantically combing the horse's leg.

Fitz wrapped his arms around her, whispering in her ear. "Easy, girl." He gently pulled her to a stand. "It's my turn to try."

She didn't fight him, only nodded and stepped aside. Fitz replaced her on the floor, his finger tracing the main artery down the left leg. Nothing. There was little to no blood on the body and chest. The sheer volume of blood meant either the main leg artery or the hoof vein was cut. He palpated the leg once more before checking for lacerations in the hoof. His hand caught on something hard. Using his shirt, he wiped the inner hoof. The horse flinched. The sedative wasn't strong enough. Fitz leaned over—a hard metal nail was stuck in the middle, blood sliding along the surface.

"Where's the farrier clippers?" Fitz pressed the outer hoof. The horse pawed at the air. The pain must be radiating from the nail piercing the inner hoof.

"I'll get them." Elsie's voice was weak.

There was rustling behind Fitz. He turned and called after her, "I need copper sulfate and a dressing."

The stableman slid more of the sedative down the mare's mouth. He gave a quick shake of his head to Fitz—the stableman didn't want Elsie to know he'd given more medicine. Fitz didn't blame him. The increased sedation would be a danger at this point. The horse had lost a lot of blood, and being unable to use a leg put pressure on the rest of the body. It'd be a rough go until she healed—*if* she healed.

Elsie handed the heavy clippers to Fitz. It'd been years since Fitz had wielded the tools. He pulled the nail from the hoof and then flipped the clippers, severing the damaged part of the hoof. With hope, the hoof would regrow. The horse wouldn't be able to eat or drink for hours—if she got to her feet at all.

Deftly, Fitz packaged the copper sulfate against the bleeding hoof and dressed the wound. A metallic burn tickled his nose, the smell of copper sulfate cauterizing the horse's vein.

The stableman gave a solemn nod. He released the lead rope and went about clearing the hay and water from the stall. Other than wiping his forehead and eyes, the man appeared unaffected by the emergency.

"Thank you." Elsie sank down, sliding her back against the stall door. Her dress and arms were stained with blood. Her eyes glassed over. She kept her profile to Fitz and blinked back tears. She wiped an errant tear with the back of her hand, smearing dirt along her cheek.

"There's nothing more that can be done." Fitz leaned over and helped her to stand. She nodded, hair from her plait coming loose. He wrapped an arm around her waist and pulled her close. "And now we wait."

Elsie's gaze was fixed on her horse and the stableman. She stepped from Fitz. "Griffiths needs help."

"No, Elsie." Her stableman shook his head. "Go inside and wash up."

"No." Her face hardened.

"She'll be alright." Griffiths pushed and pulled the horse's body, rocking it back and forth—hopefully it would help the circulation while the horse slept off sedation. "Won't you, *Direidus?*"

The name pulled a grin from Elsie's lips. "*Direidus.*"

"How long was she down?" Fitz asked.

Griffiths didn't meet his eye. "I'm not sure."

"Were you here when she was found?" Elsie's voice caught.

The horse was sedated, but her left legs flexed while her bottom right legs appeared frozen. The longer the horse was down, the greater chance of never getting up. The weight of its body would cut off circulation, killing organs and limbs.

Griffiths moved to the head and pulled back the lips of the horse, revealing white gums—heavy blood loss. "Your brother was."

Elsie spun around, shouldering past Fitz, and marched to the barn. Fitz wasn't sure which female needed him more, horse or human.

"You better go with her," Griffiths said with a frown. "Or this won't be the only blood shed."

Fitz wiped his hands on a nearby rag and ran after Elsie. Her arms were rigid at her sides while she marched to the house. Fitz circled her. Placing a hand on her shoulder, he said, "Take a deep breath."

"I'm fine, Fitz." Her shaky voice said otherwise. "I just want to know when he saw her."

"You want to know if he did something." When she looked away, he squeezed her shoulder. "Matthew wouldn't injure her."

"You don't know that."

"Matthew's an opportunist and that mare was valuable. He wanted to sell her, not hurt her."

Elsie pushed his hand off her shoulder. "How do you know that?"

"He assumed I'd sent her." Fitz couldn't admit he'd bought the mare. He'd already been a fool and proposed on a whim. She'd think him mad if he told her anything more. "He said either way he'd have to sell her. That he couldn't afford to keep her."

"He was going to sell her?" She took two steps back, her eyes welling with tears. "But she looks so much like ..." She swallowed the rest. "How could he sell her? It was a gift to me. Shouldn't that be my choice?"

"He didn't harm her, Elsie." Fitz would guide her back to the silver lining. Matthew was arrogant and selfish, but he wasn't foolish enough to injure an asset, not with his debts multiplying.

"Then what was he doing in the barn?" She held up her hand to interrupt Fitz despite his silence. "He hates the barn. He won't admit it but horses scare him. He was thrown too many times. He thinks you're supposed to dominate them, not work *with* them. You can't—you can't—" Her lip trembled.

Fitz cautiously stepped closer. "Hey, it's going to be fine."

"Would you stop?" She retreated. "I'm not a child."

"I'm aware," he said wryly, feeling every ounce of the tension rolling between them. Gaining Elsie's trust was proving harder than her beloved horse.

"Stop acting like you know me." She hugged herself. "You don't know me. Matthew doesn't know me. No one knows me." Her hands shook. The last of her plait came loose, her hair spilling over her shoulders. "I don't want to go to London. I don't want to leave Wales. I don't want to get married. I don't want any of this."

"Is that so?" Lady Bevue's voice pierced the air.

Elsie's shoulders slumped, defeat in her eyes. Blood stained her skirt and arms. Her disheveled hair framed her delicate face. She was the very opposite of ladylike beauty, according to the *ton*. She'd never looked more captivating to Fitz.

Lady Bevue closed the gap, walking so gracefully she seemed to glide. Her eyes scanned her daughter, from the bloodied hem to her disheveled hair. "We are packing, Elsie. Despite you not wanting to leave, we have no choice."

"I can't." Elsie set her jaw.

"You can't or you won't?" Lady Bevue brushed a strand of hair off Elsie's cheek—her daughter recoiled. "Child, you will collect your wits and prepare to leave."

"I will not." Elsie's expression hardened, her lips forming a taut frown. "*Diedrus* looked just like Father's horse."

"Your father is gone and so is his horse." Lady Bevue held up a finger and paused. She took a sharp breath and said, "The earl will not feed your horse if you throw a tantrum. Do you not realize her survival rests on your temperament?" Lady Bevue eyed Fitz, clearly uncomfortable with his presence. When Fitz didn't move, she returned her focus to Elsie. "Need I remind you that your family, if you care for us at all, must do what is necessary?"

"I would not leave your side if you were injured," Elsie answered.

The admission softened Lady Bevue. "I know this is hard." She reached for Elsie's hand. "This isn't the life I would have chosen for us. Fate dealt us a hard hand, but we can make the best of it."

Elsie nodded once.

"Do not keep the earl waiting." Lady Bevue sent a searching look to Fitz, but he still refused to leave Elsie alone. After another beat, she left.

"As soon as she can walk, I'll move her to my stables." Fitz inched closer, wishing they were back on the ridge, away from prying eyes. He wanted to hold her once more, to comfort her.

"*If* she can walk. That hoof was pierced clean through." Elsie groaned. "You'll keep me posted?"

"Elsie?" He took another step. He was but a foot from her. She gave a cautious look. "You don't have to go to London."

A smirk appeared; it was infinitely better than the tears a moment before. Her emotions had turned with dizzying speed. Elsie had been in the throes of grief, then anger, and finally, resolute. "I'm not sure Scotland is the answer."

"Maybe not." He reached for her hand and held it to his lips. A curious warmth filled his chest. He pushed up her sleeves, the edges lined with straw and blood. "But what if I'm the answer?"

She inhaled sharply, giving him courage. Her lips parted to an O. He kissed her hand, holding it a moment before releasing. Never had Fitz tenderly held a woman's hand, nor had he ever wanted to. The temptation to pull her against him grew with each second.

Everything about Elsie's situation told him to run—but everything about who she was told him to stay. Jonathon was right. Fitz was a bloody liar. Kissing Elsie's hand was an attempt to court her, to make a claim he shouldn't be making.

She waved her hand toward the barn. "Keep me posted. I want to know everything. Even if she doesn't make it."

"Stay."

A smile pulled at Elsie's lips. "Even if I was tempted, you know I can't."

"Are you tempted?" Fitz cursed, hating how lovesick he sounded. He wasn't a romantic, and the notion made him ill. He just wanted to know Elsie would be taken care of—who better to take that responsibility than him? Stuck inside with a sickly constitution, Fitz had spent his summers watching her through the windows of his home. She'd run with abandon, her hand raking the tips of overgrown grass. He'd give anything to see her free once more.

She pulled her hand from him, blushing fiercely. "I am not a girl wishing for her knight in shining armor, Fitz."

"That didn't answer the question." He swallowed the rising doubt. He was well beneath her rank. "I offer you freedom."

"I've had two years of freedom." Elsie rocked on her heels and cast a wistful glance to the house. "I don't suppose it did me any good, did it? The result appears to be the same."

"But you'd be married. That's an entirely different result."

Elsie grinned, a mischievous glint in her eye. "I am not your problem to be solved."

"I didn't say you were a problem." His tone was rough. Fitz could negotiate like champ, but speaking to women—this particular woman —left him feeling wholly inadequate.

"I'm not a stray dog for you to take in." She cocked her head to the side, her smile growing. "Although, I've been known to bite."

ELISHEBA BEVUE

Under the cover of dark clouds, the Bevue family arrived at the inn in the late afternoon. Elsie descended the carriage, not stopping to make sure her mother or the earl would be helped. They'd traveled all day and she'd felt every inch of it. Elsie circled the modest building twice before entering, praying the dratted earl had already been taken to his room. She received her key and climbed the creaky staircase, her head pounding with each step. Her brother had been privileged to spend the day in the Parr's carriage while Elsie had been trapped in the earl's. The old man had vacillated between interrogating Elsie and ignoring her all together. Thankfully, he'd fallen into a snoring slumber the last hour of their trek. Elsie had never been more grateful to see an inn. She wished for nothing more than a quiet, dark room for the night.

"Elsie?" Lady Alice asked, scurrying up the stairs.

Elsie flinched. She hated that Lady Alice used the nickname without consent, her high-pitched voice adding to Elsie's already painful headache.

"You're frightfully pale." Lady Alice gasped. "Shall I send for some laudanum?"

"No." Elsie's stomach twisted at the memory of her last encounter. One dose had sent her reeling for days. "I just need to retire."

"Oh, traveling is so hard for our delicate constitutions."

Elsie held her breath. She would not have a delicate constitution. She was *not* fragile. And she refused to be a woman who complained. She straightened her back and forced a smile. "Thank you for your concern, but I'm feeling much better."

"Wonderful!" Lady Alice clasped her hands together—much to Elsie's annoyance. "We shall play a hand of cards before dinner. I'll go tell your brother." She scurried off before Elsie could decline the assumed invitation.

Elsie's annoyance with Lady Alice had grown after she and Matthew found the mare bleeding. The injury wasn't Lady Alice's fault, but there were quite a few questions left unanswered. Adding to the hurt was how her family—and now Lady Alice—would switch topics at any mention of the horse.

Begrudgingly, Elsie made it to the top of the inn's staircase before realizing she didn't remember her room number. She glanced at the key but the marking had faded. She leaned against the railing. The wooden floor beneath her feet appeared suddenly cozy. Her body was tired from the constant jarring of the carriage; her mind exhausted from the cyclical battle with Tyndeth.

She wanted quiet.

She wanted Wales.

The door ahead of her cracked open, revealing a haggard Lord Armonde. "You look about as good as I feel."

"You are an exceptional flirt," Elsie deadpanned.

He smiled wryly and tipped his head. "We're both worse for wear." He joined her against the railing, his finger lazily pointing downstairs. "How'd you escape my sister?"

"She thinks we're going to play cards before dinner."

"She thinks wrong." Lord Armonde braced his arms against the railing and shook his head. "I am the worst of brothers, but I cannot abide one more minute of them prattling on."

Elsie bit back a smile. "I had no idea my brother could prattle."

"A genuine Shakespeare." Lord Armonde clutched his chest with dramatic flair. "I'm not sure who is more prolific with their words."

The tension from her headache eased. "At least you weren't subject to the Earl of Tantrums."

"There's another man who has a way with words," the marquess said cautiously. He narrowed his gaze, searching her face. "You've struck his fancy, in a way."

The tension came back with a flourish. Elsie rubbed her temples. "I suppose I deserve it."

Lord Armonde pulled her hand from her face. "Why do you say that?"

Elsie ignored the warmth from his touch—and the wish that the marquess was Fitz. She could still feel his kiss on her hand and the feeling of safety in his arms. "You cannot strike an earl without some sort of punishment."

His eyes widened. "That was *you?*"

Elsie pulled her hand from his. "He was saying horrible things about my father. It was the middle of a dinner party, and he wouldn't stop. He kept pointing his absurd cane at me—he kept getting closer and then used his finger to point at me. And then ..."

"You're the girl who punched him?" A strange expression crossed Lord Armonde's features, not happy or sad.

"I didn't punch him." Not that a slap was any better. "But he howled like a stuck pig."

"I do not think forgiveness is something he gives." Lord Armonde gave a nervous laugh. "That's ... that's interesting."

Elsie cradled her head in her hands. "I know. I shouldn't have done it. I was just, I don't know. I was angry. My father hadn't been gone long."

Her father had dashed off to help in the Crimean War, forgetting he was no longer the spare son. Elsie couldn't fault the late baron. He'd inherited the title, land, and the responsibility. His soldier days were supposed to be a blink in his history, not the final episode of his life. Lady Bevue made no secret of her feelings of abandonment; she hadn't married the soldier. She'd only known the baron.

"I do not think you're alone." Lord Armonde shifted his weight and sighed. "I can't think of a single person who likes him. Most of us can barely stand the earl."

"Why is he tolerated?" *And not me?*

Lord Armonde shrugged. "He's an earl."

"And?"

He gave an awkward chuckle. "And he's richer than God."

"Again, why is he tolerated?" Elsie placed a hand on her hip. "Midas turned everything to gold, and look what happened there."

"Midas isn't real, Elsie." Lord Armonde drew a circle in the air. "All of this is real. The earl. You. Me. We can read stories. We can attend the theatre. But eventually we come up for air and realize we do not have happy endings. That life will never be fair."

Elsie balked. "Then why try?"

"I didn't say we shouldn't try." He turned his gaze toward the stairs, the light dimming in his eyes. "I just don't think we should lie to ourselves."

"Do you truly believe that?" Elsie touched his shoulder. Defeat covered his features. Until her father died, she'd assumed life *would* be happy and that love not only existed but that it was commonplace. She'd never been particularly close with her mother or brother, but she'd known paternal love and watched her parents exchange secret smiles.

"It's hard not to." Lord Armonde motioned to the stairs. "My sister will be starting her seventh season."

"Seventh?" Elsie had been gone for at least two seasons, and before then she'd not paid attention to the other girls. Her first dinner party had landed her two-years seclusion in Wales.

"She's never been the darling, but she's not hideous." He shook his head, sighing. "She's not had much success. Only twice has a gentleman approached my parents."

"For her hand?"

"No. Permission to court her." He patted the railing. "Her desperation is showing."

"Is that what you meant the other night?" Elsie gripped her key in her hand. "That my brother's courtship is up to your parents, not you?"

Lord Armonde frowned. "I believe my parents would be more accepting of you, not him."

"Because of my dowry?" Elsie wondered how her father had secured the dowry, and who was telling the truth regarding her family's situation. She didn't know the particulars of the law regarding finance. She assumed she'd have access soon enough.

"You do not have a reputation."

Elsie waited for the tease. This was a joke. If anyone in her family had a reputation it was most certainly her. "Sir, you jest."

He arched an eyebrow. "I do not."

"Did you not hear me?" She motioned behind her as if the conversation existed there. "I just told you I slapped the earl."

Lord Armonde grinned like a fool. "You never attended a ball. As far as the *ton* is concerned, you never came out. You're as good as a debutante."

"You jest." Dumbly, Elsie repeated herself.

Lord Armonde folded his arms across his chest, looking very pleased with himself. "You are properly shocked."

"But Matthew said—"

"I would believe only half of what your brother says." He waved a hand in the air. "Beg your pardon, Elsie. I shouldn't have said that."

"Fitz has said the same thing." She glanced at her hand, remembering the touch of him. "He called him a scoundrel and a gambler."

Lord Armonde hesitated. "Elsie, answer me honestly."

She met his gaze.

He leaned in and whispered, "Is there an understanding between you and Fitzburgh?"

"He's agreed to take care of my horse." Elsie blushed fiercely. She rubbed her upper arms, remembering their embrace.

"Nothing else?"

"He proposed, in his own way." She didn't know if it was the memory of Fitz or the embarrassment that caused her pulse to race.

"He proposed." Lord Armonde snapped to a soldier's stance, his back straight as a rod.

"It was a hasty proposal. He didn't mean it." Elsie rushed the words. Her heart beat wildly. "He was solving a problem. I turned down the offer."

"You turned him down," Lord Armonde echoed, his brow furrowed.

Her head pounded. Elsie gripped the key and made a curtsey. "Excuse me, Lord Armonde. I need to rest."

His hand shot out, grabbing her forearm. "Did he give a reason?"

"He believed he was offering freedom." Elsie kept her gaze on the floor, her embarrassment in full swing.

"And what was your reasoning in declining?"

"I didn't want him to resent me." She felt the weight of Lord Armonde's scrutiny. The truth was neither Fitz nor Elsie wanted to be caged. She risked a glance but saw the smooth, blank expression of Lord Armonde's facade. "He doesn't love me. One day he'll find love. And when he does, it would be tragic if he'd gone ahead and married me. His proposal was an act of goodwill, not a romantic notion. I don't want to be someone's charity case."

The mask slipped, revealing warmth in Lord Armonde's eyes. He released her hand and said softly, "Elsie, you are the furthest thing from a charity case."

𝔰𝔢 14 𝔰𝔢

FITZBURGH SMITH

Fitz slammed the door to his study in the rented townhome. He hated London and the wicked people in it. He'd come only to appraise a bank needing a buyer—a lie he sold himself. The real reason was the woman living four streets over. Elsie was waiting on the note in his pocket, the one he should have sent weeks ago but hadn't. He couldn't bring himself to tell her about the mare in a letter. She deserved to be told in person.

Instead of doing either, Fitz had barked and pouted like a spoiled toddler, growing more irritable at his own behavior with each passing day. His apologies to his butler and other servants were becoming so frequent they sounded rehearsed.

It didn't help that twice Fitz had witnessed Elsie in the Parr's open phaeton, sitting next to Jonathon for all the *ton* to see at Hyde Park. An announcement would follow soon—that was how their circle of life worked. If Fitz were honest, he'd acknowledge the bitterness. Jonathon wasn't worthy. But was Fitz? He cursed the day he spoke to her in the study. He should have stayed an arm's length away. The few moments Fitz had spent with Elsie had changed him, making him question his future.

The world was changing. The amount of titled gentlemen and

financial institutions begging for help was evidence enough. But beauty and titles still sparkled nicer than a mere mister, no matter the wealth. Fitz had felt it with every business meeting. There was a growing resentment for people like him, those without pedigree owning more land than the nobles. Even in America there was a shift. Families flush with wealth were dangling their daughters to English nobility in hopes of snagging the elusive prestige of a title. The dowries offered were enough to fill even the most anemic of coffers.

Fitz paced in front of the study's window, the dank street below stuffed with hansom cabs and pedestrians. New York City was just as crammed but didn't reek of horse dung and urine like London.

In America, he was sought after, businessmen clamoring to join Fitz in another investment. Sadly, not every venture was a success. While Fitz would be relatively unscathed from a sour investment, many of his fellow peers would lose their homes and businesses, their families forever affected. Fitz had watched with a guilty conscience, determined to never have a family affected by his poor choices. Even with the rising tension in America, Fitz admired the country's work ethic. They valued ingenuity more than pedigree, but Fitz had returned to his native land for the same reason he'd come to London— for Elsie.

He shook the thought. He'd returned for business, that was the reason. He folded his arms across his chest. The note crinkled in his jacket pocket, reminding him once more of the dark haired beauty.

A knock on the door was followed by his butler's low voice, "You've a guest, Mr. Smith."

Fitz sighed before turning around. He gave a nod to his servant and settled into the desk, not bothering to ask who'd come to call.

"I wouldn't believe it had I not seen with my own eyes." Matthew Bevue burst into the room, his smile wide. "Fitzburgh Smith in London. Did the queen have to summon you personally? Is that the only way to get you here?"

Fitz cursed under his breath. He should have asked the butler who'd come before allowing them in. This wasn't the Bevue he needed to see. He waved to the chair opposite the desk. "Sit."

Matthew tucked his coattails and sat with a flourish. "My good man, you must be doing well to live this close to Regent's park."

"You are not that far from here, Matthew."

The fool grinned. "So, you know where she lives, do you?"

"I know the address of all your assets," Fitz snapped. A brief image of the horrible earl flashed in his mind. Fitz rubbed the bridge of his nose, the guilt washing over him. Tyndeth might be the Earl of Tantrums, but Fitz was quickly becoming one as well.

"She is quite an asset." Matthew hadn't taken the hint. "But that's not why I've shadowed your door."

"Do tell," Fitz said with no small amount of sarcasm. He knew this dance and waited for the begging—and arrogance—to begin.

"I've a proposition for you." Matthew leaned forward, his golden hair falling forward. In that moment, he looked as naive as his late father. Both held a puppy-like quality with light brown eyes and lips that quirked toward a smile, even when frowning. "You're familiar with Hudson and Brassey."

"They are contractors for the railroad, Matthew. I do believe anyone who's read the papers knows who they are." Fitz leaned back in the chair and stared at the ceiling of his rented townhome. He should have sent the dratted letter. Anything was better than sitting in the study with this bootlicker.

"Right." Matthew stood, interrupting Fitz's view. "But there's a new railroad line being laid. And I don't mean the King's Cross."

"I'm aware." Fortunes had been made with the railroad. Fitz's father had invested small, but his tidy profit had given Fitz ample room to expand. "There are district lines going along the east coast up to Scotland."

This wasn't common knowledge, but it was old news to the investing side. If Fitz wasn't among the first few to invest, it wasn't profitable enough to care.

"But have you heard of underground travel?" Matthew whispered, his eyes dancing with excitement.

"Yes." An eager inventor had approached Fitz with a possible underground tube for New York City. That was before tensions had risen in the states. Fitz had quickly absolved himself of American assets, including firearms, and began searching elsewhere for business opportunities.

"You have not." Matthew's face drained. He slumped back to his chair. "How can *you* hear of something that's not even been invented yet?"

"You think you're the first to think of it?" Fitz scoffed and shook his head. "Are you saying that you—out of thin air—invented an underground rail line?"

This was arrogance at its finest. Matthew couldn't understand basic arithmetic—his dire circumstances underlined this fact—yet, now Matthew had suddenly become an engineer of the first order.

"I didn't say *I* invented it. Only that I know who did." Matthew sulked, his head in his hands. "We could have invested in it together."

"You have nothing to invest." The conversation had turned from odd to absurd.

Matthew's head perked up, a slow grin creeping across his face. "I have a sister."

"She's a person, not an asset."

He ran a hand through his hair, his brow furrowing. "She's a liability."

Fitz smirked. If Elsie was a liability, that meant she'd not lost her spirit. "To you or to the earl?"

"To everyone."

"Why did you come, Matthew?" Fitz tapped his fingers on his desk. Suspicion raised its ugly head. Matthew would use Fitz and Elsie to his advantage without a thought to the consequences. Fitz would never align himself with the baron. He wished there was a way to separate Elsie from her brother. His spirit sank. A man wishing to deprive a lady of her family was no gentleman.

"To partner in an investment." Matthew balked, as if the reason was obvious.

Groaning, Fitz stood and gestured to the door. "You need a viable investment. And money. Both of which you do not have."

"You're not better than me, Fitz," Matthew said quietly.

"I've said nothing of the sort." Guilt tugged at Fitz's chest. His parents were humble and hard working. They valued each other above all else. Fitz had thought romantic love was a foolish thing and that the *ton* were drunk with foolishness. But now, with his behavior mimicking the earl's, he wondered who was the fool.

"You say a lot. Even when you're not speaking."

"Matthew—"

"I need your help." Matthew's shoulders were hunched. He waited a moment before adding, "The Parr family has not yet allowed me to court their daughter."

"I cannot—"

"I've not yet given up." Matthew held up a hand. "But I do need an alternative."

Fitz opened the door, dismissing the baron. He would have no part in Matthew's schemes. The charming young man from university had come to Fitz for a reason—none of Matthew's peers would help him. Whatever plan he'd hatched was either scandalous or illegal. Fitz was a mere landed gentleman and did not have the protection of the noble class.

Matthew took two slow steps to the door. "I just need an introduction, Fitz."

"Much is implied with a simple introduction." Fitz could not recommend Matthew's character, especially to other investors.

"I know." Matthew faced him, his eyes soft, almost apologetic. "You know my family's situation. I just need an introduction at the next event."

"And what should I say when those investors ask about your debts?"

"Investors?" Matthew laughed nervously. He rocked on his heels. "I was hoping you could introduce me to some of the Americans."

"You want to meet the Americans?" The realization came slowly. "You want to marry a wealthy daughter."

Matthew had enough sense to appear sheepish. "It's an open secret what they want."

"A title, Matthew." Fitz rubbed his temples. In America, Fitz held court because of his financial success, but here in England, he was wealthy enough for prominence but not high born enough for marriage. Matthew was the opposite. "You're a baron. These families are richer than most dukes. That's the rank they're willing to negotiate for. They might settle for a viscount. You're a baron on the brink of bankruptcy."

"I am aware of my situation." Matthew glanced around before whispering, "But most of the Americans care about titles, not money."

"And the Parr family?" Fitz wondered if Matthew truly cared about his family or if this was an elaborate revenge plot. Matthew seducing an American heiress would hurt the Parr family if Lady Alice remained unmarried. "Your pursuit was rather public. I'm not sure if that was bravery or manipulative, pursuing a lady without the blessing of the family."

"Says the man who proposed to my sister in secret." Matthew narrowed his gaze.

"We are done here."

"You can pretend to me all you want, but I know you care for her." Matthew straightened his stance. "Is that why you visited that morning? Did you threaten me with collecting debts to make sure she was desperate enough to accept your hand?"

"Get out." Fitz turned from Matthew. Elsie had told her brother. Fitz shouldn't be surprised, they were siblings, but he'd thought that was a secret, a link only he and Elsie would know. Anger grew within him, not at Elsie but rather her idiotic brother.

"I can help, Fitz."

Fitz shook his head, not trusting his tongue.

"She's not smart enough to lie." Matthew forced a laugh. "Jonathon asked her if there was an understanding between the two of you. She said you proposed but that she turned you down. I can help you, Fitz. I can get her to see reason."

Jonathon asked her. Elsie hadn't volunteered the information. Relief filled him and then shame. Fitz had no claim on Elsie—there was no understanding, only unrequited feelings. He had an old memory of a brave girl, nothing more. His heart shrank at the lie.

"They would make a lovely couple." Fitz kept his tone neutral. "I believe there should be an announcement any day now."

"Fitz ..." Matthew's face drained of color. He leaned against the doorframe. "There will be an announcement. He's asked for permission."

"Congratulations to the happy couple." The words burned his tongue.

"There will be another announcement soon after."

Fitz clenched his fists, imagining the worst.

"The Parr family won't honor the engagement."

Fitz spun around. "What?"

Matthew held up his hands. "The dowry is spent. If we do not honor the terms, the engagement will be cancelled. She will be humiliated. And the family will be truly ruined."

15

ELISHEBA BEVUE

Elsie fidgeted while her maid finished her intricate plait, weaving Elsie's dark hair into an updo. Her maid stepped back and admired her handiwork. "You look lovely, milady."

"Thank you," Elsie murmured and glanced at the bed, wishing she could stay behind in the London home instead of venturing out for another engagement. The days and nights had blurred, morphing into one continuous whirlwind of dances and dinners.

Back in Wales, she'd gone to bed and risen fairly early each day. Nothing was more beautiful than watching the sun rise and set on the mountain ridge. It had been weeks since she'd seen the horizon. London wasn't as accommodating as Glamorgan, with sunsets or with people.

Leaving her room, Elsie stood and ran her hands along the fabric of her new riding habit, a gift from Lord Armonde. Both her mother and brother were shocked when it arrived, wondering if the marquess was behind the mare. The beautiful animal had come long before Lord Armonde and her family had burst back into Elsie's life. Selfishly, Elsie didn't want him to be the anonymous giver. She didn't want to feel obligated toward him. Or anyone.

In another time, Lady Bevue would be shocked at the scandalous nature. A man purchasing clothing for a lady was far too intimate. Elsie's mother had recently pivoted on most of her opinions, including Elsie's love of riding. Lord Armonde's affection had changed Lady Bevue's complete disdain of women riding to encouraging the practice —if only the weather had cooperated. Lord Armonde had asked twice to go horseback riding during his visits, but rain had cancelled their impending outing for a week. This morning Elsie had received a note. *Lovely day for a ride, Parr.* The note was the first time Lord Armonde had communicated in writing.

Elsie's new riding habit was of the latest fashion and should have made Elsie feel cherished. Instead, she felt misunderstood. And homesick.

Her old habit was modified; her legs in feminine trousers hidden under a thin skirt. Elsie would mount the horse in her custom saddle, her legs separated. She could pin or unpin the thin skirt over the top of the trousers, keeping both modesty and safety in mind.

Descending the stairs, Elsie's heart sank, each step reminding her that everything had changed. Her clothes, her family—her life.

In Wales, Fitz hadn't given her a second look when she'd mounted her mare. He'd not been bothered by her saddle either. He'd also not sent word about her horse. Both Lord Armonde and Fitz were like her family, hot and cold—good and bad. Elsie never quite knew where or what they wanted. A calm settled in her chest. Fitz had been more honest than her family. He'd admitted to relishing his bachelorhood. Her brother would have hidden that fact. But Fitz had come to her Welsh home to discuss business with Matthew. That was a mark that still created doubt. And suspicion.

On the last step, Elsie passed under the front window, the streets saturated with umbrellas and carriages. There would be no riding today.

She stood, clinging to the railing. In Wales, she'd still ride no matter the weather. The reduced number of servants allowed for hours of independence and few opinions. Yet here in London, the city of her birth, Elsie was a foreigner. She couldn't take a carriage by herself to the stables—not that she would be allowed to rent a horse without a chaperone or a gentleman present.

Her world was shriveling to nothing, the walls growing thicker. Her dress appeared to shrink, feeling far too tight, the room too warm. She tugged at the end of her sleeves, frustration rising with each passing moment. Fitz's impromptu offer of marriage had become more tempting than ever. Even if it wasn't offered from affection.

"Would you be so kind and join us?" Lady Bevue crossed the entryway. Her smile was wide but her eyes were hard, the strain obvious. She had borne the brunt of Tyndeth's demands and incessant complaints. Pity threatened to soften Elsie's feelings toward her mother—if Lady Bevue would only defend Elsie instead of reprimand. Elsie chided herself. She was no better, placing conditions on her family. Lady Bevue took a deep breath and then softly added, "Please."

"Are you ready Elsie?" Lady Alice joined Elsie's mother at the base of the stairs, her fingers wiggling into her gloves. "Shall we?"

"It's raining." Elsie paused. The note's handwriting was masculine. Elsie had hoped to ride with Lord Armonde, not his sister. Lady Alice wore a bright sapphire day dress—*not* a riding habit.

"Oh, heavens." Lady Alice wrinkled her nose. "We're not taking our phaeton. We'd be soaked through."

"I thought we were riding." A lump formed in Elsie's throat. "On horseback."

Lady Alice adjusted her hat. "Is that why you're wearing a riding habit?"

Elsie's face flushed. She was such a fool. "Your brother sent word."

"Yes." Lady Alice smiled wide. "We're to go for a ride in the park."

"I see." Elsie's spirits sank. Of course Elsie would misunderstand. She felt foolish at her silly emotions. Mistaking an outing was nothing to fret about. But a smile wouldn't appear. She desperately wished for fresh air and freedom. The fire inside her dimmed, exhaustion settling on her shoulders. "I should change."

"Nonsense." Lady Alice squeezed her hand. "Jonathon will love that you're wearing my gift."

My gift. Elsie swallowed the hurt and followed Alice to the entryway. Lord Armonde hadn't sent the riding habit. Lady Alice had. The fashionable fabric was dirtied. The day appeared less promising by the minute.

Lady Bevue had once picked Elsie's dresses, from the cut to the color. And now Lady Alice had slipped into the position. Elsie swallowed against the suffocating feeling. She shouldn't feel caged—but she did.

Lord Armonde stood at the door facing Matthew. Tension flowed between the two men.

Alice looped her arm through Matthew's, beaming up at him with complete adoration. Guilt nipped at Elsie. She couldn't look at Lord Armonde the same way.

Matthew and Lady Alice began whispering together, climbing into the carriage. Lord Armonde held out a hand to assist Elsie, whispering, "I promise we'll not spend the day with them."

Elsie breathed a sigh of relief. Lord Armonde arched an eyebrow. She blushed fiercely; she'd yet to become a master of her emotions. She shouldn't feel the way she did. A lady should be principled and able to bridle her emotions. Elsie had yet to master her thoughts, let alone her heart. Lord Armonde, a man she'd known only a few months, had guessed Elsie's discomfort correctly. It seemed Elsie would never become a lady of character. She mumbled, "Sorry."

"Why?" He tossed a mischievous smile to her. Lord Armonde had the easy confidence of someone born of privilege, his future bright and open. "It isn't every day my words take a lady's breath away."

Elsie grinned, grateful for his kind distraction. She should want his attention. And she would at least attempt to be a lady. "I shouldn't be so obvious."

"I do believe I've found a way to your heart." Lord Armonde squeezed her hand, warmth coming through her gloves.

"Oh, and how is that?" Elsie's own future didn't look so dire. Lord Armonde *was* kind. He was trying to understand her. She might not care for him the way his sister cared for Matthew but she did appreciate his kindness. Elsie's mother accused her of being stubborn. Perhaps, Elsie needed to force herself to love him.

"I just need to steal you from Matthew and flatter you incessantly."
He gave a practiced wink and helped her inside.

Elsie hoped the disappointment didn't show. She had hoped he'd
mention riding or being outside. Not flattery. She faced the window,
unable to participate in the conversation on the upcoming dinner
party. Elsie didn't give a fig about a party. Or the people attending. She
wanted to feel the rain on her face or, if the weather would accommo-
date, the warmth of the sun on her skin. She'd completely taken for
granted her independence the last few years.

"Is Tyndeth attending?" Lady Alice's voice jerked Elsie's attention
back to the present company.

"Always." Matthew straightened, his fingers fidgeting in his lap.
"The man is a shadow like none other."

"Do you think he'll propose?" Lady Alice must have missed the
somber tone in Matthew's words. "Tyndeth has a summer home in—"

"Alice," Lord Armonde warned.

Lady Alice blinked, her face awash with innocence. "Why aren't we
celebrating the union of two families? Lady Bevue and the earl are a
good match."

"They are." Matthew smiled softly, looking down at Lady Alice's
porcelain face. "I can't wait to celebrate. Lady Bevue will have no more
worries. Her life will be sorted again."

Lady Alice's eyes dimmed. She traced the intricate pattern of her
skirt.

Elsie should feel pity for Alice and her seventh season, but selfishly,
Elsie felt nothing. She didn't trust Alice even though she couldn't
explain why. Guilt nipped at her. Elsie was the one who'd slapped an
earl. She was the wicked woman—and truth be told, Elsie deserved her
frustrating family.

Lord Armonde shook his head and faced the window. Tension filled
the carriage. Elsie could only guess it had to do with Tyndeth but
wasn't sure why Lord Armonde was upset. His life wasn't strapped to
the earl, only Matthew and Elsie. Elsie's mother—if she did marry
Tyndeth—would be elevated from the lowest rung of nobility to the
upper echelon. Matthew's scandalous behavior would be overlooked

without another thought. He could marry Lady Alice or whomever he pleased.

But Elsie's fate would remain the same—unless she married.

The carriage stopped at the entrance to the park. Elsie looked longingly at the stables across the street. The rain was just a light drizzle, but she knew they still wouldn't ride. She felt foolish dressing in her habit.

Lord Armonde cracked open the window and squinted up at the sky. "It's hardly raining. Should we risk a walk?"

"Heavens, no." Lady Alice giggled. "Even if it's not raining, it's still muddy."

"I wouldn't mind a walk," Elsie blurted, feeling sheepish when all three heads turned toward her. "I was hoping to be outside today in one form or another."

"Is that why you wore a habit?" Realization flickered in Lord Armonde's eyes. "I do wish to ride with you."

Elsie fidgeted, feeling her blush all over again. She was forever assuming or speaking or *doing* things wrong. Nothing in London had been right since her father had passed. Herself included.

"We could try," Lord Armonde whispered.

"It's fine." His offering made her feel even more embarrassed. She should have changed into a day dress.

Lord Armonde opened the door and extended his hand. His scent was so different than Fitz's, a heavier perfume. "Let's start with a walk and see where that takes us."

"Jonathon." Lady Alice huffed. "You can't go for a walk."

"I believe I can." Lord Armonde kept his gaze on Elsie.

"I can't be left unchaperoned in the carriage, Jonathon. You know—"

"If you choose to stay in the carriage, that is your choice." Lord Armonde helped Elsie down, his hands lingering a moment longer than necessary. His grip was strong but didn't give the sense of safety like Fitz. Elsie silently cursed herself. Fitz wasn't here. Nor had he sent word. Lord Armonde was the one courting her. Grinning, he said, "Elsie and I are going for a walk."

"Jonathon—" The door cut off Lady Alice's reprimand.

Elsie's hands clasped then fell to her side. She didn't know what to do with them. Her hands—herself—was horribly out of place. "She's going to murder me."

"No." Lord Armonde offered his elbow. "She'll save it all for me."

"We don't have to walk." *Take me home,* Elsie almost said. *Home.* Home was Wales.

"If you make me get back in that carriage, I might cry." Lord Armonde winked at her, easing her mind. "We can give her a proper heart attack and walk toward the stables."

Elsie's spirits brightened. Her head cleared. Perhaps Lord Armonde did know the way to Elsie's heart. "That sounds absolutely delightful."

"We should walk through a few puddles to ensure we are completely dirty before climbing back in the carriage."

"She will absolutely murder you," Elsie said with a grin.

"Ah, I plan on it." Lord Armonde gave a quick shake of his head. "She might have to catch me first, but I do have high expectations for my demise."

They crossed the street and heard the carriage door open and close. Matthew and Lady Alice exited, one with a cheerful smile and the other with a considerable pout.

"Shall we see if they have any horses available today?" Lord Armonde held open the stable's office door.

Unable to speak, Elsie blinked, her heart in her throat. She wanted nothing more than to ride—to feel the wind caress her face, the horse pounding against the ground. There was comfort with horses that she could never explain.

"I'll take that as a yes." Taking a backward glance, Lord Armonde smirked. His sister glared at him and raised a pointed finger at them, her hand on her hip. Lord Armonde apparently didn't care that she was his older sibling. Elsie beamed, feeling hopeful for the first time in weeks. She would ride—*finally*—she would ride.

A young man stood at the modest table, his eyes searching both Lord Armonde and Elsie. "A gentleman's horse and a lady's?"

"Yes, please." Lord Armonde nodded.

Elsie felt the cold splash of disappointment. She should have known. The young man was preparing a lady's horse. She shook her head. She should be grateful for the offer of riding. The young man reappeared, leading a calm, slow moving gelding—a side-saddle placed on its back. The gelding was short, maybe thirteen hands high. His muzzle was wrinkled and grey. His ancient joints crackled with each step. There would be no wind, no running—no joy.

Elsie swallowed her pride. Lord Armonde had been kind. Attentive. And she'd never felt more alone.

🜲 16 🜲

FITZBURGH SMITH

itz refused to send the carriage to the Bevue estate. Matthew could find his own way to the gentlemen's club. Fitz had promised to help Matthew with one, possibly two, introductions and that was all. Matthew had balked when Fitz suggested the *Reform Club* instead of the aristocratic *Brook's* or *White's*. Fitz was not titled and did not have the membership of the prestigious clubs— although Fitz was fairly certain he'd done business with the majority of their members.

There was an entirely different reason Fitz would avoid the more noble clubs. He had done his due diligence before arriving in Matthew's Welsh home weeks before. He knew where Matthew's weak points lay; Matthew did not need to visit his old haunts. The less comfortable the baron was, the better behaved he'd be. At least, Fitz hoped.

Fitz's carriage turned toward the southern edge of clubland. Its location was indicative of Fitz's place in the world, on the edge of wealth and respectability. The more prestigious clubs were on the northern end of Pall Mall with *Brook's* and *Almack's* snuggled together at the very tip. Both buildings were stuffed with gambling and alcohol —vices Matthew would never turn down. Like most of the northern establishments, they catered toward the well-bred and bored. The owners of those clubs had no problem siphoning funds from friends and family of an indebted gentleman. Fitz would go nowhere near there—he wouldn't pay a dime of Matthew's debt. Not today or any other.

The carriage stopped in front of the *Travellers Club* and Fitz gave a deep sigh. The Union Flag waved an invitation in front of the two-storied building. Fitz was tempted to sneak inside his old haunt. This was Fitz's first time visiting London and not renting a room. He'd opted for the townhome, hoping it'd give him more respectability. Fitz tugged at his collar. He'd never cared about perceptions before.

He faced the dark door of the club and pivoted to its behemoth neighbor, the *Reform Club*. Fitz was a member there as well, but his visits were less frequent. The likelihood of Fitz running into a close friend or business partner at *Reform* was near impossible. He signed the ledger and wrote Matthew's name on the guest list, adding, *Will not sponsor—guest only.* Fitz would not be shackled to the baron in any way. He paused—knowing it was a lie. He'd proposed to Elsie, not once but twice. He would not force Elsie to choose between her family and him.

Fitz entered the grand lobby. The echoing of whispers drowned the outside traffic. He'd forgotten the sheer magnitude of the building. The curb appeal allowed for three stories to be visible but inside felt infinitely larger.

"Fitzburgh?" A gravelly voice asked.

Fitz spun around to see the lanky frame of his dear American friend, William Johnson, an exuberant smile and hand extended. "William, you're in town?"

In a thick, brassy American accent, William said, "For the time being."

"And your family?"

He nodded. "I think it safer here than home."

A wave of shame fell on Fitz. America had been kind to him, only for Fitz to abandon the country when tensions ran high. The topic of slavery—to own or to free them—had turned from controversial to lethal in a matter of months.

"Has it reached the north?" Fitz motioned to the nearest chairs, sitting in the closest. He kept an eye on the entrance for Matthew. A man by the name of Lincoln had united America's north where William lived but angered the south where William's in-laws lived.

"There's whispers." William settled into the chair, a puzzled look on his face. A darkness settled on his features. "I've been looking for you."

Fitz's pulse raced. The American was unflappable—if he was looking for Fitz, the situation was dire. Fitz had been too distracted to answer correspondence. He was a poor friend indeed. "What's wrong?"

"Nothing serious." William gave a subtle wave of his hand. "We are fine here."

"Do we need to take this conversation elsewhere?"

William frowned, aging a few decades in the moment. "No. Nothing like that."

Fitz leaned forward, his elbows on his knees. "How is your home?"

"I still have one."

"This sounds serious."

"We are luckier than most." William cleared his throat. "And we hope to not return until the dust settles."

Fitz tapped his fingers against the chair's armrest. "I have a few homes not rented out. Nothing in America though."

William waved Fitz's word away. "We won't take advantage of your generosity. We are fine. And we are staying here in London for the time being. It's been ages since we've had an English Christmas."

"What if it is only self-interest?" Fitz gave a soft chuckle. "I'm always in need of a new venture."

"Will you return?"

"To New York?" Fitz paused. He'd asked himself the same question a dozen times in the last few days. He glanced at his hands. He'd only hugged Elsie and yet felt tied to her, anchored to her in a way he couldn't explain. It was a dangerous game he played, caring for her at a distance. "I'm not sure. I don't know what my next move is. And you? What brings you to London of all places?"

"My wife is wanting Sophie to have a traditional season. Like my grandmother had." William scoffed and rubbed his jaw. "With all that's happening at home, it doesn't seem right."

"That is something I cannot help you with." *Nor do I want to.* Fitz had enough problems of his own. Matthew entered, his gait sloppy and his eyes dazed. Fitz flinched. He'd hoped meeting here would keep Matthew from Fitz's closer friends. "And neither should the man you're about to meet."

"Is that why you're here and not at *Travellers?*" William followed Fitz's gaze, turning to watch Matthew stumble toward them.

"I've rented a townhome by Regent Park."

William's mouth fell open, his eyes glinting with mischief. "You've not turned respectable on me now?"

"I've never been accused of being respectable." Fitz couldn't stop his smile. He'd missed his friend. And the confidence Fitz had once held. Being with Elsie had twisted his plans and pricked his heart.

Both men stood as Matthew approached. William held out a hand. "William Johnson."

"Lord Bevue." Matthew smiled and shook their hands. "Baron of Glamorgan."

Not once had a duke or earl introduced himself with such arrogance. Matthew had even less reason to put on airs. Fitz was even less inclined to help Matthew now. "William is a close friend of mine."

"Is that so?" Greed lined Matthew's face. He clapped Fitz on the shoulder and addressed William. "It's good to meet you. What brings you to the Motherland?"

"Matthew, really?" Fitz rubbed his temple. He mouthed *sorry* to William.

William's gaze flicked from Matthew to Fitz, questions in his eyes. "You two are good friends?"

Fitz rolled his eyes. "His family spent their summer vacations in the house next to ours. We were geographically close." *Nothing more.*

"Ahhhh." William nodded. He brushed his hands along his sides and said, "Well, Fitz, it's good to see you. I was at *Travellers* and saw you cross the street. When everything is said and done back home, I'd want nothing more than to lure you back. You could help filter the young men vying for Sophie's attention."

"The states have always been good to me." Fitz felt the pull, the temptation to pack his bags and leave on another adventure. There'd been ups and downs with their financial exploits, but overall, the partnership had enlarged his wealth. He'd added upon what his father started decades before. Fitz didn't have a wife or children to look after. Risk was easy when there was no one else to worry about. Except Elsie. Tucked in his memories, she'd accompanied him on every venture.

"What are your thoughts on Australia?" William didn't gossip nor did he abide in idle talk. He spoke deliberately—he'd followed Fitz to the club with a purpose.

"I know very little." Fitz rubbed his jaw but wondered how quickly he could be ready for a trip. "I've heard it's a land of possibilities."

"Adventure can go both ways." William frowned. He'd been burned by sour investments before but had fared well since partnering with Fitz. "Is it worth looking into?"

Fitz smiled. "You forget. I'm a bachelor. Adventures are always worth looking into."

Matthew furrowed his brow, his gaze flicking between William and Fitz.

With a nod, William said, "I'll leave you to your business, but let's look into some details soon."

"Have you been in town long?" Matthew asked, his face suspiciously serious. He threw his hands in his pockets and rocked on his heels. He apparently hadn't noticed William was bracing to leave.

"Just a week." William scratched his head, exhaustion lining his eyes.

Matthew shook his hand. "Where are you staying?"

William gave a nod to Fitz. "We've rented a townhome just a few blocks from where you're staying."

"Come to dinner, William." Matthew clapped the American on the shoulder just as he'd done to Fitz a moment earlier. "We can be one big happy family."

"Family?" William arched an eyebrow.

"Oh." Matthew grinned like a fool. "Fitz hasn't told you about my sister?"

Narrowing his gaze, William stiffened. Both William and Fitz had spent far too much time finding truth in the mouth of liars.

"Matthew," Fitz warned.

"I do not know what is happening here." William nodded curtly to Matthew. "But I do know the value of friendship. Loyalty is too often tossed aside."

Fitz watched his friend. He'd not seen William this somber. The rumors of impending war must have finally become reality. He extended a hand to William. "You are a bright spot, my friend."

William's face relaxed, a smile slowly appearing. "I've seen too much of deception. Of brother turning against brother. I've no stomach for anything of the sort." He sighed and gave a subtle shake of his head. "It's a sad state, Fitz. I wouldn't wish it on the worst of men."

"You're a good man, William." Fitz rubbed his jaw, wondering again why he'd come to London. Fitz had left America for home but had become distracted. The letter to Elsie was still tucked inside his jacket. He'd not yet delivered it. Nor had he bothered to post it. "It might be time for me to leave the city."

Matthew's head perked up. "Leave? You just got here."

"London was never supposed to be this long of a stay." The moment the words left Fitz's mouth, relief filled him. London had never been home to him. Matthew's company had made it even less so.

Fitz needed to court his courage and tell Elsie that her mare had died. He'd hoped to find another horse, not that replacing the mare was the answer. Fitz had just wanted to soften the blow. Instead, he'd done nothing.

"Just how long were you planning on staying?" Matthew folded his arms, only to unfold them.

Alarm rang in Fitz's head. "Is there a reason my coming and going bothers you?"

"No, no." Matthew retreated. "Does Elsie know?"

"About your affairs or mine?" Fitz snapped.

William grinned. "It's good to see you've not changed."

"I am as stalwart as ever," Fitz said wryly.

"Stubborn too." William's grin grew to a wide smile, appearing more like the friend Fitz remembered. "Send word."

"Will do." Fitz ignored Matthew fidgeting beside him. He watched William leave and gave into the pull. Whether his future lay in

Australia or somewhere else; it was time. His feet were itching to leave London and so was his heart. He had just one last thing to do.

"You're leaving?"

"Matthew Bevue, I do not report my travel plans to you."

"You promised you'd give an introduction."

Fitz held out his arm. "Did I not just introduce you to William Johnson?"

Matthew pouted. Like a child. "That's one person."

Fitz had planned on making introductions here in the club, but the growing headache killed the thought. "I will make one more introduction. One. Do you know how much that is?"

"Oh, come off it—"

"It's one digit more than zero. One less than two."

Matthew threw his hands in the air, looking half his age. "I know what one means."

"Then you'll understand that *one* is about twice more than I ever wanted to do." Fitz flinched at his own voice.

"You're not—"

"Better than you, I know," Fitz added softly. "I am not a baron. No do I ever wish to be. But I know that I will not be a pawn in your game of chess."

Matthew hung his head. "I am a desperate man, Fitz."

"And that is why I will give you one more introduction." And then he would be rid of the Bevues. Fitz paused, sad at the thought of never seeing Elsie again. He would still provide for her, somehow or someway. But he was done with the rest of her scheming family.

🗶 17 🗶

ELISHEBA BEVUE

Elsie paced under the cover of trees. The little sliver of a garden was tucked to the side of her London home. It was the closest to privacy Elsie could find. She fought the urge to scream and cry like a toddler as she pivoted, retracing her steps over and over again. She didn't dare walk in the back or in the front where someone could see her.

She just needed a moment to herself, to be completely hidden and forced to converse with absolutely no one. It'd been weeks since she'd left her mare, bloodied and broken in Wales. She flexed her hands at her sides. Her mother had accused her of caring more for her horse than her own family. Elsie hadn't shown enough enthusiasm coming home from her riding adventure with Lord Armonde. Her face flamed at the memory. She'd tried to smile and be attentive, but the entire ride was a complete and utter disappointment. The poor gelding refused to go any faster than a wobble, and the side-saddle was ridiculous—whoever invented the blasted contraption should be shot.

Elsie paused, the guilt piercing her once more. Her mother was right. She was ungrateful and cared more about riding than anything, or anyone, else. Elsie should have been more grateful to Lord

Armonde. He'd tried to give her an outing, a wonderful, delightful adventure that most ladies would swoon over.

She leaned against the fence, wishing once more that she was with *Direidus*. She lifted a boot and untied it, and then the other. She slipped her feet free of the stockings and felt the cold, wet earth. The act was rebellious—even scandalous—but her heart lifted. She wriggled her toes, the day appearing brighter by the second.

Taking a step back, Elsie felt homesick all over again. She missed the animal's impatient pawing while Griffiths hurried to saddle her. Elsie missed the feel of the cold morning wind and missed the independence. And the quiet.

Most of all, she grieved for the Elsie she was in Wales. Her confidence was nowhere to be found. And she saw no end in sight.

With a sigh, she began pacing again, this time more careful, her boots in her hands. Being a lady in London was so much harder than she remembered. The earl's punishment had been the sweetest reward. She smiled, wondering what she could do to incite another two-year seclusion.

She heard the muffled yell of her mother. By the tone, Lady Bevue was speaking to a servant. Elsie hoped she wasn't the cause of the scolding. She'd not been gone long enough to warrant a search party. Glancing at the sky, she guessed she'd only been gone half an hour.

Wrapping her coat closer around her shoulders, she debated on her route. If she returned to the house through the back, chances were her mother was in the sitting room but if she returned through the front, her maid would see her and the fussing of hair and dress would begin anew. Or worse, she could accidentally be spotted by Lady Alice or someone of her ilk. Elsie didn't need anyone's judgment.

Another muffled scold from her mother made her decisions—through the front.

Peering around the corner of the house, she glanced up and down the street. Both views were blocked by hedges. She glanced down at her feet and frowned, not wanting to cage her feet just yet.

Gripping her boots, she opened the gate, wincing at the squeaky hinges. Tyndeth's carriage came to a sudden halt in front of her home. She froze, one hand on the gate, the other clutching her boots.

The footman jumped to the carriage door. Matthew burst through, not waiting for the servant. Elsie gripped the gate, wondering if Tyndeth would be next. Scowling, Matthew clutched an envelope in his hand. The carriage hurried away before Matthew took two steps toward the house. He swayed—Elsie narrowed her gaze. He was drunk.

Brushing off her feet, she shoved them into the boots, the stockings tucked into her pocket. "Matthew."

He stiffened—then shoved the envelope behind him. "Good morning, Elsie."

"It's well into the afternoon, Matthew."

Nodding, Matthew gave a Cheshire grin. He was up to another scheme. "But did I wish you good morning yet?"

"What are you hiding?" Elsie slid in front of him, cutting off his escape into the house. Her mother would cover for whatever he'd done.

"Nothing." He scoffed, adding, "Why would you think that?"

"The envelope in your hand."

A flicker of shame crossed his features—it'd come and gone so quick Elsie wondered if she'd seen it at all. He shrugged. "Oh, that's nothing. Just something for Fitz."

"Fitz?" Elsie's heart dropped. Fitz had visited Matthew. He was in league with her brother—a man who, by Fitz's own admission, was a scoundrel. What did that make Fitz? She'd waited for word—for any sign from him. He'd promised to take care of her mare. "You've something for him?"

"Uh, no. Not really." Matthew retreated. "No, I just need to check something for him. That's all."

"What do you need to check?" Fitz had made it very clear what he thought of Matthew. They might do business with each other, but Fitz didn't trust him. They were no closer to friends than Alice and Elsie were.

"Some business things."

"Business?" Elsie folded her arms. "You're lying."

"Believe it or not, Fitz and I are long time business associates." Matthew lifted his chin.

"And just what service do you provide?" She fought the smirk. "As the accomplished business associate that you are."

"It's not about actual accomplishments, Elsie." Matthew rolled his eyes, arrogance in every breath. "Business has just as much to do with pedigree as wealth."

"You are aware that we have neither." Elsie arched an eyebrow.

He puffed out his chest, bringing the envelope forward. "I am the Baron of Glamorgan. There is nobility in my veins."

Elsie's gaze flicked to the letter. *Elsie Bevue* was written on the front. "But nothing in your brain."

Matthew growled and leaned forward. "You will—"

She stole the letter from his hand and held it up. "Would your lovely brain like to tell me why your eyes think this is for you? It's clearly addressed to me."

"As your male relative—"

"So neither your brain nor your eyes can help you?" Elsie gave a firm nod. "It is a sad state of affairs when your own body betrays you. I'm sure it's almost as hurtful as when your family deceives you."

Matthew's mouth hung open. He snapped it closed. Only to open it once more.

Elsie folded her arms. "This is where you apologize."

"For what?" Matthew shook his head. "Don't answer that."

She lowered her gaze. "Why would you keep this from me?"

"You don't even know what it is." Matthew jutted his chin, sounding more like the younger sibling than the older brother.

"And I never would have if you'd kept it a secret."

Matthew rocked on his heels, shrugging. "I wasn't going to keep it that way."

"When were you planning on giving me the letter?" she asked softly, knowing the answer. Her brother would have destroyed the letter after reading it. He loved holding information hostage—he'd boasted two years ago about sending Elsie to Wales, hiding the truth of Tyndeth's involvement. Knowledge was power and the only true control Matthew had over Elsie.

"I needed to make sure the correspondence was proper." Matthew's posture straightened with each word, believing his lie as it grew.

Elsie flipped the envelope, her heart racing. *F. Smith* was written across the back. "He sent word."

"An unmarried gentleman sending letters to an unmarried lady shows an attachment, Elsie." Matthew sniffed. "Lord Armonde would be devastated."

The envelope shook in her hands, the seal not broken. "It's about my mare."

Matthew softened, the arrogance melting away. "I'd forgotten."

"I don't know if I can open it." She cradled the letter to her chest.

Matthew held out his hand. "Do you want me to?"

"No," she snapped. "How can I possibly trust you now?"

Matthew flinched. "It's not like he posted it."

Elsie held her breath, flipping the envelope back. There wasn't postage. Fitz hadn't sent the letter. "How did you—"

"He was fumbling with his jacket. It slipped out." Matthew rubbed his jaw, glancing over his shoulder. "I saw your name and grabbed it."

"He's here." Fitz was in town. The revelation pierced her.

Matthew shifted his weight, shrugging again. "He's been here for a while."

"What is *a while*?"

"I don't know, Elsie. He's not exactly forthcoming with me." Matthew took off his hat, brushing it against his trousers. "I'm not his nearest and dearest."

"I am nobody's nearest and dearest."

Matthew froze, his hat on his thigh. "That's not true."

"Fitz promised to look after *Direidus*. And to send word as soon as possible. You deceived me, not just with this letter but with my two years in Wales. Mother has kept her secrets too." Elsie turned from him, allowing only her profile to show. "You and mother confide in each other and support one another. Who do I have?"

"Lord Armonde cares a great deal about you." Matthew drew closer, his words soft and gentle. For a moment, he would play the part of beloved brother. He had done this dance as a child, luring Elsie into a false confidence. "And despite what you think, I do believe Fitz cares for you as well."

"Not enough to keep his promises." Elsie tapped the envelope, wishing her brother was truly the devoted sibling, and Fitz—what did she want from him?

"We don't know that." He placed his hat back on his head. "I can't exactly ask him *why he didn't send the letter I stole.*"

A grin tugged at Elsie's lips. "I suppose that would be rather improper."

"Maybe I should try it. He seems to like the unpredictable." Matthew elbowed Elsie playfully.

She forced a smile. Matthew was trying to cheer her up but it fell flat. He was only playing a part to assuage his guilt. This was the closest their relationship would ever be. Not that Matthew was the only offender. Elsie *was* unpredictable. And improper. She slid a finger under the lip of the envelope, breaking the seal.

She didn't make it.

I meant what I said.

—Fitz.

Heavy disappointment settled on her shoulders. Two sentences were all he'd written. Her only friend in the world had given her a few words—and hadn't bothered to post them. Fitz was no different than her family. Or even Lord Armonde. Elsie was an afterthought. An inconvenience.

Matthew said over her shoulder, "I'm not an expert on the female mind, but even I know he's made a mess of delivering bad news."

The note shook in her hands. *I meant what I said.* Fitz had proposed twice, promising freedom. He'd also promised to send word about her horse at the soonest possible moment. Elsie's heart sank, rereading the first line. *She didn't make it.* No explanation. No words of solace. A tear fell, staining the note.

"Hey ..." Matthew cooed, reaching for her.

She retreated. "Why did you go to the barn?"

"What barn?" Matthew snapped to a stand.

"You hate horses—"

"That's not true." He folded his arms, his lips curling to a sneer. He was caught and on the offense. "I don't gallivant with Fitz through the countryside like you, but I can ride."

Elsie's cheeks burned. Matthew knew more than he let on. He must have seen Elsie riding with Fitz. "What happened to the mare?"

"How should I know?"

"You were the last—"

"Now is where you say *thank you*," Matthew snapped. "I saw your blasted horse and grabbed Griffiths. The animal was bloody before I ever touched it."

"I doubt that."

Matthew pointed a finger at her. "And yet Fitz just happened to be at the house that morning. Funny, I hadn't invited him. He just happened to be in the area?" He narrowed his gaze. "You might want to make sure you know who your enemy is before—"

"I know guilt when I see it." Elsie dropped the note and ran inside. She needed a plan. She needed to escape—she needed Wales.

18

FITZBURGH SMITH

With his valet searching his room upstairs, Fitz upturned his desk for the second time. He'd lost the letter for Elsie. He abandoned the study for the smaller secretary desk in the sitting room, the only area of the townhome not disheveled. William would be arriving any moment with more information on Australian markets. It didn't matter; Fitz had already made his decision. He was ready for his next business venture. He'd made the decision late last night and had hoped to send off the letter to Elsie if he could find the blasted thing.

He sat in a huff at the secretary desk. The lost letter served him right. Fitz had a knack for numbers, not words. He rubbed his temple and pulled out a fresh sheet of paper. The blank page stared at him, taunting him like Matthew had done as a boy. With pen to the paper, his mind blanked. How could he tell her the mare had died? It seemed too cruel through a letter but too intimate in person. Fitz tried to remember what he'd written in the original missive but doubted it was more than a word or two.

The poor animal had nicked an artery in her hoof. The farrier had deemed it an accident. Elsie had been suspicious of Matthew, but her stableman had found more nails in the abandoned paddock just outside the barn. Why the horse was in the outer paddock was a mystery, but the Bevue estate didn't have enough servants to keep the maintenance up—for once, Matthew was relatively innocent.

Fitz blinked. None of these thoughts made it to the letter. He'd only written *Elsie*. At that, the letters were shaky. He was ridiculous. This was Elisheba Bevue, the woman he'd known his entire life. He swallowed. He'd only known her from a distance. He glanced down at his hands. He'd held her. The memory warmed him, softening his heart.

A knock echoed through the thin walls of the house. The butler answered the front door, and Fitz stood, knowing William would enter any moment.

"Ah, always working, are you?" William ran a hand through his hair, his hat with the butler. "Are you sure you're not American?"

The nervousness Fitz had felt a moment ago shriveled at the sight of his friend. This was who Fitz was, confident. Capable. "How did your daughter take the news?"

William gave a sheepish smile. "I haven't told Sophie we're leaving just yet."

Disappointment fell heavy on Fitz. Leaving had given him hope—and direction. Moving forward in some way, financial or otherwise, gave him a goal. Something he could attain.

"You look like my dog when I've taken her bone away." Chuckling, William sat on the sofa. "I have not decided if my family is coming to Australia. I can't in good conscious take them from America only to place them in danger on another continent."

"What do we know?" Fitz had poured over the maps he'd acquired, each one slightly different. The gold rush towns in the north were consistent, but the rest of the topography differed. Fitz and William would be entering Australia blindly. They knew sheep and horses were fairly profitable and well known—meaning, they would not venture in either. They needed a new venture to grow, then sell just before saturation.

"We know gold is aplenty." William folded his hands over his middle, looking more like the middle-aged man he was. "And that New South Wales is slowly being tamed."

"I've not heard much of the southern tip." Hope blossomed.

"There's quite a lot of robbery and thievery going on." William eyed Fitz. "Your country sent the worst of your lot there for a long time."

"And now there's money to be had." It was a recipe for complete and utter chaos. The offspring of criminals had found gold, and now thousands of British patriots were arriving to try their luck at the riches—easy targets for robbers and thieves. Fitz wondered how Elsie would fare in Australia. He winced—he was a fool. She wasn't part of his plan. And he wasn't a part of hers. He'd never accept her family, and she deserved more than a mere mister.

"Something bothering you?"

Fitz shook his head. "Nothing, just needing to tie up some loose ends."

"It's done then? Australia is our next venture." William pulled at his collar, his lips frowning.

"Are you hesitant?" Fitz eyed his friend. William was the more conservative of the partnership. Fitz had always assumed because the man had a family, three daughters and a wife to think of. "Is there a reason we should not go?"

"I am worried about Sophie." He crossed an ankle over his knee. "I don't want fortune hunters to come calling while I'm away."

"I can go on my own." Fitz knew of one scheming fortune hunter who would have no problem draining the Johnson family coffers. Matthew was beyond desperate. "I can send word with what I've found."

William's frown deepened. "That's a bit cumbersome. By the time I'd receive the information, it'll be too late to do anything about it. I can't very well send word back fast enough."

"Can you send her on a Grand Tour?" Many English ladies took a year tour on the European continent before they entered the marriage market. His parents went on holiday for months at a time to Europe; they were doing just that now. Christmas in France was a tradition they loved.

Cocking his head to the side, William gave a playful smile. "That's a very English thing to do. That just might work." He leaned forward. "My grandmother did the same thing at Sophie's age."

"Your wife could travel with her."

"That could buy me time." William shook his head. "I cannot believe I'm sending my daughter on a frivolous holiday. Back home ..." He sighed. "Home is a mess, and I'm trying to entertain my family."

"You're trying to protect them." Fitz sat next to his friend. "It's an admirable thing to do, William."

He smirked. "It doesn't feel admirable."

"Well, no deed goes unpunished." Fitz shifted on the couch. He'd given Elsie a mare and now must tell her of its fate. He'd given her joy without a thought but couldn't bring himself to tell her the tragedy.

"Always a cynic." William chuckled and stood. "Shall we go over the maps?"

"If cynic keeps money in the bank, then a cynic I shall be." Fitz motioned for William to follow him. "Apologies for the mess you're about to find."

They stood at the threshold. Papers and books were everywhere. Fitz had torn apart every nook and cranny trying to find the blasted letter. Before Elsie, Fitz had been the epitome of order and simplicity. In such a short time, he'd imploded.

William shook his head. "Fitz, you need a woman to sort out your life."

"A woman is the reason for all this." Fitz scowled, feeling the weight of William's gaze. "Don't read into that comment."

"I'm not reading—I'm diving right in."

Fitz grunted and stepped over boxes to the large desk in the center of the room, the maps rolled on top. "You mentioned South Wales." Gingerly, he unrolled the first map, searching the southern tip of the continent.

"I also mentioned a woman, but you've not shown me that either."

"I've no intention of showing her." Fitz rubbed the back of his head. The room had become deucedly hot. How had the conversation taken such a turn? He was tying up loose ends, Matthew being one. He swallowed hard. He wasn't ready to say farewell to Elsie. That was evident in his reluctance to send the first letter. He wished he could take her with him, far away from her family.

"Even the great shall fall." William whistled. "Fitzburgh Smith, the bachelor of the century, has been pierced by cupid's bow."

Fitz braced his hands on the top of the desk. There was affection for Elsie, he'd confess only that. Nothing more. It was pointless to dwell on the impossible. "Marriage is not in the cards for me. Not today nor apparently ever."

"Apparently?" William gingerly entered the room, his long legs carrying his lanky frame over the rolling hills of paperwork. "That means you've tried?"

"Yes. No." Fitz growled again. He was not going to divulge his proposals to anyone. William was a friend, but Fitz didn't understand what he'd done nor why—how could he explain it to someone else? "Not really."

"It's a simple question." There was entirely too much cheerfulness in William's voice. "Did a lady catch your eye?"

"No," Fitz lied and then rubbed the bridge of his nose. This was William. He couldn't lie to him. Fitz sank into the chair behind his desk. "I knew a girl from my childhood. She is an old friend."

"And this old friend is the sister to the drunken fellow at the club?"

"Unfortunately, yes."

William shrugged. "We can't choose our relatives."

"Technically, we do." Fitz tapped the desk. "Isn't that what your in-laws are? Chosen by default."

"Are you rethinking your attachment because of the brother?" William arched an eyebrow.

"There is no attachment."

"I see." William gave a knowing grin.

"There isn't." Fitz folded his arms and then glanced down. He sounded—and acted—like a disgruntled toddler. "Even if I was tempted, she's well above my rank and is being courted by a marquess."

"And yet she still managed to unnerve you." William motioned to the boxes in disarray. "I'd say she's an accomplished woman of the highest order."

"She's oblivious."

William *tsk*ed. "Women are never oblivious."

"This one is."

"Make her un-oblivious."

Fitz scoffed. William didn't know Elsie or her confounded behavior. She was not the average lady. She was fire and ice, an eternal battle of opposing forces. "I have no intention of marrying. She knows that. That's why she turned down my proposal."

William's mouth fell open, his eyebrows nearing his hairline. He was properly dumbfounded.

Fitz cradled his head in his hands. The conversation had taken an absurd turn. "It's not how it sounds."

"Oh, do tell," William said dryly. "I had no idea you were so diverting. You've been holding out on me, Lord Byron."

Balking, Fitz's head shot up. "I am no Lord Byron." He was nowhere near the dratted poet and had no desire to be.

"Then by all means, tell me how your no-attachment proposal with a girl who hasn't caught your eye truly happened."

Fitz was a fool. He'd unwittingly played a game without knowing the rules. "I ... don't know."

"That is the only sensible thing you've said." William nodded, amusement tugging at his lips. The man was fighting a laugh at Fitz's expense. "Now, when do I get to meet this woman?"

"Never."

"You realize I have a daughter very much entrenched in London society." William softened the threat with a good-natured chuckle. "Sophie could tell me more about your lady love than you'll ever be able to."

Fitz leaned forward, touching his forehead against the desk. "I hate London."

"But you love the girl."

"I love no one." Fitz stood and unrolled the map. *I love no one.* The thought pierced him. Love was all-encompassing, his mother had taught him that. Love would look past Matthew and Lady Bevue. No, Fitz did not love Elsie. *I love no one.* The thought fell heavy on his shoulders. For the first time in his life, Fitz felt alone. And empty.

William placed a hand on the map. "As much as I love to see you squirm, I will drop this conversation after I say one thing more."

Fitz felt the dread.

"Oh, come off it." William smirked. "You've gone pale. It's only advice."

"I'm fine."

"You're nothing of the sort." His friend laid a fatherly hand on Fitz's shoulder. "I'll say this and be done. Love and women never make sense. Money can be counted and tracked, but it can't keep you warm at night, nor can it give you purpose."

I'm a bachelor, Fitz almost said, but the tenderness in his friend's eyes silenced him. William was a good man—a good friend and husband as well. Fitz had no intention of being a father or provider for anyone. The image of Tyndeth's scowl entered his mind. Tyndeth was a father and a husband three times over. Marriage hadn't made the earl better, not in the slightest. If Fitz could love Elsie—shove her family to the other side of the world—and love her and all her emotions, he'd do it. But life didn't work that way, not here.

William squeezed his shoulder. "You could use purpose, Fitz."

Nodding absently, Fitz ran his finger along Australia's southern coastline. William droned on about the towns, but Fitz heard nothing, his mind on Elsie and her mare.

19

ELISHEBA BEVUE

Elsie climbed into Tyndeth's landau, bracing herself for the usual barrage of insults from the earl. She'd perfected the art of ignoring the ill-tempered man. He grumbled, his hands clenching the blanket with tight fists. Lady Bevue fussed over him like a harried mother. She'd aged in the few weeks since her sudden arrival in Wales. Watching her mother, Elsie felt a twinge of sympathy. Her mother was once loved and doted upon; now she was barely above a servant, living only for the comfort of her master.

The carriage lurched forward, tossing Lady Bevue into the seat beside Elsie. The earl frowned at Elsie, blaming her mother's slip on Elsie. He narrowed his gaze. "Out with it."

Elsie looked to her mother whose chin was tucked. She'd become the shell of the woman Elsie had known. The sight of her defeated mother ignited a fire in Elsie's chest. She returned her attention on the earl. "What am I allowed to speak of? Would you prefer to write a script? Perhaps I can borrow the words you've written for my mother to speak. Surely she could use a break from her servitude."

Lady Bevue's head shot up, her eyes wide with fear. She glanced from the earl to Elsie, her eyes pleading for her daughter to stop. The sight fed the fire in Elsie. She would not back down. Not now.

Elsie had nothing to lose. How could she possibly feel worse? Her one friend had broken the very promise she clung to. She groaned. Elsie was foolish, silly even, to put so much stock in her brief friendship with Fitz. He was the spring of water in her parched landscape of affection.

"I would prefer silence than the abuse you serve." Tyndeth glared at her, his knuckles turning white in their clenched state. "You are ungrateful—"

"And you are no gentleman, sir." She leaned forward. "Your pride is wicked. So is your temper. Yet you think you are above those—"

Lady Bevue placed a hand on Elsie's forearm. "Child—"

"I'll not be muzzled by the Earl of Tantrums."

Lady Bevue recoiled as if she'd been burned. She covered her mouth and sank back in her seat.

The earl snarled. "You need more than a muzzle, you insolent child. Earl of Tantrums? This will not go unpunished, mark my words."

"I should mark more than your words." She scooted to the edge of her seat. She'd given him a simple slap last time. Perhaps the old man needed more punishment for his unending cruelty. He'd clipped her mother's wings and made her family into puppets. "You're nothing more than a sniveling cripp—"

The carriage came to a stop, cutting off her words. The carriage door was opened and Elsie shot out, not waiting for the servant's offered hand. She didn't turn around to see the earl or her mother descend the carriage. The reality of what Elsie had said fell on her shoulders. Because of her sharp tongue, her family would pay dearly.

She picked up her skirts and rushed to the entryway, ignoring the shocked looks of her peers. Elsie slipped past the announcement line and found a quiet corner in the back of the dance hall. Her hands shook as she peered around the wall, waiting for the impending arrival of her mother and Tyndeth.

A tall brunette woman blocked her view, her brown eyes pleading. She whispered in a distinct American accent, "Is there room for one more?"

Elsie nodded, moving over.

"Is it always this crowded?" the woman asked, her hands pulling at the ends of her curls. She was nearly as tall as a man and her coloring was freckled. She was the very opposite of what the *ton* deemed beautiful. The young woman nibbled her lip. She had more than likely been teased by her English competition.

"I'm afraid I don't really know." Elsie flattened her back against the wall. "I've only been to a handful of these."

"You're always with the Parr family." The woman stood on the other side of Elsie, her hands clasped in front of her.

"They are family friends, yes." That was all Elsie would admit. She knew what was expected, her mother and brother had made that perfectly clear. Lord Armonde was nice enough, but he cowered to both his parents and Tyndeth. Both their families had hinted about a match, but Elsie felt just as alone at his side than by herself. She was tired of feeling alone, a nagging thought that shadowed her every move.

"I had to memorize all the families before we arrived." She shrugged, her cheeks blushing.

Elsie rolled her eyes. "The art of man hunting is a dangerous sport."

The woman laughed and shot out a hand. "Sophie Johnson."

"Elsie Bevue."

Her eyebrows rose. "As in Lord Bevue?"

"Matthew Bevue is my brother." *And a blasted fool.*

"Interesting." Sophie scanned Elsie head to toe.

"What were you expecting?" she blurted, hating how defensive she sounded.

"You just look nothing like your brother." Sophie nodded toward the floor.

Elsie spun around and froze—standing next to Matthew was Fitzburgh Smith, smartly dressed in a well-tailored suit. She gripped the wall, drinking in the sight of him. Her cheeks heated. She'd spent days on end with Lord Armonde and just one innocent sight of Fitz sent her blushing. Another feeling altogether wriggled in. Betrayal.

Fitz was Matthew's friend first—or business associate, according to Matthew. She shoved the thought away. Fitz *had* written a letter; he'd just neglected to send it. His sudden appearance made her question his other promise. And their connection—if there ever was one. She shook her head, wishing she could disappear. What if she had accepted his proposal? Would he have forgotten the agreement the moment she left the room? Perhaps Elsie was indeed only an afterthought, another problem that Fitz had happened upon. Just another silly woman in need of help.

"Are you alright?" Sophie asked. Despite her boldness, there was kindness in her eyes.

"I just saw an old friend. Someone I haven't seen in a while."

"Mr. Smith?"

Jealousy pierced Elsie's heart. "You know him?"

"Not personally." Sophie pulled at her gloves, wiggling her fingers. "My father knows him. They spent a great deal of time together back home."

"Oh." There was entirely too much relief in that one word.

Sophie arched an eyebrow, a knowing look in her eye. "He introduced me to your brother."

"Fitz introduced Matthew?" Elsie's mouth hung open. She didn't know who to trust. Fitz had disparaged Matthew—not that she could blame him. But what did Fitz say about Elsie when she wasn't near? A chill swept across her neck. Fitz probably didn't even speak or think of her. "How colorful was this introduction?"

Sophie giggled. "Aren't the English proper at all times?"

"I'm rarely proper." Elsie smiled, feeling the tension fall from her shoulders. She'd already pricked Tyndeth's temper—why should she worry about any other man's good opinion? "My father said I was more like a Welsh wind than an English tea."

Sophie cocked her head but before she could ask what Elsie meant, Lord Armonde appeared at her side. Sophie acknowledged his arrival with a nod. "Shall I leave so you two can have a moment of privacy?"

"No." Elsie's hand gripped Sophie's forearm. Being alone with Lord Armonde would lead to either a proposal or a stolen kiss, neither of which she wanted. Her lips tingled. They wanted a kiss but not from Lord Armonde.

He gave a short bow to Sophie. "I came only to deliver Elsie to her mother, Miss Johnson."

"You've met?" Elsie waited for the jealousy to come but she felt nothing.

Sophie gave a curtsey. "We have. Mr. Smith introduced us last night."

"How long has he been in town?" Anger welled in Elsie. She hoped it didn't show. She'd asked her brother the same question, but like her correspondence with Fitz, she'd been found wanting.

"I believe a few weeks." Lord Armonde's facade slid in place.

Elsie regretted—again—that she'd told him about Fitz's sudden proposal. Jealousy didn't look good on him, especially when it wasn't deserved. Fitz admitted he'd proposed only to solve a problem, not for affection. The notion twisted Elsie's stomach. It shouldn't affect her so. She had written off love the moment she tried—and failed—to secure a governess position. Her heart rebelled, not buying the lie.

"Are you alright?" Sophie asked, a touch too loud.

Elsie waved away the question, feeling the weight of Lord Armonde's scrutiny. "Fitz was supposed to send me word about my horse. Apparently, he's been too busy."

Lord Armonde relaxed, the mask melting away. "I'm sure his arrival means good news."

"I would have taken any news." Elsie flinched at her bitter tone. She caught the smirk on Lord Armonde's face. He was far too delighted at her frustration with Fitz.

Sophie stepped to the side, waving her fingers at Matthew. Elsie groaned and shook her head. If the earl thought Elsie improper, he would die from the American's lack of decorum.

Matthew grinned and headed toward them—Fitz in tow.

20

FITZBURGH SMITH

Fitz refused to introduce Matthew to Koch's niece, one of the wealthiest men from America. Her father was some sort of diplomat, but Fitz couldn't remember her or her father's name. Matthew was aiming too high. Fitz had given an introduction to a Scottish baron. That was enough. He would now excuse himself and leave—not just the party but the blasted country.

A tall brunette stepped from the back corner, waving her fingers at Matthew. He grinned like a fool, pulling Fitz along. A few steps closer and Fitz recognized Sophie Johnson, the spitting image of her lanky father. Closer still and the forms of both Lord Armonde and Elsie came into view. Lord Armonde stiffened and Elsie gave a slight shake of her head. Fitz understood the message—he wasn't welcome. He carried his new letter he'd written for Elsie, transferring it from one jacket to the next. He swallowed hard. Giving her this letter felt wrong, worse than when he'd written the first, wherever it was. William's advice had slithered into his head, his hand obeying. Fitz feared he'd written too much this time. And like the coward he was— he'd not yet posted the missive.

"I believe I'll take my leave," Fitz whispered.

"What are you afraid of, Fitz?" Matthew grinned, his haggard eyes crinkling. He was looking worse for wear more every day. "Her bark is worse than her bite."

"So you've told her she has no dowry?"

Matthew's face fell. He tugged on his collar. "Not yet."

"The longer you wait, the worse it'll be." Fitz felt every inch of his hypocrisy. His chest warmed where the letter lay.

"Procrastination is my greatest strength." Matthew forced another grin not a moment too soon.

"That is the one and only truth you've ever spoken," Fitz murmured.

Sophie curtseyed to Matthew. "My lord."

Fitz steeled his features. Only a naive American would give such deference to Sir Matthew Bevue. Any other baron would have more prestige but not Matthew. He was a lowly, bankrupt nobleman scraping the barrel for an easy prize.

And yet, Matthew beamed—like a child being told his scribble is worthy of a museum. "Miss Johnson."

Sophie nodded to Fitz. "Mr. Smith."

"Oh, you must call him Fitz." Matthew wrapped an arm around Fitz's shoulder. "He's an old family friend."

"Is he now?" Elsie asked in a low voice filled with warning.

Lord Armonde looked entirely too pleased with himself. He wore his pedigree and a smartly tailored coat. He was the picture of respectability. Fitz soured at the thought. Jonathon smiled and shook Fitz's hand. "You're looking fine this evening."

Elsie arched an eyebrow, her gaze steady—and focused—on Fitz.

Guilt nipped at him. He was no better than her foolish brother. "Elsie ..."

Sophie glanced between the two, then launched into a discussion with Jonathon and Matthew, peppering them with questions about other guests.

Grateful for the strike of mercy, Fitz came to Elsie's side. She didn't face him but kept her back to the wall. "I should have sent word."

"I kept hoping ... you promised." Her voice was small, tugging at Fitz's heart. She shook her head, a dark strand of hair pulling free of her updo. The imperfection suited her—endearingly so. "I assumed the worst."

Something had happened. He wasn't sure exactly what, but Elsie didn't seem angry—she appeared numb. And cold. William had warned Fitz, telling him that a woman needed security and reassurance. Fitz had given Elsie none of that. "I am sorry."

"Are you?" She didn't meet his gaze. "I should have known better—"

Fitz recoiled, her words a slap to his face. Something *had* changed. "Than what?"

In an eerily calm voice, she said, "It was only a silly mare. I shouldn't have asked so much of you, a stranger."

"A silly mare?" Fitz wanted to shake her from this stupor. A *stranger*. He had thought of her every day since she'd left for London. "It's more than that."

"Not enough to warrant—"

"It felt wrong saying it in a letter." This wasn't how Fitz had imagined the conversation would go. He'd thought there would be frustration but not emptiness. He'd expected sorrow, not cold despair. "The mare didn't make it. And every time I tried to write, it just—I didn't know how to break the news. I felt awful. I wanted to bring you joy. Bring you hope. Not grief."

"Thank you for telling me." She brought a hand to her cheek but keep her profile to him. She was lost to a sea of nothing, out of his reach and without emotion.

Fitz pulled the letter from his jacket. Elsie shook her head. The paper stood between them in his offered hand. He didn't know what to do—his world consisted of men and money, not women and feelings. "You were the reason I came."

In a slow pivot, she faced him.

"But I suppose I'm not as brave as I thought." He offered the letter again. "I should have sent it. Or come earlier."

"Or come at all."

He nodded, feeling foolish and simple. "I'm not good at this."

The admission tugged a smile from her lips. "This is true."

"I am sorry, Elsie." Fitz leaned closer, his side against the wall. He opened the envelope and pulled out the letter.

Elsie hesitated, eyeing her brother and Lord Armonde. Gingerly, she accepted the note and read, "'Elsie, I do not know how to tell you. I have stayed away in fear I would make a mess of this.'" Her gaze flicked to Fitz. "'But *Diedrus* passed away the day you left. It's not right. Nor is it fair. This is not how I hoped, how I wanted it to be. She was perfect. She was beautiful for you. You deserve more than this.'" She swallowed hard, whispering, "'With love, Fitz.'"

He inched closer. He'd written *love* without thinking. He'd written to his mother weekly and enclosed the same endearment. Elsie was the only other woman he'd written. He waited but she stared at the letter. He gathered courage and said softly, "I meant what I said."

Jonathon shot him a questioning look. Fitz straightened, as did Elsie.

She folded the letter with trembling hands. "I shouldn't be this sad. I didn't have her that long."

"You and I both know there's more to it than that." He stiffened. He confessed more than he should. Hurrying to cover his mistake, he added, "A horse is freedom."

"That." Elsie searched his face, her eyes narrowing. "Just a moment ago, what did you mean?"

Fitz wanted to disappear, melt into the wall and fade away from her scrutiny. "I just know what it means to lose a horse. An ally."

"Let me know when you're ready to be brave." She pursed her lips. "Or honest."

"Can't you be merciful for once, woman?" He groaned.

"No. I can't." Elsie motioned to the dance floor crammed with people. "It's one of my many flaws. Perhaps you and the earl can compile a list."

"I am not the earl," Fitz growled.

She flinched but didn't cower. "Then stop acting like him."

He leaned closer. This woman found insult in everything Fitz tried to do. A better man would walk away and free the woman from constant pain. But Fitz was no gentleman. "The earl cares for himself and no one else. He would never have taken care of the mare. He wouldn't have taken the time to know you or even know what type of horse you'd need. Or better yet, what you would desire in a horse. He wouldn't know what the animal needed to look like. He wouldn't—"

Elsie placed a hand on his forearm. "You."

"Yes, me." He was confused at her reaction. "Not the earl."

"You." She blinked, her dark eyes filling with moisture. "You gave me the mare."

Jonathon was at her side in an instant. "Are you alright, Elsie?"

Elsie. The intimacy in Lord Armonde's voice sent Fitz reeling. He gave an awkward bow and left, opening and closing his fists at his side. Elsie's words echoed in his ears, *You.* He'd made a grave error and needed to be a world away from the Bevue family. Matthew would corner Fitz and demand a fortune for his sister's reputation. Fitz rubbed the bridge of his nose. Her voice taunted him, repeating again and again in his mind, *You gave me the mare.*

His head clouded, Fitz nearly walked into Tyndeth's wicker wheel-chair. The earl cracked his cane against the side of the chair and snapped at the attendant pushing him forward. Fitz wondered if his fate would mirror Tyndeth's—alone and despised by all who surrounded him. Tyndeth's attendant pushed him forward to where Matthew and Elsie stood, dispersing Sophie and Jonathon with a wave.

Fitz had finally given the message to Elsie; with his confession, two messages. The dratted mare. How had Fitz let that secret slip? He groaned. Any other woman would wrangle a proposal out of him but not Elsie. She'd rejected him. Twice. His confession in giving the mare should have changed everything. He flexed his hand into a tight fist. He could not survive another mistake like this.

There was nothing left for him in London. He'd never truly needed to conduct business in the city. Elsie was at the center of his motiva-tion. He watched from across the room, hoping the earl was delivering his judgment to Matthew and not just Elsie. She didn't deserve ill treatment, from the earl or otherwise.

Matthew gave a solemn nod to the earl before Tyndeth's attendant pushed the wheelchair, back toward the center of the dance floor. They stopped for a moment to give an order to Jonathon Parr. Fitz turned, unable to watch the family work through its troubles. He once thought

Elsie just needed a bit of freedom, that her happiness would be complete if she could race along the countryside on horseback. But she was a grown woman. And Lord Armonde was better suited as her savior. She deserved the heart of a nobleman. Not the coward Fitz had become.

Tyndeth banged the end of the cane against the floor, gathering attention from the surrounding attendees. "Well, Parr what say you?"

Lord Armonde blinked, his surprise evident. "I'm sorry, what?"

Fitz paused, wondering if he was needed. He hadn't publicly courted Elsie, and he wasn't family. He slipped to the shadows to watch. He'd heard rumors of Tyndeth's pettiness. Public or not, the earl got what he wanted.

Tyndeth bellowed, "Are you deaf? Lady Bevue gives her consent. You may now announce your engagement."

"Shouldn't I at least ask?" Lord Armonde forced a laugh, eyeing Elsie. The crowd immediately surrounding the couple grew. Whispers grew.

Elsie gave a subtle shake of her head. She was being coerced—she couldn't willfully participate in this. Not the Elsie Fitz knew. Fitz stepped forward. *Please, no.*

Lord Armonde's gaze flicked between her and Tyndeth, and like the coward Fitz believed he was, Jonathon gave a little nod and whispered, "It'll be fine."

Fitz felt the dread. She couldn't reject Jonathon here, not in front of everyone. Fitz could intervene but not publicly. He'd have to bide his time. He would not leave for Australia until he knew Elsie was safe.

Tyndeth banged the cane again. The crowd surrounding them quieted. "I have the great privilege of announcing the engagement of Lord Jonathon Parr, Marquess of Armonde and Elisheba Bevue."

A fury filled her eyes, her hands shaking. Fitz sighed in relief. If Elsie was furious, she wouldn't submit. She would still fight for her freedom. As would Fitz.

Clapping and shouts of congratulations erupted in the center of the floor. The crowd thinned, revealing Elsie's pale face. Jonathon stood next to her, an adoring smile on his lips. Elsie searched the crowd, settling on Fitz—piercing him to where he stood. She seemed to disappear before him, despair in her gaze. He stepped forward again, his resolve crumbling. He would come if she called. He could not abandon her.

Alice Parr sidled up next to Fitz. "Have you congratulated the happy couple?"

The last person Fitz wanted to have this conversation with was a Parr sibling. Fitz would come up with a plan—on his own. "I will send my regards tomorrow."

"Will you?" The naive persona was dumped and the keen eye of Lady Alice emerged. "I know you've been in town for weeks and yet you've not stopped by the Bevue townhouse."

"Are you training for a magistrate position, Lady Alice?" It'd come across gruff but Fitz was past caring. He lost sight of Elsie and Jonathon as a new wave of people eager to congratulate cut off his view. Fitz wanted out of this dance hall and out of this city. He would help Elsie and then he would leave. His heart lay on the floor, hurting for Elsie. He'd always known she would marry and that Fitz would never be her choice. He should be happy that soon she *would* marry— preferably someone she loved and not a spineless man that Tyndeth dictated.

"I am not a fool, Mr. Smith." Her voice was low and sure. Faint wrinkles framed her eyes and lips. "I am aware of your generosity." She nodded to Matthew and once more toward Sophie. "Americans with wealth can be tempting."

Fitz eyed the blonde lady. She knew about Fitz's introductions. She was not the empty-headed debutante she claimed to be. "I am sorry to cause you—"

She gave a subtle shake of her head. "My parents did not approve. I hold no ill will toward the Bevue family."

"Neither do I." Fitz narrowed his gaze. She was after something. The little patience he held, fled the room.

"I am not a silly debutante. I heard the whispers before Matthew came calling. Tyndeth only confirmed what I already assumed."

"I will not discuss—"

"My parents do not know." She leaned closer, a smile plastered to her lips. "They rarely make an appearance and refuse to indulge in idle gossip."

Fitz dropped all pretense—the little he possessed. "Speak plainly, madam. What is it you're wanting?"

"Once Matthew's financial ruin is known, my parents will no longer approve of her." Alice eyed him. "She is in an impossible situation."

"How is it that you know of her predicament?" He was aware of how daughters and mothers strategized marriage, but he would not be a pawn to Elsie's pain. Alice gave this information as strategy—and Fitz would have no part of it. "Your brother would still propose knowing she was without a dowry?"

Alice smirked—and Fitz realized his mistake. Alice hadn't known for sure until Fitz unwittingly confirmed her suspicions. The earl had been far too vocal when criticizing the Bevue family, fueling rumors that Alice could now use to her advantage.

"I would be careful, Lady Alice." Fitz had brought enough bullies to their knees in his life, Matthew being one. Alice Parr would be no different. "There is a ripple effect with scandal, and women bear the brunt of it."

"I have no intention of being anywhere near the scandal." The gleam in her eye said otherwise.

Fitz crossed his arms. "A cancelled proposal would taint your marriage prospects."

"Thank you for your concern, Mr. Smith. I shall take them to heart." She batted her eyelashes. She clasped her delicate hands to her chest.

"It is not your heart that I worry about."

Alice smirked. "Your heart is the one in danger."

❧ 21 ❧

ELISHEBA BEVUE

Elsie searched the dance hall for Fitz. The emotional highs and lows of the night had kept her nerves on edge. Fitz had confessed to giving her the mare, only to disappear in the crowd. She had placed herself in a dangerous situation when she'd lashed out at Tyndeth in his landau on the way to the dinner party. Her wicked tongue had tied a noose around her neck.

Elsie hated Tyndeth and his tight-fisted influence on her family. She knew Tyndeth would enact revenge, the reason she'd hid on the far side of the dancehall. Elsie could have been safe had Sophie Johnson not invited Matthew and Fitz over to join them. The crowd grew from the earl's announcement. The horrible man was purposely loud. She swallowed hard, forcing herself to smile at the growing crowd.

Lord Armonde cupped her elbow, his smile wide and genuine. He'd cowered to Tyndeth. Lord Armonde hadn't bothered to properly propose. Elsie struggled to breathe. Her legs trembled. Her head pounded. She needed to escape.

An older couple, both hunched and covered in wrinkles, hobbled forward. In a shaky voice the older gentleman offered, "Congratulations, to you both."

The guilt of the announcement made Elsie heart shrink. Tyndeth had cornered Matthew and her, berating Elsie for her behavior earlier in the carriage and announcing her subsequent punishment. She would apologize and become someone else's concern or her family would be cut off. Elsie thought she had days to fix her problem—but Tyndeth had been a step ahead of her. And Lord Armonde had fallen in line. He hadn't even attempted to stand up to the earl. Tyndeth's public speech had turned everything upside down.

Elsie tried to pay attention to the congratulations coming their way. Lord Armonde deftly weaved a path through the floor. The entire proposal was a sham, and Lord Armonde was an unwitting accomplice. He cared for her, that was obvious. Elsie had waited for him to drop his pursuit at every barb Tyndeth had thrown. The earl had made no secret of the Bevue's financial upheaval—the more public, the more vocal Tyndeth would become. For a man so eager to rid the family of Elsie, the earl had worked double time to destroy her one prospect.

Tyndeth sat at the end of the dancehall in his wicker wheelchair, his lips curled to a smirk. He had a front row seat to Elsie's humiliation —soon, she would have no one. And Tyndeth would watch it all.

In a blur, men and women came and went, each with jubilant smiles and handshakes. At long last, an exhausted Elsie was deposited into the earl's landau, opposite her mother and Tyndeth. Just before the carriage lurched forward, Matthew opened the door, sitting beside Elsie in a tired huff.

Lady Bevue's face warmed at the sight of her son. Elsie felt a pang of jealousy. Her mother had never given her the same affection.

Matthew tilted his head back. "That was a long night."

"You've had quite a few long nights of late," Lady Bevue murmured.

Tyndeth scoffed but said nothing. The festivities had taken its toll on the ancient man as well. His frailty offered little consolation to Elsie, her heart full of nothing but pain.

"I've missed you too, Mother." Matthew leaned forward, his elbows on his knees.

Collectively, the Bevues eyed the earl and said nothing until they were dropped off at their house, the earl staying several houses down at his magnificent estate at the end of Regent Park. Stepping into her childhood home, Elsie glanced back at the landau where Tyndeth was alone. She'd lived by herself in Wales and, despite the peace, there were moments of intense loneliness. Her heart squeezed, wondering if Tyndeth's anger came from his isolation. The sympathy was chased away by thoughts of her own future.

"I do not believe I've given you my own congratulations, Elsie." Lady Bevue squeezed Elsie's hands, her smile weak.

Matthew paused at the foot of the stairs, a hand on the railing. "You deserve happiness."

"Does Tydneth speak the truth?" Elsie had to know, everything depended on it. She didn't trust Matthew's sudden concern.

"He abhors falsehoods," Lady Bevue offered gently.

"Is our situation as dire as he says?" Elsie would not back down. "Are we truly at his mercy?"

Matthew tossed over his shoulder, "It's been a long night. This can wait."

"If I do not marry, can we draw from my dowry?" Elsie tugged her gloves from off her hands. "Would that help?"

Matthew turned around, his face long and his eyes downcast. "There is no dowry."

Elsie gripped her gloves in her hand. She was tired of Matthew's arrogance, insisting he knew more than she ever would. "Father set aside—"

"Father said a lot of things." Matthew looked passed his sister, his focus on his mother. "We have nothing."

"That's not possible." Doubt crept in. Elsie's father had promised he'd provided for her. He'd said it again and again the summer before her season. This wasn't happening. Tyndeth couldn't be the only one telling the truth. The lack of dowry made her a fraud.

Matthew held out his arms. "This house will be sold to pay debts. I've still not heard back about the Glamorgan estate."

"Do you realize what this means?" Elsie glanced between her mother and brother. Neither met her gaze. "How could you offer congratulations when you both knew I had nothing to offer the Parr family? How am *I* the improper Bevue when you two have deceived me? And what of Jonathon Parr? What of his parents? They believe I come with a dowry. They can cancel the engagement."

"Sophie Johnson has a dowry that puts our worries to shame." Matthew shrugged, still not looking his sister in the eye.

"You never planned on telling me." Elsie closed her eyes briefly. She shouldn't be surprised. Matthew couldn't admit defeat. "Your solution is to pour more money into a bleeding wound."

Lady Bevue stepped forward. "Elsie—"

"Do not placate me, Mother." Shaking her head, she retreated from them. They were her family. They were supposed to help her, support her. Protect her. They'd done none of it. "You've become the earl's slave. That is your choice. Matthew can chase whomever he pleases, but I will have no part in this."

Matthew folded his arms across his chest. "If you break off this engagement—"

"What?" Elsie threw her hands up in the air. "What could possibly happen to make this worse? How can you provide records of a dowry that doesn't exist?"

"We've survived this long, haven't we?" Matthew ran a finger along the staircase railing. He hiccupped—another night for Matthew to overindulge.

"If you break the engagement, we will fall from grace," Lady Bevue whispered. Her shoulders hunched. "I've tried. After everything I've done, it wasn't enough."

"We've already fallen," Elsie cried. She reached for the staircase, her legs shaking. "The blame is not with me. If Tyndeth truly cared for you, Mother, he would not have pushed for the proposal. He would have—"

"Elsie," Matthew warned. He could assign blame to Elsie because he never took responsibility, even when her father was alive.

"If he was like Father, he would have married you two years before." Elsie hugged herself. "Not strung you along and tormented your daughter."

"If you had held your tongue, we would not be in this mess." Lady Bevue's face hardened. Her dark hair and eyes became foreign, all maternal affection gone. "You are the reason Tyndeth postponed our engagement. We have been limping along because you thought only of *your* pride. *Your* hurt. I miss your father, but he cannot help us from the grave."

"I have read Father's ledger." The lie came easy. Elsie hadn't touched the book. She'd held them close to remind her of Wales, but her brother's face drained of color, Elsie's suspicion was confirmed. "Father is not the reason for this family's failure. Neither am I."

Matthew swallowed hard, his head lowering. Elsie picked up her skirts and marched past him. He shot out an arm, holding her shoulder. "I will fix this. I swear it."

Elsie pulled from his grasp and ran up the stairs. She slammed her bedroom door and let out a frustrated yell. She sat at the vanity and stared at her reflection. She would not let Tyndeth win—nor would she simply stand by while her family let her reputation sully. They'd made a liar out of her. This was how the world worked. Elsie had no control of her dowry or finances, but a broken engagement—prompted by either the Parr family or Elsie—would reduce Elsie to a castaway, a lady without character.

Her two year stint in Wales had sharpened her perception. She'd applied for dozens of positions, both as a governess and as a lady's companion. Without consent from a brother or father, she'd been rejected by one and all. And now with a potential broken engagement on the horizon, her prospects were even darker. No matter where she turned, she was trapped. Holding her head in her hands, she fought for a clear mind. If she were to be caged, she might as well choose her captor.

The soft, quick knock of her maid pulled Elsie from her thoughts. Mary offered a sympathetic frown and made quick work of Elsie's dress. "It'll work out, my lady. Your brother will see to it."

Your brother. The words were fire in Elsie's mind. Her family would not help, but Elsie knew one person who would. Her hand shot out, holding Mary's. "I have a favor to ask of you."

Mary stilled, her face sober. "It has to do with the engagement?"

Elsie nodded. "I have not been told the truth about my family. Lord Armonde deserves to know."

The maid's eyebrows rose. "You wish to end it?"

"I wish to tell him the truth." Elsie hesitated, testing Mary's loyalties. In Wales, Doris and Griffiths would have Elsie's best interest in mind. Mary was still new—and hired by Matthew. "It is the honorable thing to do."

"You do not wish to end it, then?" Mary asked again.

A pang of loneliness hit Elsie. Mary was a simple maid—a girl who more than likely couldn't read—but if her loyalties lay with Matthew, Elsie's impromptu plan would have to change. "No, not at the moment."

Mary's shoulders fell in relief—answering Elsie's suspicion. Her plan to send the truth in a letter to Lord Armonde would have to wait. Elsie's trusted circle of friends consisted of only one. The image of Fitz appeared in her mind, his voice echoing in her ears.

Elsie's face flushed, remembering Fitz's beautiful confession. He'd given her the mare, the spitting image of her late father's horse. Tyndeth had turned a beautiful night into a painful terror.

Mary began brushing Elsie's hair, humming softly. "Oh, love looks good on you, my lady."

22

FITZBURGH SMITH

Fitz entered his London townhome to find Matthew Bevue in his sitting room, swirling a glass of brandy in his hand. The baron's eyes were hooded, dark circles revealing a night of little sleep.

"To what do I owe the pleasure?" Sarcasm saturated Fitz's tone. He was both angry and anxious to see Matthew. Dozens of questions rang in his ears, all of which had to do with Elsie. He took his time, walking slowly to the hearth.

"No congratulations?"

"Did she agree to the marriage?"

Matthew raised his eyebrows and hesitated. "They are still engaged. There's to be a marriage."

Fitz wouldn't count on it, not with the crumpled shirt and blood-shot eyes of his visitor. "Then why are you here?"

Matthew held out a letter, the seal broken. "My sister wishes to see you."

"You opened a letter addressed to me?" Fitz shouldn't be surprised.

Matthew tapped the envelope against the armrest of the sofa. "Opening the letter doesn't change the contents."

"You broke into a pillar box?" Fitz stood before the arrogant baron.

Wisps of blond hair fell across Matthew's forehead, reminding Fitz of the late baron. The Bevue family had been unanchored since the man had passed away. Fitz didn't know the best approach. Losing a parent wasn't something Fitz had experience with. "Stealing the post is still a crime no matter your rank."

"You assume the envelope made it to the box." Matthew scoffed and tossed the letter to Fitz. "Check the front, there's no stamp."

Fitz ran a thumb over where the adhesive should have been, confirming Matthew's statement. The world had gone mad—or at least, the Bevue family. Elsie's brother had intercepted the envelope before the stamp could be placed. A delicate feminine hand had written *Fitz Smith* but no address. Elsie—or perhaps Lady Bevue —had either waited for his address to be given or had known the letter would be intercepted.

"You've been summoned." Matthew pushed himself to a stand, wavering a moment, before setting his glass on the end table. "My job here is done."

"Dare I ask why you opened a letter addressed to me?" Fitz knew of Elsie's engagement to Jonathon Parr. He was there when the congratulations had begun. And yet, Elsie had written to him. She'd called out to *him,* not Jonathon.

"My sister is not in her right mind of late." Matthew stretched and wobbled to the door. He'd either not been to bed or was recovering from a night of celebration.

"Says the man who cannot walk." Fitz was missing something.

Matthew scowled and straightened his posture, only to rub his eyes with shaky hands. "I'm not the one ruining everything."

"Do not place the blame on your sister." Fitz felt no guilt when Matthew flinched.

"I blame Tyndeth." Matthew shrugged. "And Elsie."

"Do not—"

"You have your blasted letter." Matthew threw both hands in the air and stumbled out the door.

Staring out the window, Fitz waited until the baron appeared on the street before reading the note.

I have exciting news. Please let me tell you in person. Regent Park Entrance. Noon. —*E. Bevue*

He refolded the note and sat. Elsie was well aware of Fitz's attendance last night. He had confessed to giving her the mare. There was no reason for them to meet. Granted, Fitz had not congratulated Lord Armonde. He'd rather punch Jonathon than give him a clap on the back. How the marquess had managed to snag Elsie baffled Fitz. She was in a tough position but still, it was hard to imagine Elsie agreeing to the marriage. She'd looked terrified last night. He had to be missing something. That, or Matthew was lying.

Fitz slipped the note in his jacket pocket and went to the fireplace, her brother forgotten. He leaned against the mantel. He would be lying if her acceptance of Lord Armonde's proposal didn't bother him. Fitz had offered marriage—more than that, he'd offered freedom. He would never demand decorum or give into whatever the *ton* dictated as proper. She could come and go as she pleased. Jonathan Parr caved both to society and his parents; the marquess was no closer to becoming a man than Matthew Bevue.

A quick glance at the mantel clock told Fitz he was short on time. If Elsie was planning on heading to the park, she'd have to walk, her maid in tow. She wouldn't dare ask for the earl's carriage or the Parr's—especially not to meet Fitz. She would be on foot, meaning she'd leave at half past eleven. Matthew had opened her letter and would no doubt be watching the park. Whatever had made the sniveling baron panic enough to break the seal of an envelope was significant enough for Matthew to keep watch.

Fitz rubbed the back of his neck, not fully convinced of his paranoia. Elsie could in fact just want to tell him about her proposal. Nothing more, nothing less.

There was only one way to find out. In little time, Fitz waited inside his carriage down the road from the Bevue townhome. At exactly half past eleven, Elsie left the home, her maid two paces behind her.

Fitz descended from his carriage directly in front of a surprised Elsie. "Would you prefer a ride to the park?"

Elsie nibbled her lip and glanced back at her maid whose head was obediently tucked. "I believe we would appreciate the ride."

He offered a hand. She shoved a thick envelope toward him. He quickly tucked the envelope inside his jacket and prayed the maid hadn't seen the exchange. Elsie and her maid sat opposite him in the carriage, an awkward silence filling the space between them. The maid kept her gaze on her clasped hands while Elsie stared out the window, her face full of longing.

"Are congratulations in order?" Fitz asked carefully. Speaking in code was not his forte.

Elsie nodded slowly, cautiously. "A proposal was announced."

A bitterness filled him—followed by surprise. Fitz already knew the proposal had happened but having the woman confirm it felt different. "Your brother visited me this morning."

Elsie's gaze flicked to his. "My brother?"

Fitz watched the maid but she gave no hint of betrayal. He pulled the opened letter from his jacket, careful to not disturb the new envelope Elsie had just given him. "He dropped this off."

Elsie took the letter, her face blank. She leaned closer to her maid. "Mary, do you know how my brother could have received this?"

"No, my lady." Again, no reaction.

With a tight smile, Elsie turned over the envelope. Her eyes didn't widen. Her mouth didn't part. There was no hint of surprise. "Where is the postage I'd given you?"

The maid shrugged, never lifting her chin.

Fitz cleared his throat. "The seal was broken, Elsie."

She ran a finger under edge of the fold. "It seems I have no one to trust in my own home."

Mary raised her head, her eyes wide. "I've no choice, my lady."

"There is always a choice," Elsie murmured, turning back toward the window.

"You do not seem shocked."

Elsie closed her eyes for a moment. She sighed, her face relaxing. With a subtle shake, she opened her eyes and said softly, "Fitz, would you mind terribly if we returned to my house? I feel suddenly out of sorts."

Fitz gave the order but didn't buy the lie. The woman's disposition hadn't changed, unlike her maid who shifted nervously next to her. The sealed letter in his pocket warmed his chest. Fitz would tear into it the second the women were returned. No one spoke. Each hoof step closer, the tension grew.

At the estate, Matthew greeted his sister and maid. Each gave a curt nod and walked past him to the house. To Fitz, Matthew mouthed, *What happened?*

Instead of answering, Fitz climbed back into the carriage. Matthew ran to the carriage. Just as Fitz was about to close the door, Matthew yanked on the handle.

"You never made it to the park." Matthew's breath reeked of alcohol.

"Your sister no longer wanted to meet." Fitz was tempted to shake Matthew by the shoulders, but the man's bloodshot eyes begged for mercy. Pity at the very least.

Matthew shifted his weight. "Did she say why?"

"I believe it had to do with her maid." Fitz hoped the annoyance showed in his tone. He tapped the inside of the carriage, signaling his driver that he was ready to depart.

Matthew opened his mouth to say something but shook his head, deciding against it. He ran his fingers through his golden hair and turned around. There was a note of hopelessness in his stance.

Fitz felt a twinge of sympathy. He'd known what it was like to be found wanting, left on the outskirts, dismissed simply because of who he was. Or rather, who he wasn't.

Matthew was once in the very center, taunting Fitz and everyone else without a title. Matthew, like most boys on the cusp of manhood, fought for his place in the world by setting down lesser boys. Fitz was once a scrawny ginger, both flaws garnered scorn and teasing from children. Not until Fitz had begun to grow—both in stature and in wealth—did the teasing fade.

Except Elsie. She'd never teased.

23

ELISHEBA BEVUE

Matthew had stood in the front garden when the carriage arrived, and again, Elsie shouldn't have been surprised. But she was. Elsie hadn't said a word on the short ride back to her house, her maid shifting uncomfortably next to her. *As she should.* Elsie had little sympathy for Mary. She had known Matthew hired her in Wales and that her loyalties should lay with him, but Elsie had hoped, or rather assumed, that Mary would be Elsie's friend. Or at least an ally.

The second betrayal cut as much as the first. Matthew usually didn't get out of bed until past noon, but today of all days, he'd been to Fitz's house and now appeared to be ready for an outing—more than likely to spy on Elsie.

The thought sent a rush of anger, her cheeks and neck flushing red. She climbed the staircase with all the ladylike sensitivity of an elephant. She pulled the door shut behind her, spinning around when it caught.

"Please, Miss Bevue." Mary stuck her shoe between the frame and the door. "I'm sorry. I'm so sorry."

"Leave me be, Mary." Elsie needed the maid to believe her, time was not on Elsie's side. She had much to do—assuming Fitz read her letter and was willing to help.

Mary shouldered the door open. "Please, I can't lose my position."

"I've said nothing of the sort." Not that Elsie had the authority to release the maid. "Your employment belongs to my brother."

Mary hung her head. "I have to obey him, milady."

"I've not spoken a single word against you." Elsie sat at the vanity, eyeing the clock on the wall. There was much to do and little time granted. Hope and doubt swirled in her head.

"My family depends on me." Mary wrung her hands together. "I can't ... can't lose—"

Elsie hoped she was giving a reassuring smile. "I know the predicament you are in but I need to be alone."

After a moment of hesitation, Mary left. Elsie waited for her footsteps to fade and then sprang into action. She packed her worn riding habit and a threadbare day dress, followed by her father's ledger and journals. She was grateful she'd stolen them from her Welsh home. She'd given two letters to Fitz, one for him and one for Lord Armonde. The marquess deserved to know the truth, the whole of it. He would understand the reason for breaking off the engagement once he read her words. Either way, she would never see him again.

She had to be careful. She needed to cause a scene with her family. So many pieces needed to fit together—she wrung her hands. She'd asked Fitz to meet her at the party tonight. If Fitz didn't help her ... her hands shook. He had to. He was her only hope.

Hours ticked by until the family's appointed departure came. Elsie snuffed all but one candle and slid under her covers, her day dress still on.

Mary knocked and quietly entered. "Miss Bevue?"

"Not now, Mary." Elsie rolled over, groaning. "I have a terrible headache."

"Your family is preparing to leave," Mary murmured.

Elsie tucked her head under the covers, saying nothing. Mary paced beside the bed and then left. The maid tried once more—only to leave again.

A harder knock on the door came, muffling her brother's voice. "Elsie?"

Elsie waited for him to enter but he neither opened the door nor knocked again. Soon enough, the slow, deliberate knock of her mother came. Elsie felt her pulse race. No matter her age, deceiving her mother would always make Elsie nervous.

The door opened with a squawk, followed by the rustling of fabric. The mattress shifted as Lady Bevue sat and pulled back the heavy covers. "We do not cower when life gets hard. It's time to face the world, child."

Elsie gingerly sat up, making sure to sigh and groan as she did so. "I am not the one cowering, mother."

"And yet you hide."

Elsie grabbed her mother's hand, placing the palm against her neck. "Do you feel that racing pulse?"

Lady Bevue pulled on her hand. "Settle your nerves. We leave soon."

"Settle my nerves?" Elsie recoiled from her mother. "That is all you can say to me? My brother has spent my dowry—made me a liar to my betrothed—and all you can say is, *settle your nerves?*"

"Elsie—"

"No." Elsie folded her arms over her legs, shaking her head. "I will face the world but not today. Not tonight."

"You are a lady—"

"Who was set up to fail by your beloved earl and my brother." Elsie spat the words. Strength filled her bones. She could leave—she *would* leave. It was time. "You betrayed your own daughter. Tyndeth knew the dowry was gone but wants to see me suffer. You knew as well but said nothing."

Lady Bevue snapped to a stand. "Elisheba Bevue, you are not blameless."

"I slapped the man." Elsie launched herself from the bed, facing her mother. "Why not take a sword and run me through? That would be a better option than living with the deceit and contempt of my own family."

Lady Bevue covered her mouth, her eyes wide. Slowly, she collected herself, her back stiffening and her face stilling. She let her hands fall to her side and whispered, "Your nerves have got the best of you. Tomorrow you will see reason. Tyndeth will be here any moment. We will speak as a family then."

"He is not family."

"We announce our engagement tonight." Lady Bevue held up her hand, revealing a large emerald ring. "You will be there."

"I would rather rot than ride with that man."

Her mother opened the door, revealing a penitent Mary. Speaking to the maid, she said, "Miss Bevue will need help readying for tonight. Please hurry as we do not want to keep the earl waiting."

"Unless you strip me down and change me yourself, this is how I am going." Elsie folded her arms. The larger her protest, the easier she could disappear.

"If you wish to embarrass Lord Armonde, that is your choice." Lady Bevue left the room, slamming the door behind her.

Elsie felt a twinge of satisfaction. Her mother had never slammed a door, or any other unladylike behavior. But tonight, Elsie's words had hit their mark. The satisfaction fled, replaced with the guilt of what she was about to do. Elsie had hoped she wouldn't be forced to attend. She allowed Mary to dress her, keeping her comments to a minimum.

Before Mary left the room, Elsie asked, "Will you please grab me two parcel wraps?"

"For what?"

"My engagement is days away from ending, I'd like to give Lord Armonde something while he still cares."

Mary nodded slowly and returned with two parcel wraps. As soon as her maid was gone, Elsie wrapped her riding habit and day dress between the journals and ledger. She addressed the outside to *Fitzburgh Smith* and quickly covered the name with another wrap, this time without a name. She didn't know who to put on the outside. If she was forced to hand over the parcel she would have to think of someone to trust. Her brother had already proven he'd open her letters.

Hugging the parcel to her chest, Elsie descended the stairs and was greeted by a seething earl and silent mother. Matthew was nowhere to be seen. He would conveniently—again and again—be missing when the earl gave his lecture during another uncomfortable carriage ride.

Tyndeth smacked his cane against the wicker chair. "You will apologize for the late hour."

"How long will you hold this family hostage?" Elsie's heart pounded in her chest. She ignored her mother's glare. This would be the last time she saw her mother and hopefully the earl. She wanted her words to be heard.

"Your wickedness has held your family hostage." The earl gripped his cane, his knuckles white. "I've saved your family from your father's recklessness."

"This family's misfortune was not my father's—"

"Elsie," her mother warned. She patted Tyndeth's shoulders. "My daughter has always idolized her father. I pray she will be equally devoted to her husband."

The earl smirked. Elsie's cheeks warmed at the set down from her mother. The entire proposal situation was unfair, just as the blame of financial ruin was unjustly given to her father. She clutched her parcel and, giving the earl's wheelchair a wide berth, marched to the carriage.

"Why are you taking a package to a dinner party?" Lady Bevue followed her daughter.

"It's a gift, mother." Elsie refused to speak another word while her mother and Tyndeth were helped into the carriage.

They arrived at the curved entry. Elsie didn't wait for an attendant; she threw open the door and jumped to the ground.

Lady Bevue shouted, "Elisheba Bevue—" Her mother's word were cut off with the carriage door slamming shut.

Elsie scurried up the stairs with the footmen eyeing her hurried ascent. Instead of entering the main hall, she slipped toward the powder room, waiting for a bigger group to enter. An older couple entered—they weren't large enough to hide behind, but Elsie was running out of time. She snuck behind them and hunched her shoulders, hoping to appear as a humble lady's companion. With her head bent, she followed them to the matron's corner, where silver-haired men and women gossiped about the young debutantes. She tucked herself between the matrons and the wall, sneaking toward the back. Her heart pounded in her chest. She neared the back door.

"Elsie!" Matthew shouted from behind her.

Three more steps. Elsie quickened her pace.

"Elsie!" Her brother sounded closer.

She rushed to the outer courtyard, her arms aching from carrying the parcel. She heard a rustle from the side and ran toward it, down the steps into the dark garden. Arms wrapped around her, covering her with a black robe.

"This way," Fitz whispered and pulled her into an enormous bush.

"Elsie!" Matthew's voice carried to where Elsie and Fitz stood.

Through the branches, she squinted, watching Matthew's blurry shadow zip back and forth across the courtyard. He descended the same steps she'd just walked down, his face shadowed by the night. Elsie inhaled sharply.

"Elsie," Matthew hissed to the night air. "Stop this."

She trembled, her arms weak from carrying her father's journals and ledger. Matthew groaned and marched down the darkened path away from the house, calling her name.

Fitz wrapped his arms around Elsie and gently pulled the parcel from her hands. His presence calmed her, lulling her heart to a steady rhythm. His nearness quieted her fears. Warmth spread through her. With his lips brushing against her temple, he whispered, "We wait until he goes back inside. Then we run."

Elsie could only nod and then felt silly, realizing Fitz couldn't see her in the dark. She was vulnerable with her father's books in Fitz's hands. Of all the things she could have taken with her, she'd chosen his journals. Fitz more than likely thought her a foolish girl, but those journals had her mark as well. As a child, her father would trace her hand on a page and let her scribble. Later, when she was learning to write, her father would pretend to look the other way while she wrote a sentence or two for him. The letters were never quite right and the spelling was questionable. Only in her father's journals could she be both imperfect *and* beloved.

❧ 24 ❧

FITZBURGH SMITH

itz was hiding in an oversized bush—with Elsie. In the dark.
If they were caught, her reputation would be utterly
ruined. She was already flirting with disaster. He'd come to
help and convince her of another alternative. He'd not yet given her
letter to Jonathon Parr. Fitz had read—and reread—the letter she'd
addressed to him. He'd been torn. She'd admitted to knowing her
future was bleak and that her only escape was through an elopement.
Fitz had been tempted to destroy the letter right then and there.
Jonathon wouldn't agree to run off and marry her. Neither would his
family. The mere suggestion would force the Parr family to turn on her.

You offered your help once before, I need you now, Elsie had written, the
words echoing in his mind.

Matthew hissed again, directly in front of them. She flinched and
Fitz stifled a groan. Nothing good would come from Matthew catching
them. Her brother turned away, following the garden path, calling after
Elsie. Fitz leaned closer, her scent of rose water making him pause. He
swallowed hard—realizing all over again that he was alone with a lady.

In a bush.

In the dark.

He silently cursed himself. Every uncomfortable moment in the past few weeks had involved the woman next to him. And yet, he found himself leaning closer. He felt an overwhelming urge to wrap his arms around her—and then froze. He'd *actually* wrapped his arm around, the other arm holding her parcel. He couldn't give in to the burgeoning desire, the wanting. She was the girl who'd visited the country as a child, the younger sister of Fitz's university bully—not someone to seduce in a dark garden.

Matthew raced back through the path, rushing up the stairs and into the house. Elsie exhaled, shifting next to Fitz. He grabbed her hand and together they kept to the shadows, running along the side of the house. The parcel in one hand and Elsie in the other, Fitz guided them to his carriage tucked at the edge of the entrance. He helped Elsie inside and climbed in after her. The carriage lurched forward, tossing them together—smashing the parcel between them.

"Oh," Elsie murmured, appearing to be more concerned about the package than of Fitz's nearness.

He sat next to her, wondering how he'd come to this moment, sneaking a lady out of a dinner party. He should feel guilty but instead felt a rush of protectiveness. Elsie—his thoughts were always of her. "I think my grandfather is rolling in his grave."

Elsie paused, cradling books to her chest. "I shouldn't have involved you. I just didn't know who I could turn to. Who I could trust."

"I am not sorry." Again, he found himself smiling. *I'm a fool.*

"But you will be. Eventually." A piece of clothing fell with the parcel wrappings.

"What is this?" Fitz reached for it. The streetlamp offered more shadows than light.

"My riding habit." She seemed to shrink.

Fitz's heart sank. She was too naive, innocently thinking Jonathon Parr would elope. Jealousy pierced him; Jonathon didn't deserve her. He never would. "He won't do it, Elsie."

"It's the right thing to do." Her voice came small, clenching his heart. "He'll have no choice in the end."

Fitz pulled the letter addressed to Lord Armonde from his jacket. "I didn't deliver the letter. If you ask me to, I will, but I need you to know that just asking Jonathon for an elopement is enough for his parents to intervene."

Elsie tucked her chin. "You didn't read it, did you?"

Fitz scoffed. "I would never."

"I wasn't asking him to elope." Elsie curled away from Fitz.

"Then what were you asking him?" Tension had filled the space between them, and he didn't understand why. She'd been both vague and clear. She'd written to him of her lack of dowry and how that fact would cancel her agreement. She kept stating an elopement was her only way out. Fitz had to think of another solution for her. The dinner party would be over in just a few hours. He had until then to convince her of reason.

"I wasn't asking him for anything." She shifted in the dark. "I was telling him the truth. Everything."

Relief washed over him. He was grateful Elsie had reached out to him and felt the first spark of hope. "He will see reason, eventually."

"And what is the reasonable thing to do?" Elsie faced him and with despair etched in her tone, she said, "We're circling downtown London."

"I'd asked my driver to—"

"—go in circles until you could convince me of my foolishness." She buried her head in her hands. He placed a hand on her shoulder; she recoiled. "Don't. Just don't. Everyone has a plan. Everyone is a just a piece in a game of chess. You are no different. Neither am I."

"I thought you were going to ask Jonathon to run away with you. I couldn't stand by and let you throw your life away." Fitz was completely lost. She'd just admitted she wasn't asking Lord Armonde to elope.

She gathered her things, hastily rewrapping the clothes and the books in the torn wrapping. "I need to go."

"What are you doing?"

"I thought I was so clever." Elsie sniffed, wiping her cheeks with her hand. "It's all fallen through."

"Hey ..." Fitz cooed. "What were your plans?"

"To elope, Fitz." Elsie cried out.

"He won't—"

"You, Fitz." She banged a fist on the seat between them. "I was asking to elope with you."

You, Fitz. The details fell into place. Her words in the letter raced in his mind. He was an utter fool. He ran a hand down his face. This was his fault. He'd given the suggestion weeks ago. She'd asked for him, not out of affection but rather desperation. He was both flattered and wounded.

Silence stretched between them, punctuated by the horseshoes clapping against cobbled stone streets.

"Did you mention me in the letter to Jonathon?" Fitz asked quietly. He could not walk away. He would do everything to protect her, whether she cared for him or not. Perhaps this was the love his mother spoke of.

"No." Elsie turned back toward the window, her hands wiping the tears running down her cheek. "I told him about the dowry and how sorry I was that he would be embarrassed. That I was going to fix it the only way I knew how. And ..." She hiccupped. "... that I hoped he'd find love someday."

"Does he know you plan to elope?"

She shook her head. Fitz lowered the window and shouted for the driver, handing Lord Armonde's letter to his servant. "This needs to be delivered to Lord Armonde at the dinner party, but first, return to the townhome."

Elsie whispered, "Please don't make me go home."

Fitz pulled her hand between his. William Johnson was right. Fitz needed a woman to sort out his life. The lady next to him was just fiery enough to help in his adventures. "Elisheba Bevue, will you run away with me?"

"You don't have to."

"It would be an honor." Fitz felt the twinge of guilt. He wasn't just helping a woman in need. Deep down, he felt smug. Elsie was well above his reach. He wasn't the romantic like his mother, but he felt twice as tall snagging Miss Bevue.

"Thank you." She pulled her hand from his and lowered her gaze.

"Elsie?" When she didn't answer, he asked, "Have I ever lied to you?"

"Not that I'm aware of." There was doubt in her voice.

"So when I say it's an honor, it *is*." The words fell flat. Fitz had been more confused in her presence than at any other time in his life. He thought she'd be happy. Or at least content. His mother reminisced about his father's proposal every Christmas. If both parents weren't still traveling the continent, they'd be tipsy with congratulations.

"You are an honorable man."

"An honorable man wouldn't meet a lady in a dark garden. Or ask her twice to run away with him."

"I hate this." Elsie groaned in frustration. The sound offered relief to Fitz; her irritation more like the lady he admired than the broken woman a moment before. "I'm not a damsel in distress—"

"I'm fully aware of what I'm getting into."

"Are you?" She turned in a huff, sitting sideways on the seat and faced him. "I cannot paint a thing. My musicality is abominable. I cannot sit or do needle work."

The carriage came to a stop. Fitz descended and offered his hand. Warmth flowed from the touch. He didn't need the *ton*'s version of a lady. He needed Elsie, untamed and free. "You can ride."

Stepping down, she smirked. "That is the one and only talent I have."

"You convinced a determined bachelor to marry."

"That is not a talent, Fitz." Elsie lowered her eyes. "That is a fault."

"Not if the bachelor is me."

25

ELISHEBA BEVUE

W alking to Fitz's front door, Elsie wrapped the robe tightly around her. She tucked her head under the borrowed black hood that Fitz had brought to the garden. He'd been more prepared than Elsie, giving her another round of apprehension. He'd been in business with Matthew. Duplicity might be in his nature. Fitz had mentioned the townhome was rented. The amount must be staggering with the proximity so close to Regent's Park. Her stomach tightened. Fitz was wealthy and could have snared an accomplished lady or better yet, a pretty American heiress. He was a gentleman and had money, both of which Elsie wished for. If she were a man she could have entered a profession, or if she had money she'd be free and content as a spinster.

The streetlamp flickered, casting eerie shadows. Elsie gripped Fitz's hand tightly. He wrapped an arm around her, his other arm carrying her battered parcel. The warmth of safety filled her. She'd felt it before in her father's study and again when her mare was injured. He dropped his arm as they entered the townhome. She shivered from the loss of contact and realization of her decision. She had just walked into an unmarried man's house without a companion or chaperone of any kind. Her reputation would be shattered. There was no turning back.

She risked a glance at Fitz, his face unbothered as if this was just another night. What kind of life did he live where this kind of adventure was ordinary?

"Are you still ..." She took a deep breath. "Are you still in business with my brother? Will this complicate matters?"

Fitz paused—a foot in the air. "You think I would enter into business with Matthew?"

"You were in my family's study. Back in Wales."

He shook his head. "So that's what Matthew calls being in business? I'm not that foolish."

Relief filled her. "Then what were you doing?"

He tucked his chin. "To be honest, I was checking on you."

She froze. *I was checking on you.*

"And the mare. I could lie and come up with another excuse, but there it is."

Guilt burrowed into her. She'd taken advantage of Fitz. He cared for her. *She* was the duplicitous one. She had shackled him to her. And yet, his touch soothed her.

Fitz deposited her father's books and clothes on the sofa. She grimaced. He'd touched her clothes. Everything about this moment was both intimate and inappropriate. Yet there was nothing she could do. She would repay him, somehow. In some way.

"We need a carpet bag for her things." He spoke to the butler and then sat on the far end of the sofa. He was calm without a hint of distress. Nothing at all like the storm inside her. He waited for his servant to leave and then scooted closer. "It will take two days, possibly three to make it across the border. Or we could hide out for three weeks and marry in Wales."

"You cannot have the banns read if we're in hiding." The heaviness in her chest eased despite the topic. Somehow the discussion of what to do relaxed her. Sheepishly, she wished he'd touch her. She wanted the steady feel of him.

"True." Fitz smirked. "Forgive me, but how old are you?"

"Nineteen." Elsie squirmed. She was about to marry a man who didn't know her at all. She'd only known him a few months, and most of that time, she'd been courted by Lord Armonde.

Fitz grinned and cocked his head. "That's how old my mother was."

"Oh." Elsie was England's most wretched lady. She'd conned a motherless man. "I'm sorry for your loss."

"When she got married, Elsie." Reaching over, he squeezed her hand once before releasing it. "She's alive and well."

"Oh."

He arched an eyebrow. "You don't have to go through with it. I can take you back this instant."

Elsie shook her head. She inhaled slowly and said softly, "I'm not of age. I suppose Scotland it is."

Fitz hesitated and ran a hand down his face. "Why do I feel like I'm taking advantage of a lady?"

"I believe I am the one taking advantage."

"You're a lady." He pulled her hood back. "I'm the lowly mister."

"I have to ask." She prayed for courage. "Is there someone ..." She swallowed hard. "Is there someone you were hoping to—"

"Elsie." Fitz took both her hands in his. Her heart raced. "If I wanted to court someone I would have. I'm closer to thirty than twenty and have never courted anyone."

"You're older than Matthew?" Elsie sat up. She'd assumed Fitz was closer to her age, not Matthew's.

Fitz let go of her hands and pulled at his collar. "I was a sickly child and entered school later than most."

"You're *years* older than him?" Elsie winced. For the love of all that's holy, why couldn't she shut her dratted mouth?

"That I am." Fitz's neck and cheeks flushed an adorable pink. He walked to the stack of papers on a table near the mantel. "I need to send a letter to my solicitor. I know only of Scotland's laws regarding debts, not marriage."

"I didn't mean to embarrass you." She didn't want to admit it, but there was something sweet about his sudden shyness. He'd been attentive in the carriage and on the sofa, but the topic of his age had sent him across the room. She wanted him near. She would never admit it, but she was very much the damsel in distress. She felt safe when he was close, when he gave even the lightest of contact.

"May I suggest we leave within the hour?" He shuffled the papers, fumbling with pens and ink bottles.

Fitz must not entertain often. The townhome was tidy and well-kept but not at all functional for society. The furniture was hardly used and placed close to the fire—appearing to be meant for comfort instead of social calls. The room had a bare quality, as if he either had never really moved in or was readying to leave.

"Fitz?"

He paused, his hands on the desk. He seemed nervous. Dread filled Elsie. She would try one last time. "Are you absolutely certain?" Elsie held her breath, wishing he'd answer honestly but praying he wouldn't.

"Are you?" Fitz straightened, meeting Elsie's gaze. "You do not have to marry me. I will do everything in my power to protect you, regardless of your answer."

There was a pleading in his voice, as if he cared—no, Elsie shook the thought. She was reading into what she wanted to see, not what was before her. Elsie was difficult, a fact she knew and wouldn't fault anyone for their frustration. Least of all, Fitz. She paused. What *did* she want? She swallowed. She wanted the impossible, freedom and Fitz. "I don't want you to resent me."

Searching her face, he came to her slowly. She felt curiously exposed under his scrutiny. He took her hand and took a knee before her.

"No, Fitz." She pulled on his hand. "Please, don't kneel."

He didn't move, his eyes still scanning her. With a sigh, she kneeled, mirroring his stance. Fitz grinned. "You have no idea how happy you're making my mother."

"Your mother ..." Elsie jumped to her feet. She'd forgotten about his parents once again. Her decision impacted everyone.

"Elsie, what is wrong?" He circled her. "She is alive."

"Yes, but I didn't think of how this will affect her. Or your father. Or—do you have any siblings?" Her stomach twisted. Elsie knew nothing about Fitz, save his parents were alive. He could be one of a dozen children who would rightfully crucify Elsie.

"I do." A curious expression came over Fitz. "And I assure you, they will think you a miracle."

"No mother wants a sham of a marriage."

His face fell. "A sham of a marriage." Gone was the cheerfulness. His eyes became heavy.

Elsie wrung her hands together; she was making a mess of his life. "I didn't think about your family."

"I'll see to the arrangements." Fitz took a step back.

"Wait." She swallowed her pride. "I promise I'll do my best. I won't embarrass you. I promise I'll behave."

"That's a pity. We wouldn't be here if you had." He turned to leave.

Elsie rushed forward and wrapped her arms around him, her head against his back. He stiffened, then relaxed and covered her intertwined hands with his. She closed her eyes briefly, pretending for a moment that Fitz was doing this from affection, not pity.

He twisted to face her and lay his head on hers. "Promise me you won't behave."

A nervous laugh escaped. She looked up and saw kindness in his eyes. His face was so close, just a few inches away. If she were to stand up on the tips of her toes ... The thought sent a shiver through her. A thrill coursed through her. She leaned forward. He leaned in—did he wish to kiss her? She swallowed hard. He blinked—she panicked and stepped back. "Be careful what you wish for."

"I am." He snapped to a straight stance. His eyes became blank. There was a steel quality about him. He felt far away, similar to how Lord Armonde would act.

"Please don't." She was making a mess of everything. Her father had loved her wild ways, but now more than ever, Elsie knew what was expected of her. She would be the demure wife. She could bridle her tongue—she *had* to. She owed it to Fitz. "Don't disappear like that."

Fitz lifted her chin with a finger. The stoic expression was gone, only gentleness remained. "Shall we promise? You promise not to behave, and I promise not to disappear?"

"I promise." Elsie meant it. She'd been alone in a family before, she couldn't bear to spend the rest of her life in the same, cold manner.

Fitz rubbed a thumb across her jaw. Delicate shivers ran down her spine. His gaze flicked to her lips. He stiffened and dropped his hand like he'd been burned. "We need to leave."

❧ 26 ❧

FITZBURGH SMITH

Exhausted and sore, Fitz stretched his cramped arms and legs, careful not to wake Elsie. He cursed to himself. He'd been tempted to kiss her last night. He was no better than Matthew.

Elsie curled against the seat of the railway car. Fitz was an average-sized man but felt infinitely larger over the past few hours. Back in London, he'd braced himself in the hansom cab as it bobbed and weaved through downtown London. With Christmas next week, London was awake, not able to sleep until the new year. Pedestrians and larger carriages swerved out of their way, throwing Fitz and Elsie closer together. The lithe cab allowed for quick movements but little comfort.

In the snug cab, Fitz's awareness had heightened, his pant leg touching Elsie's dress. He'd tried distracting himself by checking his pocket watch every few minutes. Thankfully, when they boarded the last train for Liverpool, Elsie immediately curled away from him and toward the wall.

He flexed and stretched again. She'd been uncharacteristically quiet. He didn't want her to feel grateful, he wanted her to feel free. He'd telegraphed William, delaying their Australian adventure. Fitz had also sent word to his longtime solicitor, asking about Scotland's marriage laws and how to protect Elsie from her family. Once married, Fitz knew her family would try to guilt money from her. Their imminent elopement left Elsie vulnerable to blackmail, and Matthew would take advantage however and whenever he could. Fitz would not cave to her family. He loved Elsie enough to overlook them, but he would not enable their recklessness.

Fitz risked a glance, her arms cradling a book. He had given her a carpet bag. There was no reason for her to carry anything. He'd even given her pocket money, which she'd hesitantly taken. They were to be married. And if there was anything Elsie hated, it was dependence. He didn't want her to ask him for anything. He wanted her to take—to *act* without thinking. Like she had as a girl.

The railway car rumbled, knocking the book from her lap. It fell with a thud and slid under the bench in front of them. Fitz kneeled down and pulled it back. The book in hand, he sat, wondering if he should return it to her now or wait for her to wake.

"It's my father's journal." Her voice was gravelly from lack of sleep.

He held out the book. "We should be arriving at the station in an hour."

She nibbled her lip and opened the book, flipping toward the middle. She showed him the rough sketch of a girl on horseback, the horse's head twice the size of its body and the girl's hair longer than the horse's. "I told you. I can't draw."

"That's better than what I can do." He was grateful for the conversation, *any* conversation. He tapped the drawn figure. "At least the pen is the same color as your hair."

She smiled and traced the decade-old artwork. "Only because the black has faded to a dark brown."

Fitz tugged on his hair. "It wouldn't have worked with my hair."

She quirked an eyebrow. "Let me guess, you were blond."

"Only in my dreams." He rolled his eyes dramatically, wanting this moment to last. "I was a ghastly, ginger-haired boy."

"Ghastly, is it?" Amusement tugged at her lips, a gentle laugh escaping.

Fitz shrugged, his chest warming at the sound of her laughter. And the thought of her lips. "It was my burden to bear."

She flipped a few pages over to a child's attempt at writing. "Any guesses on what I'm trying to say here?"

Most of the letters were crossed out. Fitz imagined a frustrated Elsie scribbling, her childhood brow furrowed in concentration. "Haven't the foggiest idea, Elsie."

"Neither do I." She pursed her lips. "I know it's odd, carrying these things around. But I just feel like I have to do something to keep him with me. I've known my father my whole life and in a matter of years, I can't remember his voice. And his laugh."

"I am sorry, Elsie."

"I'm not sad." She gave a lackluster smile, pulling at Fitz's heart. "The grief has come and gone, but I can't move on like Matthew. Or my mother." She looked back to the journal in her hands. "It's like they just flip the page in a book while I keep going back to the beginning."

"Just because you are not like them, does not mean you are wrong."

"I'm afraid they will never see it your way." Her gaze flicked to his. "I can't go back, but I worry about what Tyndeth will do once he finds out."

"Tyndeth is his own master. He will grant mercy when, and only when, he sees fit. He does the same with his own twisted idea of justice." Fitz covered her hands on the book. "You are beholden to no one. Including me."

"Fitz." Elsie closed the book and faced him. "Why did you give me the mare?"

Fitz cursed under his breath, bringing a smirk to her lips. "You needed a horse."

Her smile grew. "And you knew this how?"

Fitz pulled at his collar and swallowed hard. "I was just being a good neighbor."

"Oh." Her shoulders slumped and she spun back around to the window.

Fitz took a deep breath. William had told him to make Elsie un-oblivious. Now was as good a time as any. "I knew you were in Glamorgan. I knew there was a scandal but didn't know the details. Nor did I care."

She turned her profile to him but said nothing.

"I used to watch you from my bedroom." He laid his head back on the seat. "I'd watch you run through the overgrown grass. Your hair ... it'd wave free in the wind."

She fidgeted, her dress rustling next to him.

He didn't risk a glance but spoke straight ahead. "I was not only a ghastly ginger but ghostly white." He grimaced dramatically, rewarded with her soft giggle. "You were a little thing running along the ridge separating our lands. I was a scrawny boy and always, always sick. And there you were, riding your father's hackney mare while I was bound to a bed."

"Matthew hated that horse."

"He hates anything he can't control." Fitz *tsked* and shook his head. "It's a common sin."

"I loved her," Elsie said breathlessly.

"I know." Fitz could feel the weight of her stare. "I'd returned home for the summer from St. Peter's."

"That's where Matthew—"

"Went to school." He cleared his throat. "We did not get on." That was an understatement. Images of Matthew and his friends pummeling Fitz ran through his mind.

"That is not surprising." Elsie sighed, relaxing into the seat. "I rarely *get on* with him either."

Fitz smiled, eying the woman next to him. "He was surprised when I grew several inches that summer and the ginger turned to brown."

Elsie wrinkled her nose. "I suppose that's a rather large problem for boys?"

"Very large." He folded his arms across his chest and crossed his ankles. "The week before we had to return, I woke up early. I'd finally decided to talk to you."

Her gaze snapped to his. "To me?"

"I'd been practicing to ride and had hoped to meet you on the ridge." Fitz had thought it silly, wanting to impress the young lady. He was not yet a man. But he'd watched her every day for every summer while he lay bed ridden with a persistent cough or fever. He was only one of two children who lived long enough to leave the nursery.

"I loved riding her." Elsie's tone turned wistful. "My father had that mare for ages."

"I know." Fitz nodded. "When your view is confined to windows, you tend to memorize everything you see."

Elsie gave a sheepish grin. "I'm afraid you probably should forget some of those things."

"You were not an evil child." *Far from it.* He'd witnessed it all, her brother's incessant teasing, her untamable hair, and her daily riding. All of it. "I wanted to ride with you. I wanted to feel what I thought you felt."

She rubbed her neck, her face seemingly lost in thought. "Why can't I remember you?"

"I looked different." Fitz turned on the seat, propping his tired head up by his hand. "And to be fair, I never actually rode with you. Your brother saw me coming and started taunting me."

"I'm so sorry."

Fitz waited for Elsie to defend her brother or at least gently suggest a reason for the torment. "It wasn't right. His actions or mine."

"What did you do?" Her eyes widened, reminding Fitz of his mother's lapdog. The little thing was deceptively adorable at times—other moments her bite was as fast as her bark.

"He wouldn't stop, and I saw you coming. I knew if you saw Matthew, you'd turn the other way." He chuckled at her sudden flushed cheeks.

"I hated riding around him. Matthew thought it funny to try and spook her."

"He tried the same with my gelding." Fitz rubbed the bridge of his nose, fatigue setting in. "I fell and he laughed, along with his friends. I can't remember their names."

"They were probably my cousins on my mother's side." She frowned and grimaced. "You'd think having a priest as a grandfather would rein them in."

"Blood isn't everything." But even Fitz knew the lie he'd spoken. Elsie was well above his rank—would he still feel a marriage to her was a gift if she wasn't a lady? Had he truly descended in his line of thinking—had he become like the earl?

"Tell that to society."

A rush of courage washed over Fitz. He would tell society a thing or two. In a way, he already was. He twirled a finger in the air. "Isn't that what we're doing? This goes against everything society has to say about marriage and family."

"My family has a lot to say about marriage."

"Soon, they might have more to say." He cast a conspiratorial grin. "Did you name your horse Mischief for yourself or for her?"

"*Direidus.*" Elsie sighed and closed her eyes for a moment.

Fitz wrestled out of his coat jacket, wrapping it over her like a blanket.

In a sleepy voice, she said, "You never finished your story." She blinked, fighting to stay awake.

"Sleep, love." He tucked the ends of the jacket around her. She relaxed, her head bobbing against her chest. He leaned against her, nestling her head against his shoulder. Warmth spread from the touch. Her hand fell next to his. Without thinking, he intertwined their fingers. His chest grew heavy, not from concern or nerves but rather with another emotion altogether.

Fitz didn't quite understand what was happening, nor did he really care. All he knew was that her misfortune had been to his benefit. He should feel guilt or remorse for her situation, but all he felt was relief. And peace.

Perhaps, he'd already become as selfish and cruel as Tyndeth.

❦ 27 ❦

ELISHEBA BEVUE

Brakes squealed to life, slowing the train and waking Elsie. Disoriented and confused, she blinked at the early morning light and with a jolt, remembered the earl and the dinner party. And Fitz.

She became all too aware of the man to her left—and his hand in hers. His fingers twitched. She froze, her mind blank. Regret and shame took turns washing over her. She'd spent the night with a man. Her maid was back in London, along with her family. She was ruined. Tyndeth would make sure of it. Her lot was cast.

With a stiff neck, Elsie glanced at Fitz's sleeping face. Her heart lifted, her pulse steady. His eyelids fluttered and a soft, subtle snore escaped. The morning light bathed his brown hair with an auburn tint. He'd confessed to being a sickly, scrawny boy. Her brother had once joked gingers were inferior and was known to take a jest too far.

The hurt from Matthew's taunts had stayed with her but did Fitz harbor the same pain? His hand twitched, drawing her attention to the ink stains on his thumb and forefinger, evidence of hours spent hovering over accounts and ledgers. Matthew probably never bothered to look at a ledger. Not that there was much to count. His foolishness and her temper had made a fertile field for Tyndeth to strike.

The earl would never forget Elsie's slap. He'd done his best to ruin her.

The nagging doubt took hold, refusing to back down. Would Fitz—a boy cruelly teased by Matthew—would he seek vengeance with the same thirst? Fitz was running away with Matthew's little sister. It would prove a point and give Fitz the upper hand. Sadly, that made more sense than Fitz's willingness to overlook Elsie's faults.

Gentle and slow, she slipped her hand from his, careful to not wake him. She didn't remember Fitz from her youth. Her first memory of meeting him was in her father's study. He'd come to speak to her brother. There was obvious tension between them, but Matthew had insisted he stay for dinner.

Elsie rubbed her temples. None of it made sense. She was exhausted and worried ... and scared. For two years she had lived in a relatively predictable bubble. And now nothing was stable. She was to marry a man she hardly knew in a country she'd never been—to a family she couldn't remember.

The brakes quieted, slowing to an abrupt halt. Elsie gripped the seat while Fitz jumped to a stand, banging his head on the low hanging baggage shelf.

"What in the devil." Fitz rubbed his head. He twisted and turned, the realization of where they were creeping across his face.

Elsie waited for the look of regret. Or of revenge. She'd been on the receiving end of Tyndeth's wrath and believed she could spot it in anyone, even Fitz.

He blinked, his eyes adjusting to the growing light of morning. "Liverpool looks a bit different this early."

Elsie pursed her lips. That wasn't what she was expecting.

"How stiff are you?" He gave a lopsided smile and yawned.

"A little." She'd already asked twice if Fitz was certain about marrying her. She couldn't do it again without a reason.

"We have to take a cab across town to the other station." He pulled both their bags from the overhead shelf. "I should have received a telegraph by now."

Elsie nodded dumbly, her mind both tired and racing. She'd crossed from London to Glamorgan throughout her life, from east to west and back again. Her family had stopped in the same towns along the same roads every year. But Liverpool was a town she'd never seen. Stepping from the railway car, Elsie was surrounded by busy movement and the loud racking of an incoming train. Despite the early hour, she winced at the onslaught of sounds, including the rushed accents of northern England.

"This way, Elsie." Fitz carried both bags in one hand, the other guiding her through the station.

She clung to his hand, his touch steadying her. A pang of homesickness hit and she wished for something familiar. Even Fitz's own speech wasn't Welsh enough, his words filtered by his travels.

In a blur, they traveled in another carriage to a station on the east end of Liverpool, but for all Elsie could tell, she was a world away from London and all that she knew. She clenched her fist and shook the thought. She'd brought this on herself. She should be celebrating, not indulging in a fit of melancholy.

"For how long?" Fitz's raised voice pulled Elsie from her thoughts.

The man behind the ticket counter shrugged. "Sorry, sir. It's a crack in the gauge. We don't know how long. Could be a few hours to mend or a couple days."

Fitz glanced back at Elsie, his face screwed up in worry. "I'll need a runner to the nearest inn as soon as the train's back on schedule."

Nodding, the man gave Fitz a paper with a list of hotels. "These are the closest but they might be full. You're not the only stranded passenger."

Fitz mumbled a thanks and sat with Elsie on a nearby bench. "We can try the stagecoach or wait for the train."

"It wouldn't take Tyndeth long to find out where we are." Word would spread quickly. Fitz and Elsie didn't look similar enough to be siblings. Any stranger at the hotel or train station would easily identify her and Fitz. Elsie still wore the dress she'd left the dinner party in. They hadn't travelled with a maid or a valet. They were on the run, plain as day.

"We would have to rent one room. It'll make us look married and settled, instead of a couple running from relatives." Fitz cleared his throat. "But I don't think he's looking yet."

"Oh." Elsie's hands shook. In a day or two, sharing a bed and room would be expected. She'd not thought through the entirety of marriage. Had Fitz?

"I've slept on plenty of floors," He offered a touch too cheerfully. "But Tyndeth and Matthew aren't who we need to worry about."

Before Elsie could ask, Fitz gave her the telegraph slip from the attendant. *See you in Liverpool. Parr.* She let out a gasp, the paper drifting to the ground.

"Do you remember what you put in his letter?" Fitz grabbed the paper, shoving it in his jacket pocket.

"I didn't mention you. Or Scotland." Elsie leaned forward, her elbows on her knees. Her bones ached from the train's jarring and night of little sleep. "I just ... I just wanted him to know the truth. That's all. I didn't mean for him to come."

"He knew about my proposal."

Elsie sat up with a snap. Fitz must have spoken to Lord Armonde. "He thought there was an understanding between us."

"You could have said yes." Fitz's eyes crinkled, a grin forming. "Would have saved us all a bit of trouble."

Elsie brightened. "Oh, and what agreement was there?"

Fitz held up three fingers. "One, take care of your mare. Two, keep you posted and three, runaway to Scotland."

"Only one of those is about matrimony."

"Not necessarily." He grabbed the bags and helped her to a stand. They walked to the outer platform where he threw up his hand to hail a carriage. "I did gift you a horse. That implies a great deal."

"Why didn't you tell me?" She climbed in and waited for Fitz to give the driver an address.

"I didn't need tongues wagging." Despite having two benches, he sat next to her. "Your brother was ready to wed us in the study and your mother at dinner that night."

"And now I've forced you." Guilt tugged at her heart once again. She placed a hand on his forearm. "I don't know why you gave me that mare. And I'm not completely sure why you're doing this now. But you truly, honestly don't have to. I'll find my own way out of it."

His gaze flicked to her hand. "Do I strike you as a man who is coerced easily?"

"You clearly dislike my brother yet you visited him in Glamorgan. And then introduced him to who knows how many people."

"I am not fond of your brother. Or, to be honest, your mother." The passing streets pulled his gaze. "I did introduce him to a few Americans. He was desperate, and I was worried you would take the brunt of his foolish behavior again."

"Again?"

Fitz pulled at his collar. "The day we met in the study. I was giving him a gentleman's warning."

Elsie's pulse raced. She vaguely remembered Fitz mentioning a sibling. Her brother was no saint and now she worried he'd caused harm to a younger—or older sister. She had no doubt that Matthew was capable of putting his desires ahead of a woman's reputation. "A warning?"

"I'd just acquired Glamorgan Bank—"

"A *bank*." Elsie briefly closed her eyes, relief pouring from her. "I thought you were calling him out. That he'd ..."

Fitz grinned, motioning to her face. "You've blushed from pink to scarlet in half a second."

Leaning back into the seat, she sighed. "Oh, Fitz. I thought it was something awful."

"Elsie, it is." His sobering face invited tension into the snug carriage. "Your family's in debt. More than even the earl knows."

"I know."

The carriage stopped but Fitz waited, motioning for the driver to wait. "No, Elsie. It's worse than even Matthew understands. Because he's been borrowing money to pay other debts, his interest has skyrocketed. It would take him a lifetime, two lifetimes, to pay it all back. Selling both homes isn't enough."

"What happens if he can't pay it back?" Elsie had heard her father talk of tenants owing money and how scared he was for them. He'd refused to send them to debtor's prison but would evict them off the land. Sadly, the families would wind up in debtor's prison with the next landlord.

"The entire family will be affected." He worked his jaw.

"He's a baron."

"That won't help his case. He can't afford a bankruptcy fee." Fitz reached for the door. "Your brother needs to marry well, or he'll be shipped to the nearest debtor's prison."

"What would happen to us? To the house?" When he wouldn't look at her, she pulled on his jacket. "How much does he owe?"

"I only know what he owes Glamorgan Bank."

"Which is?"

Softly, he whispered, "Over thirty thousand pounds."

Her throat tightened and the world shrank. *Thirty thousand pounds.* She'd applied as a lady's companion in hopes to secure a mere five pounds a month. The tenants in her late father's ledger paid less than that. The Glamorgan estate would never make enough to pay down the debt.

"It was foolish of me to give you a horse. I knew your brother's growing debt but still purchased her." Fitz held her gaze. His ordinary brown eyes held an intensity—a command of Elsie's senses. Her skin prickled and her breathing slowed. He blinked, softening the pull.

Elsie's heart raced with anticipation.

His gaze flicked to her lips and then to her hands. "I would have provided for the horse. And for you. No matter what befell your brother."

28

FITZBURGH SMITH

Fitz and Elsie rented the last available room, their window facing the newly opened museum. They kept their answers to a minimum, posing as a newlywed couple. Fitz hoped they blended in with the other stranded passengers. Half waited for their return train to southern England and the other half anxious for Scotland.

Fitz sent inquiries with a local runner asking for prices and schedules of the stagecoach. He wanted to be prepared if the train's gauge wasn't fixed in time. He was already disheartened with what his solicitor had telegraphed. He hadn't told Elsie yet. She was distracted with news of her brother's debt. In truth, Fitz hadn't realized the extent until he'd met with the board at the bank. A much wiser businessman would have met with the board *before* meeting with Matthew and accidentally meeting Elsie.

He'd encouraged Elsie to lie down while he made arrangements. In truth, he'd only sent one runner and sat in the corner of the lobby, rereading the solicitor's telegraph once more. The declared marriage over an anvil that his parents had done decades before was no longer allowed in Scotland. Four years earlier, according to his solicitor, Scotland had changed its marriage laws. Both parties must be over the age of twenty-one or have resided in the country for three weeks prior to the marriage.

The final kicker was the solicitor's warning—the *Person Act of 1828,* a law allowing Matthew, or his mother, to sue Fitz for damages. Fitz was guilty. He would gladly admit to the magistrate that he stole Elsie from a dinner party. He'd do it again if faced with the same opportunity. The only doubt lay in Matthew's ability to hire a competent solicitor—even the cheapest retainer fee would be difficult for Matthew to manage. But Tyndeth. He could afford an army.

Fitz swirled the brandy in his glass, not remembering when he'd ordered it. He knew he had to tell Elsie but dreaded the idea. Fitz was selfish. He cherished the moments when Elsie asked for help, first with the mare and then with her elopement plan. She might only look to him as a savior instead of a beau but he'd take it. Around Elsie, Fitz was no longer the scrawny nobody. He became Fitzburgh Smith, a taller, stronger version of who he was at birth. He hoped in time, she'd grow to love him.

He slipped the telegraph back in his pocket and tossed a coin to the bar attendant. Gripping the railing, he trudged up the staircase with the energy of a sleepy elephant. At the top of the stairs, he heard Elsie's voice rising into a panic. Rushing to their room, he swung open door.

Elsie stood by the window, her shoulders hunched in defeat.

Fitz raced to her side. "What is it?"

She shook her head. "Don't."

The hairs on Fitz's neck stood on end. They were not alone.

"Good morning, Mr. Smith." Lady Alice's low voice carried to where he stood. "Or should I say afternoon?"

He straightened but did not turn around. He stepped closer to Elsie. She gave a subtle shake of her head. He tried once more. "Talk to me, love."

"So it's come to that now?" Lady Alice laughed softly, the sound grating to Fitz's ears. "Friendship has blossomed to love, has it?"

Fitz spun around and pointed to the door. "Get out."

Lady Alice didn't move. Fitz hadn't the foggiest idea how she had found them, nor did he care. Elsie was near tears and Fitz placed the blame squarely on Lady Alice's delicate shoulders. Despite traveling—probably all night like Fitz and Elise had—Lady Alice looked every inch the lady, rings on her finger, silk ribbons in her hair. She lacked the dark circles and tired eyes that Elsie wore.

"I'm not leaving without Miss Bevue." Lady Alice sat on the edge of the bed, her ankles crossed and her back straight. Her chin was lifted but not too high to be lofty and her neck upright without appearing rigid. She was the consummate nobleman's daughter. And everything Elsie was not. The contrast pulled at Fitz's heart.

"You can leave of your own accord or I can remove you." He folded his arms. He'd drawn a line and would not hesitate to enforce it.

Lady Alice's eyes widened only a fraction before resuming the placid, stoic expression. She called to Elsie. "Are you ready?"

"She's going nowhere." Fitz shouldn't have left Elsie alone. He'd been overcome with his failures and like a fool, had unwittingly let a wolf in the den. "Least of all with you."

"Oh, silly, Mr. Smith." A simpering grin crept across Lady Alice's face. "I didn't travel alone."

The telegraph. Jonathon Parr had made it clear he'd see Fitz in Liverpool. He'd just neglected to mention his sister would be here as well.

"Come, Elsie." Lady Alice went to the door, her hand waving for Elsie to join her.

"She's not going."

Lady Alice arched an eyebrow. "So not only have you ruined her, but you'll keep her captive as well?"

"She is not ruined." Fitz cast a worried glance to Elsie. She'd said nothing in her defense. Not an insult. Not even a glare.

"Perfect." Lady Alice smiled wide. "No one's the wiser and we'll be on our way."

"I said no," Fitz growled. He didn't care how bad it looked, Elsie would stay with him. She'd asked *him* for help, not Lady Alice. And not her brother.

In a defeated voice, Elsie said, "Matthew's debts were called in."

"That's impossible." Fitz rolled his eyes. "I gave him 'til Lady Day." Most creditors gave debtors at least a quarter to pay, collecting rents and interest on Michaelmas, Midsummer Day, Christmas Day, or

Lady's Day. Fitz had left England for only a few years, not enough for an entire country to abandon their traditions.

Lady Alice *tsked* with a shake of her head. "Your friend, the Earl of Tyndeth, has called the loan."

"Tyndeth?" Fitz groaned. He should've known the jackal was up to something. "His generosity was a loan?"

"It's time to go." Lady Alice motioned once more for Elsie to join her. "We hired a coach."

"Matthew's fate is sealed regardless of what happens here." Fitz inched closer to Elsie, worried if he moved too quickly he'd scare her off. He couldn't reassure her with Alice Parr in the room. Jonathon's sister was a snake, and Fitz didn't know if the lady was here of her own accord or helping Tyndeth.

"If I return home and face the humiliation, Matthew's loan will be forgiven." Elsie took a tentative step forward. And then back. This wasn't the girl Fitz had grown up watching. That woman spoke with her heart in her throat.

"I don't believe you. Not for a minute." Fitz pointed an accusing finger at Lady Alice. "You don't give a fig about Elsie or Tyndeth. You're not here out of the kindness of your heart. Tyndeth wouldn't forgive a loan so easily. There's more going on here."

The tension in Elsie's shoulders fell. The despair and exhaustion lifted from her eyes, replaced with a familiar spark. She furrowed her brow, her gaze flicking between Fitz and Lady Alice. "Why are you here?"

"On behalf of our brothers." Lady Alice gave a deep curtsey, batting her eyes innocently. "Yours would like to avoid prison and mine would like his fiancé returned."

"And what exactly does your brother know?" Fitz pulled a chair from the corner desk to the center of the room. "Sit, Alice."

"I'm afraid, I don't have time." Lady Alice's smile was anything but scared. "I need to get Elsie home."

"She is home," Fitz snapped. He winced, knowing full well he sounded more like Tyndeth than ever. "Elsie is none of your concern."

"I could just walk away. Pretend I never saw her." Lady Alice smiled sweetly and opened the door. Her eyes widened in surprise. She seemed to have expected someone to be there.

"You have nothing I want." Fitz wouldn't make a deal with the devil nor would he make a deal with this female, fair-haired version.

The sound of footsteps echoed into the room.

"*Au contraire.*" Lady Alice held out her hand.

James and Tilly Smith walked in. Fitz hid his shock and caught the open-mouthed look of Lady Alice. She had thought someone else was entering. Fitz tugged at his collar. Facing his parents was inevitable but he'd hoped to already be married. The threat of another surprise made Fitz's head pound—he glanced at Alice, her eyes flicking back to the door.

"Fitzburgh." His mother's auburn hair spilled over her shoulders in thick curls. Her crisp, blue eyes took in Elsie, Fitz, and then the room. Her green dress rustled in the otherwise silent room. "You've been busy."

Fitz's father was next, his expression as unreadable as his wife's.

"And to what do I owe the pleasure of your visit?" Fitz wouldn't be cowed. He loved his parents but his heart hammered away in his chest. This was not how he'd planned to tell them of his elopement—he glanced at Elsie's pale face. His worry rose. She'd never been this quiet. She'd disappeared inside herself.

"We received a frantic telegraph." Fitz's father spoke so quietly Fitz leaned forward.

"I never sent you a telegraph." Fitz stared at Lady Alice whose doe-eyed expression, parted lips, and blinking gaze was everything that was pure and innocent—as much as a wolf donning sheep's clothing could be.

"This appears to be a family matter." Lady Alice beckoned Elsie. "We should leave them be."

Fitz stepped in front of Elsie, sheltering her from Lady Alice's planned humiliation. "It is a family matter. All the more reason for Elsie to stay."

Tilly Smith's mouth fell open, her eyes doubling in size. She grabbed her husband's arm, her knuckles white. "Did you hear what your son said?"

"I'm not deaf, dear." James gently pried his wife's fingers from his arm and faced Lady Alice. "And your name is?"

Lady Alice purred, offering James a genteel smile and curtsey. "I am Lady Alice Parr."

"Ah, the Parrs," his father said in the same soft tones meant for an infant. "Excuse my indelicacy, but what is your connection in all of this?"

Without a tremor or a pause, Lady Parr clasped her hands together. "Oh, so thoughtless of me. I'm to be Elsie's sister."

James and Tilly looked to each other and then to their son, confusion filling their faces.

"I'm Elisheba Bevue." Elsie didn't curtsey. Nor did she bat her lashes and simper for Fitz's parents. She was again the woman Fitz had admired for years.

"My brother's fiancée." Lady Alice was at Elsie's side, wrapping an arm around her shoulder. "We should leave you to your family."

"Fitzburgh Smith, what is happening?" His mother held out her hand when Lady Alice opened her mouth. "I would like to hear from my son."

Elsie's gaze shot to Fitz. She didn't budge despite Lady Alice's subtle pull toward the door. Questions filled Elsie's eyes, staring into Fitz. His heart shrank as Lady Alice tried once more to get her to the door. What he said next would determine how his parents viewed Elsie.

"I kidnapped Elsie." Fitz held Elsie's gaze, ignoring his mother's gasp. "She's engaged to Jonathon Parr. I grabbed her outside of a dinner party in London. We—*I* am waiting to hear from the station. As soon as the gauge is fixed, we'll be on our way to Scotland."

"This can't be happening." Tilly paced, a hand on her forehead, another on her chest. "Do you have any idea what you've done?"

A single tear fell from Elsie's eye. She mouthed, *thank you,* and stepped from Lady Alice's grasp. Elsie straightened, the fire back in her eyes.

"You went to a dinner party?" James searched his son, then Elsie and then Lady Alice.

"I did." Fitz felt the weight of his father's stare. James Smith had taught Fitz to watch and listen, not just for flaws in a business venture but in people as well. More importantly, James had taught his son the delicate art of finding a lie.

"And did you plan this, or was it an impromptu adventure?" James tucked one arm under the other, his words measured and soft.

Lady Alice shifted her weight, pursing her lips. Her gaze kept drifting to the door as if she was waiting for something. Or someone. Fitz pulled at his collar. His parents were enough of a surprise.

"Fitz?" Tilly had stopped her pacing, her voice rising. "What happened? Where is the son I raised? Was there a reason for this? Was she coerced into the engagement—"

"She was excited to marry my brother," Lady Alice snapped, then quickly smiled. "My brother is a marquess. She would be a marchioness."

Tilly and James looked to each other. An unspoken conversation snapped between them.

James nodded. "And where is our beloved marquess?" He held up his hand. "Wait, where is your companion?"

❦ 29 ❦

ELISHEBA BEVUE

E lsie stood with fear in her throat. Her mind had blanked when James and Tilly Smith walked into the room. She waited for them to call her out, label her a strumpet and dismiss her just as quickly. They would ban her from marrying their son. She was ruined. That's what her mother and brother would say and do. Lady Alice was here to ensure they drove a wedge between Elsie and Fitz. Lady Alice was not the dull-witted debutante Elsie had once thought. All of this—Fitz's parents and Lady Alice's appearance— was Elsie's fault. She'd started this mess with a slap to Tyndeth and completed it with her botched elopement to Fitz. She was a failure. She couldn't even end her engagement to Lord Armonde properly.

Fitz held her gaze. She waited for him to admit all that she'd done. Instead, he'd lied and told his parents he'd kidnapped her.

The walls blurred. Voices erupted. Elsie saw and heard nothing, only Fitz. He'd lied for her. A single tear fell down her cheek. Her family had never lied *for* her, only *to* her. Her heart warmed—followed by guilt. She couldn't do this to him. Fitz was good and kind. And honest—at least, until Elsie had changed him. She'd made him a liar.

Elsie side-stepped beyond Lady Alice's grasp, her mind begging for another solution. She couldn't let Fitz take the brunt. He maintained his gaze until she mouthed a sheepish, *thank you*. Fitz deserved more than silent gratitude.

Lady Alice fidgeted, pulling Elsie's attention. His father had stepped closer with quiet authority in every motion, from his soft voice to his serious eyes. Mr. Smith held up his hand, silencing the room. "Again, where is your companion?"

"How kind of you to remember." Lady Alice beckoned Elsie to join her. "He is waiting."

"Who is he?" Mr. Smith asked, his voice so low, Elsie leaned closer.

"We need to leave, Elsie." Lady Alice ignored Mr. Smith, her smile strained.

"We received an urgent telegraph." Mr. Smith clasped his hands behind his back. "Our son was involved in a catastrophic accident—"

Fitz glared at Lady Alice.

Elsie needed to intervene. She couldn't be the fracture in his family. "There was no accident."

"No, apparently there was nothing accidental about this at all." Mr. Smith's tone was firm, as if he was shouting without raising his voice. "My son's apparently kidnapping young maidens."

"Mr. Smith, I can explain." Elsie held her head high. If she could face Tyndeth, she could face Fitz's parents.

"Tilly." Mr. Smith extended his arm toward the door. "Would you please escort the ladies below? You might need to explain to Lady Alice's chaperone the reason for her lateness."

Fitz slid in front of Elsie. Her heart broke at his protective stance. She didn't deserve him. Elsie had hurt too many people—Lord Armonde, her family, and now Fitz. "She's not leaving this room."

"You cannot hold her hostage." Mr. Smith turned his attention to Elsie. "My dear lady, I will need to speak to your family and rectify this situation."

"I am not a hostage." Elsie's voice wavered. With Lady Alice in the room, every word she spoke would be held against her.

"No," whispered Fitz.

"I came to Fitz for help. This is my fault. All of it."

"All is forgiven, Elsie." Lady Alice rushed to Elsie, reaching for her hands.

Elsie shook her head, her face flushing. "Lord Armonde is good and kind. He is everything a lady would wish for. But because of me, he will be humiliated."

Fitz pleaded; his gentleness squeezed her heart. "Elsie—"

"Let the lady speak," warned Mr. Smith.

"I tried to fix things. And I've just made a mess of everything." With each word, Elsie became stronger. She would walk away, she had to. Fitz deserved more than her lies, more than her deceptive, desperate family. She had brought disaster to everyone she cared about. She was at fault—always.

"Dearest, will you please escort Lady Alice downstairs. We'll join you in a moment." Mr. Smith turned from his wife and Lady Alice. He offered a gentle smile to Elsie and motioned to the bench by the window. "Please, sit for a moment."

"I really—" Lady Alice's protest was cut off by Tilly closing the door.

Fitz sprang into action, reaching for Elsie's hands. "How did she know we were here?" He bent down, searching her eyes. "Are you okay? What did she say before—"

"Fitzburgh." Mr. Smith placed a hand on his son's forearm. "I need to know everything. And I need to know now."

Fitz gave a subtle shake of his head. "No. It's not my story to tell."

"But it *is* mine." A plan unfurled in Elsie's mind, stretching out the details for her. She would save Fitz, even from himself. She would never forget him and his tenderness. He deserved a woman, not a hurricane. "Mr. Smith, would you be so kind as to wait outside the door? Only for a moment. I will tell you everything after that."

Mr. Smith hesitated, narrowing his eyes.

"None of this is your son's fault. I just need a moment to convince him—"

"Are you mad?" Fitz balked. The calm man with soft brown hair and kind eyes was replaced with haggard frown lines and a disheveled attitude. "After all this, do you have any idea what's going to happen? You'll be ruined. If I kidnapped you, I pay a fine. More than likely a large one because it appears your brother has Lady Alice wrapped around his pathetic little finger. But you, you'll never recover from this."

Fitz's raw affection tugged at her heart. He was committed to his role of savior, even at the expense of his character. She didn't know if this was love. She didn't have enough experience to truly decide. She only knew that Fitz felt like home.

"Telling me how dire my situation is won't change the facts." Elsie's throat went dry.

"Dire?" Fitz pulled off his jacket and tossed it to the bed, apparently unaware that his father was still in the room. "This is past dire, Elsie."

Mr. Smith stood quietly. Still as a painting, his eyes captured everything.

The less control Fitz had, the harder it was to watch. He was supposed to be a friend, someone who could grant her freedom, but the longer they stood, the more she realized he truly cared. She doubted Fitz even recognized it. After all, she was the neighbor girl who rode past his window, not a living breathing woman who was almost his wife.

She blinked. His heart wasn't the only one in jeopardy.

"Thank you." Elsie barely managed to speak.

"Thank you?" Fitz's eyes bulged, his jaw clenched. He pulled at his collar, his hands trembling. "For what? I haven't done anything yet. We've been stuck in this blasted—"

"Fitz," warned Mr. Smith. He was apparently unaware of his son's filthy mouth.

"Oh to blazes with propriety, Father." Fitz tossed his hat to his jacket. "We need to reside in Scotland for twenty-one days. After that, none of this will matter."

"And what of Matthew?" Elsie whispered.

Fitz paced. "I don't give a fig what that bootlicker—"

"Fitzburgh." Mr. Smith raised his voice. Elsie flinched.

Fitz ran a hand through his hair, groaning. "He deserves what he gets."

"And my mother."

"She's not innocent in this, Elsie." Fitz nodded toward the door. "I wouldn't be surprised if she was Lady Alice's confidante."

"For what purpose?" Defending her mother felt wrong but nothing about this situation felt right to Elsie. "What could my mother possibly gain from this?"

"She knew what Tyndeth was years ago. She chose him over you again and again. And again." Fitz's voice rose. The guests in the surrounding rooms could undoubtedly hear him. "Your brother tried to sell you off to the highest bidder."

"Except no one wanted me."

Fitz stumbled back. His mouth hung open, his face draining of color. Elsie felt her face warm hotter still. His father watched with little emotion. Elsie wondered if it was from disinterest or shock. Her ears rang with her words, the truth cut deeper than she'd thought.

"After everything ..." Fitz wiped a hand over his face, his breathing labored. "After everything, that is what you think?"

Elsie closed her eyes. She needed to finish the job. Her heart ached, watching Fitz's distress. "The earl was unkind and so I slapped him. That single act has somehow pierced Tyndeth in such a way that I do not think he will ever forgive or recover. I wish I could say that is the beginning and end of my poor behavior, but I have a lifetime of speaking without thinking, of rushing over fences and into trouble again and again. I've been the bane of my family's life. And now, when my family is needing me most, I've betrayed them once more." She opened her eyes but looked straight ahead at the regal museum framed in the window. "My brother spent my dowry and who knows what else. But in truth, did he really think I would marry? Why keep a horse you cannot ride? That is what I'm good for, is it not? If I'm not marriageable, why keep me around?"

Fitz scoffed. "Elsie—"

"Tyndeth wants to see me humiliated, to feel the same pain he felt when I assaulted him. I'm not a fool. I know he will not forgive my brother's loan. I know that my mother will still be little more than a servant to him. Tyndeth holds all the power. I've failed at securing a husband. I've failed at being complicit in my family's schemes. I completely acknowledge that but you, Fitz." Her voice wavered. "You don't have to."

"So, you just give in?" Motioning to Elsie, Fitz glanced at his father for help. "Help her see reason."

The door opened and closed behind her. Elsie couldn't face whoever entered the room. Not yet.

"I am not giving in, Fitz." Elsie lifted her chin and straightened her posture. "And I'm not giving up."

"Is that what I am?" Lord Armonde's voice cut through the room. "I am nothing more than a scheme, a means to an end?"

Elsie's lungs froze. She gasped silently. Lord Armonde approached her, standing directly in her sights. Dark circles accented his blue eyes and flaxen hair. He'd traveled all night—probably with his sister. This was why Alice Parr had been so insistent. Elsie internally flogged herself for judging Lady Alice's behavior. She'd come to help her family. Lady Alice was a better woman than Elsie would ever be.

"We will be downstairs." Mr. Smith cupped his son's elbow, guiding him toward the door.

Fitz jutted his chin. "I'm not leaving."

"Yes, you are." Mr. Smith went to the door. "The discussion is far from over, Fitzburgh. You and I need to speak privately just as much as Miss Bevue and Lord Armonde do."

"I will be right outside—"

"We will be downstairs," Mr. Smith corrected him.

"Fitz, go," Elsie whispered. "I'll be down soon."

He stepped closer and whispered, "You are *not* unwanted."

Elsie blinked, emotions twisting and turning inside her. She couldn't meet his gaze. He pulled the jacket from the bed and wrapped it around her. He paused as if to speak but then left without a word, his father closing the door behind them.

30

FITZBURGH SMITH

Fitz's pulse screamed at him, pounding in his chest and head. He'd lost his temper and the respect of his father—and yet all he cared about was the woman in the room. He stomped down each step, becoming angrier with each passing second. They were so close to being married. He'd love to get his hands on whoever invented the dratted broken gauge. And Tyndeth. And Lord Armonde who was speaking with Elsie alone.

"Are you quite finished with your tantrum?" His father's even tone belied the fury below. Fitz knew his father was beyond disappointed. Fitz was completely wrong—and didn't care. "It would bode well for both of us if you could tell me exactly—*exactly*—what happened."

Fitz stalked to the corner booth behind his father. He didn't glance around the dining area for his mother or Lady Alice. He already knew his mother would give him an eternal tongue lashing and he couldn't give the satisfaction to Lady Alice. That chit needed a set down, not a victory.

"It's not as bad as it appears." Fitz felt childish sitting at the table, his father arching his eyebrow like he'd done a decade before.

"I've gathered the lady was in distress, but what I need to know is whether or not she was compromised."

"No." Fitz smacked the table. "I would never. Not her."

James raised both his eyebrows. "But you'd kidnap her?"

"Yes," Fitz said with too much force. He was caught. His father knew. "I won't let her go."

"Is there true regard for her as a woman, or is she the newest prize in your struggles with Matthew Bevue?"

Fitz sat back, his father's words shocking him. This had to do with Elsie and her future. "This has nothing to do with Matthew."

"He beat you soundly for years." James raised a hand when Fitz started to protest. "I just want to know if there is any other motive at play."

"If I wanted revenge on Matthew, I would have foreclosed on his assets months ago." Fitz clenched his fists and then paused, watching his hand flex and relax. "I don't know what's happened to me. But I can't get anything right. Not when it comes to her."

"By *her*, you mean the dark haired beauty you kidnapped?"

Fitz winced, his nerves settling and allowing the guilt to finally do its work. He let his hand drop to his lap. "It's all my fault."

"That I have no doubt." A soft smile crept across James's face, further confusing his son.

"I found a hackney filly, just like the one she used to ride."

James frowned. "This is appearing more and more like a childhood grudge."

Fitz pulled again at his collar, wondering if his father was right. "It looked just like the one her father used to ride."

"You knew what type of horse her father rode?" James pinched the bridge of his nose. "This goes beyond kidnapping."

"It's not what you think." *Or maybe it is.* Exhaustion wrapped around him, regret on its heels. Fitz sighed and sat back in the booth. In an instant, he was transformed back to his childhood, once again the scrawny boy, bloodied from Matthew's fist. Barely able to breathe, Fitz hadn't backed down, taunting Matthew for his fear of horses. Matthew had waited until summer to exact his revenge, and there—on the ridge, Matthew had spooked Fitz's horse and pounced on Fitz.

"She's not a prize you can set on your shelf." James tapped his fingers on the table, a faraway look in his eyes.

"I know," Fitz lied. She *was* a prize. And a lady. "She was the friend. The one from all those years ago."

"What friend?" His father leaned forward on the table. He, like Fitz and everyone else involved, was exhausted. Fatigue was in the vacant look of his eyes and in the strain of his voice—and lack of patience.

"The friend who saved me." The memory pulled Fitz back in time. He'd fallen, narrowly escaping the spattering of rocks. His horse had kept running while Matthew stood by and laughed. His hand touched his side, feeling the sticky blood. He had gasped, his senses revealing the sharp pains. The knife he'd hidden in his belt had cut him during the fall, a few inches above his hip. It wasn't deep, but enough blood for Matthew to panic and try to disappear. Elsie—to his eternal embarrassment—had watched him fall. She'd come in a blur of wild hair, screaming at her brother for his foolish behavior. Fitz had stayed on the ground, completely enthralled at the tongue thrashing she delivered, her eyes lit with a fury he'd never known. Her stubborn defense, despite being just a slip of a girl, had given him a strength he'd not yet forgotten. She'd run back to her house and brought a servant to help carry Fitz home. Matthew never again bested Fitz, in or out of school.

"Fitzburgh, you've built up this story in your mind of who this woman is and what she is to you." James folded his arms across his chest and leaned back in the chair. "She's not yours. She never was."

"She needs me." Fitz jutted his chin, hating that he sounded like a child. *I need her.*

"Does she?" His father's face softened. "Or do you want her to need you?"

"It doesn't matter if I want her to, the fact remains the same. She needs me." The moment the words left his mouth he knew he'd lost. His father wouldn't help him. "I don't need your permission."

His father raised his eyebrows and sat back. "I won't let you steal someone's fiancé, Fitzburgh."

"She asked me." Fitz didn't want to admit that the idea was hers but he needed his father's help. "I'd asked her to run away with me after I gave her a mare—"

"You gave her a horse?" James's face paled.

"I didn't tell anyone that I'd given it to her. I know what that would imply."

James rolled his eyes. "And yet you did it anyway. I've been married to your mother for over thirty years and *I've* never given her a horse."

"Mother doesn't ride."

"Fitz—"

"Her family was taking her to London and she was miserable." Fitz narrowed his gaze when his father scoffed—the man who'd never lost his temper until today. "I offered to marry her—"

"Of course you did." James shook his head and looked around as if the surrounding strangers could provide an answer to their situation.

"She turned me down."

"Smart girl."

Fitz winced. "Father, her brother spent her dowry. She entered into an engagement with the Parr family thinking she was saving her family and providing financial gain to Jonathon Parr."

"Marriage is often viewed as a business transaction."

"I have spent my life under my mother's romantic notions. I know what marriage is and what it isn't." Fitz paused. He'd proposed to Elsie as a means for freedom, a trading of one roof for another. His hasty proposal before Elsie had left London was very much a transaction. Perhaps that is why she felt unwanted. Fitz needed to be upstairs. He needed to convince her she *was* wanted. And needed. "Elsie knew Jonathon's parents would cancel the engagement once they found out. He'd be humiliated. So would she. She sent a letter and ended it."

"And you became her savior from there?"

"I was hoping we'd be married by now." Fitz groaned. "Or at least closer to the border than Liverpool."

"Lady Alice didn't send us the telegraph." His father gave an apologetic shrug.

"Drat," Fitz cursed, knowing exactly who'd hauled his parents from the continent—their shared solicitor. "I'm firing him."

"He's a good man, Fitzburgh." James's lips curled to a genuine smile, his eyes twinkling with affection. "We were already on our way home. We'd just landed in Dover."

"Ah." Relief flooded Fitz.

"Is the engagement truly over?"

"She wrote a letter." Fitz's focus drifted to the staircase across the room. "I don't know how well he's taking it."

"Does he love her?"

Fitz blurted, "No."

"Are you sure?" James asked quietly.

"He doesn't know her." Fitz's voice rose. "She can't be cooped in a house. She can't be caged. She hates drawing or needle work. She abhors the pleasantries and pretending of the *ton*. She's the happiest at home. In Wales. Not in London or in a crowded dance hall."

"Does she know?" James reached across the table, placing a hand on Fitz's.

"Know what?"

James squeezed his son's hand. "That you love her."

✲ 31 ✲

ELISHEBA BEVUE

Fitz and his father had gone downstairs, Fitz's words echoing in Elsie's ear. *You are not unwanted.* The sentiment pulled at her heart. As much as Elsie knew Fitz believed the words, there was little proof that Elsie was wanted anywhere. The greatest evidence was Lord Armonde's furious face in front of her. She gripped the edge of Fitz's jacket he'd draped over her before leaving.

"You lied to me." Lord Armonde's gaze flicked to her fingers clinging to Fitz's jacket. He held out Fitz's letter Matthew had stolen days before. "You've been corresponding for months."

"He never sent the letter." She swallowed hard, hating the pain she caused. "My brother took it before Fitz ever posted it."

"I asked if you had an agreement—"

"I didn't lie." Elsie felt half her size. Lord Armonde had every reason to be angry with her. So did Fitz. Her thumb rubbed the seam of his jacket. "He'd proposed as a solution—"

"And how is that working—your *solution?*"

"I'm sorry." She didn't rush to comfort him. She did nothing like the fool she was.

"Why didn't you tell me?" Lord Armonde sat on the poorly made wooden bench tucked under the window. "I could have helped you."

"How?" She hoped her tone was sincere. Reality painted a different picture than Lord Armonde's. "How could you have helped me?"

"I could have talked to my parents. Told them your problems. You're family—or would have been." He smacked the bench. "Your brother has made his intentions toward my sister very public, much to my parent's dismay, and now this. How can I get them to overlook you running away—"

"I don't expect them to." She pulled the jacket tighter, not for warmth but for the feeling of safety, the scent of Fitz. She was an utter fool. Her heart belonged to the foul-mouthed man downstairs. "I didn't want you to bear the brunt of my fallout. I didn't know about the dowry."

"Of course you didn't." Doubt dripped from Lord Armonde's words.

"You don't believe me."

"How can I?" Lord Armonde shook his head. "You sent a letter practically begging me to elope with you but then run off with Fitzburgh Smith."

"I wasn't asking you to elope, Lord Armonde." Elsie's cheeks flushed. She clearly had a knack for miscommunication. "I knew your parents would cut you off."

Lord Armonde clenched his jaw. "You broke your engagement with me, to elope with a steward from Wales?"

Elsie narrowed her gaze. "Fitz is not a steward and we never eloped."

Lord Armonde put a finger in the air. "There. Right there. I should have seen it."

"Seen what?"

"Jonathon," he whispered. "I've asked a dozen times or more for you to call me Jonathon. But you can't because Fitz is the one you've chosen."

The truth settled between them, the farewell in the air. Elsie would fix this—she knew the source of the problem was her.

"I'm sorry I hurt you." Elsie let her hands fall, the jacket slipping to the edge of her shoulders. "I was hoping to spare you from the pain. From all of this. I've hurt everyone. You. Fitz—"

"And just how is Fitz hurt?" Lord Armonde snorted, appearing more like his sister than himself. "He is the hero. Although, I'm sure it's costing him a pretty penny with your brother in the family."

Elsie swallowed hard at his words and the greed in his smile. He wanted her to hurt. She wasn't fond of Matthew, but Lord Armonde's jabs cut all the same. "I do not think he will give anything to Matthew."

"He saves the lady and doesn't have to deal with your family." Lord Armonde stood and smacked his leg, forcing a laugh. "Where do I sign up?"

Elsie said nothing, unable to confess anything more. The less Lord Armonde—or anyone—knew, the greater chance she had at succeeding.

He quieted, searching her. "The only way Fitz gets hurt is if you don't marry him."

Guilty. Elsie lowered her chin. "He doesn't deserve this."

"Oh, Elsie." The tension fell away. Lord Armonde pulled her hand between his. "You didn't know, did you?"

Tears fell from her cheeks. She wiped them with the back of her free hand and stepped from Lord Armonde's grasp. Kindness was back, his face soft and open.

"I *am* sorry."

"So am I, Elsie."

"What will your parents do?" Her words were barely above a whisper.

He shrugged. "I think they're more concerned about their eldest daughter than me."

"You're lying."

"Not completely." He smirked with a twinkle in his eye. "I would have helped you. I would have tried."

"Thank you." Elsie wished it were true, but he was just as powerless as she, both not yet of age. Family and traditions still bound them to someone else's will.

"I hate the idea of you marrying him." Lord Armonde threw his hands in his pockets. "But I hate the idea of you *not* marrying him more."

Elsie's heart was on the verge of bursting. Lord Armonde giving his support for Fitz was too much. She had to be strong—she could not, *would* not be selfish this time. "Lord Armonde—"

"Oh." He pretended she'd landed a bow to his chest.

"*Jonathon.*" She smiled, grateful for his humor.

"I know what it feels like." Lord Armonde stepped closer. "It's an awful feeling knowing someone you care about is off and alone. I admit it, I was angry when I found out you were with Fitz but at least I knew you were safe."

"I will be fine."

"Talk to him before you do whatever it is you're thinking of doing." When she opened her mouth to lie, he shook his head. "You don't hide much behind that pretty face of yours. You're a beauty, oh, don't close yourself off again, Elsie. You're beautiful, but I wonder if the life of a marchioness would be a cage."

"Being a sister is a cage." Elsie pulled the jacket tighter, flipping the collar up to hide more of her face. "Being married is just another cage."

"Leaving doesn't change the cage any more than running can keep you dry when it rains."

Elsie's heart warmed, remembering her stableman's words. "But maybe I can learn to dance in the rain."

"I cannot in good conscience allow you to run, Elsie." Lord Armonde enveloped her hands in his once more. "As much as I want to scream at you, I cannot deny the affection I still hold. I cannot watch you get hurt, even if the pain is self-inflicted."

"You are a good man."

"Not good enough." He squeezed her hands and pointed to the luggage in the corner. "Shall we take those down? We should probably telegraph your mother. Let her know what's gone on. Definitely, Tyndeth. This might be enough of a shock to send him to the grave."

"Only in my wildest dreams." Elsie burst into laughter. She covered her mouth with both hands.

"Oh, come, now. Do you really think anyone likes that dreadful man?" He tugged the end of the jacket, his smile playful. "We'll get this sorted, Elsie. I promise."

Lord Armonde's tendency was always to succumb, to defer to parents and authority.

Elsie was the opposite. The very thought caused her to feel small and stifled. She began this journey by acting without thinking. And that was how she would end it. "Thank you. For everything."

"Always." Lord Armonde touched her hand, raising it to his lips. He kissed her hand and said, "Shall we?"

"I need a moment." Elsie glanced around the room, wondering if her plan would work. "Let me gather my courage before I face everyone."

"It'll work out." He let go of her hand and tossing one last look, left the room.

Elsie sprang into action. She opened Fitz's luggage, pulling out a pair of trousers. With shaking hands she changed, his clothes several inches too long. Stuffing her dress back into her luggage, she felt for her journals. She wouldn't be able to take them. The last piece of her father she would leave behind. Fitz had been kind, insisting on giving her pocket money. She counted the coins and paper. It was enough for a one-way ticket for the coach.

She slipped from the hotel, the hood of her borrowed jacket covering her head. Across the street she watched Fitz and his father argue at a table. Without Elsie, the discord would mend and the Smith family would return to bliss. She fought the rising emotion and boarded the stagecoach, her heart as dark as the storm brewing overhead.

32

FITZBURGH SMITH

Fitz stared at his father across the table, reeling from his father's words. *Does she know?* Fitz had not thought of himself as a romantic, nor was he drunk with love like the famed Lord Byron. His affection for Elsie was quiet and steady. He'd not thought of any other woman. But did Elsie know? Romance was his mother's obsession, not his. He was practical. Thoughtful. Was it enough to convince Elsie of his love? He'd given a hasty proposal to Elsie. Twice. He might have run away, or tried to run away, to Scotland. Was that enough evidence for Elsie? Or did Fitz only prove he could provide a practical solution to her plight.

Fitz rubbed his temples, replaying his conversations with Elsie. Had he not declared his feelings to her?

"Fitzburgh." His mother's voice pulled Fitz from his thoughts.

"Mother?" Fitz hadn't noticed her arrival.

She glanced between her husband and her son. "Produce her. Now."

His father reached for his wife's hand. "Your son needs our perspective."

Tilly pulled back and with a warning in her voice, asked, "Where is she?"

His father smiled. "She's upstairs speaking with Lord Armonde. I thought it best she—"

"That Lord Armonde?" His mother nodded toward Jonathon Parr speaking to his sister, both waving their arms in a heated discussion.

Fitz narrowed his gaze. Lord Armonde had suddenly become a man a touch too late. He should have stuck to bowing to his parents and the *ton*. His arrival in Liverpool didn't mean he deserved Elsie; it was the polite thing to do. Both he and Lady Alice needed to board the next train to London. "He has got—"

"Fitzburgh, you will sit down." His mother gave no room for argument. "We will not make a scene."

"Elsie is upstairs by herself." She'd spent the last few years alone and the last month as a pawn for her family's gain. Fitz would show her she was more than a puppet. She was wanted. She was needed.

"She is not in the room." His mother kept her voice low as she glanced around the room. "I've checked the garden and the other lobby. There's no sign of her."

"She could be hiding in the garden." Fitz wouldn't disclose how he'd once hidden in an overgrown bush. He eased to a stand, careful to not alarm his mother.

"I must ask." Tilly leveled her son with a mother's piercing gaze. "Is there anyone who would harm her? Was there an injured party besides her betrothed?"

Panic threatened to erupt. Tyndeth couldn't travel as fast, but he could employ a runner to drag Elsie back to London. He'd nursed his wounded pride for the last two years. He would not give up so easily now. "We have to find her."

James grabbed Fitz's arm. "Who is it?"

"The Earl of Tyndeth." His parents hadn't kept up with society since shunning them decades before. They'd chosen love over tradition —over family—and had kept their distance since. "She's defied him and he aims to see her humbled."

"A garden has many hiding spots," his father offered, eyes wary.

"We don't know if she's left of her own accord or if she's been taken." Tilly *tsked*. "Does she have someone she could reach out to? Close friend? Maid?"

"Me." Dread filled Fitz. Elsie was gone—or hiding—with no one to turn to. "Her maid was loyal to her brother. Her mother did Tyndeth's bidding. She was alone."

"How would she reach you, when she needed you?" James stood, slowly shuffling his family toward the staircase.

"Through a letter she knew her brother would open." Fitz felt a swell of pride. The panic was still very much alive but Elsie had outwitted her brother at least once. "She won't go home, not if she can help it."

Tilly shook her head. "That is a vulnerable place to be."

They climbed the staircase feigning smiles as other guests descended the steps. If Tyndeth had traveled to Liverpool, he wouldn't be able to reach her room. Fitz paused at the top of the railing. "Tyndeth is bound to a wicker chair. That is, if he traveled this far north."

"I don't believe there are any rooms on the lower floor," James added, reassuring his son. "Let's check the room once more and then split up."

Fitz opened the door. The sight of the empty room clenched his heart. Just a few moments before, she'd stood in the center, believing she was unwanted. He'd not yet convinced her otherwise. He wouldn't have given her a dratted horse if she was such a despicable person. He wouldn't have kneeled over the mare, elbow deep in blood if he'd not wanted to be near. Fitz had been drawn to her since the day he'd watched her ride along the ridge, the breeze combing her hair.

"The luggage is still here." James nodded to his wife's old carpet bag on the bed.

"James." His mother pushed the carpet bag over, showing the hem of a dress—the same dress Elsie had worn not an hour ago. "She's gone."

"No." Fitz ripped open the bag, exhaling when he found her father's journals. He held one out to his father. "She wouldn't leave this. It meant too much to her."

"Or maybe she knew it'd be safe with you." Tilly walked to the window. "If she's clever enough to plan an escape once, she'll plan another one."

"I am the escape." Fitz shoved the dress and book back into the bag. "I am the one she goes to. I am the one who saves her. I am ..." He blinked, anger growing with each breath. "I am the one who listened to her. I ... I am still here."

"Oh, my dear." His mother threw her arms around her son. "She needs to hear those words."

Fitz pulled back. "She knows. How can she not?"

Tilly lowered her head, James coming to her side. He wrapped an arm around her waist. "Fitz, it's a bit different for a woman. They need to know with more certainty that you'll be there. If her family has given her only broken promises, she might not know who is safe."

"I'm safe." Fitz jutted his chin and then growled at his own immaturity. "I'm not a blasted child."

His father chuckled. Fitz glared. Tilly sighed and grabbed her son's hand in her left and James's hand in her right. "I cannot pretend to know all that has gone on, but I know love when I see it." Fitz groaned. She squeezed his hand. "She might not know what love feels like or even what it looks like. We need to find her. You need to tell her, hopefully with less cursing."

Fitz smirked. "She already knows I've a foul mouth."

"No wonder she's running." James flinched at the look his wife sent. "He's spent too much time as a bachelor."

"What if Tyndeth got her?" Fitz would pummel the man. He didn't care that the earl was ancient or that a simple assault could land Fitz in prison.

"Your father and I will head to London. We can make discreet inquiries." Tilly arched her eyebrow when James opened his mouth. Obediently, he closed it and nodded. "If she left her father's journal, she was saying goodbye. Is there anyone she considers a friend? Anyone?"

"No," Fitz whispered, feeling the fatigue and despair return.

"What about Lord Armonde?" James asked, wincing again at his wife's poking. "It's an honest question."

"No." Fitz stepped from their circle. "If she trusted him, she would have asked him to elope. Not me." Doubt crept in. Did Elsie truly trust Fitz or was he a convenient savior—one without a loyalty to the *ton* and its ridiculous rules.

"We'll see you in London." His father paused, clapping his son on the back. "I cannot say I am proud of what transpired or that I condone your behavior. But I am proud of the man you are becoming. I'd thought you were determined to never marry. I hope you remain open to matrimony no matter how this adventure ends."

Fitz could only nod. His parents split their time between traveling the continent and visiting their daughter living in the southern tip of England. They loved their small family but had spent more time prodding Fitz toward marriage than anything else. Fitz had stubbornly braced himself against the idea. Titled families didn't want their daughters to marry mere misters, and lower gentry saw Fitz as nothing but a bank. His financial success had placed him in an untouched area, wealthy enough for prominence but not high born enough for true respect. He prayed he was enough for Elsie.

Fitz gathered the bags and slipped from the hotel, careful to not run into the Parrs. He paid the shipping cost for the bags to be parceled. Across the street, he watched a groomsman saddle a dark hackney horse, a spitting image of Elsie's mare. The memory of her tear-stained face caused a lump in his throat. She'd loved that horse just as she'd loved her father.

He pulled a telegraph paper from the wall. He was properly addled but there was still one more thing Fitz had to try.

33

ELISHEBA BEVUE

Elsie ducked under the awning of the train station, her head down and ears tuned to the surrounding conversations. Wrapping the jacket she'd stolen from Fitz tighter around her shoulders, she followed an elderly couple to the waiting benches. Whispers of Christmas and family surrounded her. She was no stranger to spending the holidays alone—but at least before, she'd had a place to call home.

It'd taken two stage coaches to get to Birmingham station, the tickets far cheaper than she'd anticipated. She'd tried to purchase when there were at least five other people in hopes the attendant wouldn't look too closely. It'd take only a glance to notice her trousers were too big and her face too feminine to pass for a man.

Her hand wrapped around the rest of her money. When her father was alive, he would walk Elsie to market and let her buy a sweet in one of the London shops. He would hang in the background, allowing Elsie to make her purchase on her own. It'd take a few trips before the shopkeeper would realize Elsie was paying. She'd not paid for anything in ages, the accounts always settled by a man in another county—Elsie shook her head. She'd thought her brother, or rather his steward, was the one settling the Bevue accounts. Not Tyndeth.

The gray haired couple sighed, their hands clasped to each other. The gentleman wrapped a sheltering arm around the woman's. Elsie's heart twisted. A day before, Fitz had guided her through the Liverpool station, his hand on the small of her back. She prayed leaving helped mend Fitz's relationship with his parents.

A young woman in a green dress stood waiting, her eyes flitting about. Elsie eyed her, recognizing her as one of the women Lady Alice would watch. Alice appeared to be jealous of her—which meant, she could be an ally. Matthew hadn't bothered with her, at least, that Elsie knew. She must be a widow to have the freedom of no companion. Elsie scooted along the bench to allow room.

The young woman didn't seem to notice. Two men rushed toward the row of waiting benches. She quickly sat down next to Elsie—*right* next to Elsie, as if they were traveling together. The older of the two men walked slowly toward each of the passengers, his eyes dark and searching.

The younger slid in front of the ticket line counter. "Have you seen a young lady traveling alone?"

The woman next to Elsie reached out and gripped Elsie's forearm.

The men at the ticket counter whispered to each other.

The woman leaned over to Elsie. "Stay calm."

Elsie's heart warmed, she wasn't alone. "How did you know ..." She let the question hang, not wanting to admit she was running.

The woman placed a finger to her lips and tucked her head.

The man slid a paper across the counter. "Here's a likeness."

Her new friend's fingers dug into her forearm and whispered, "Can you see the paper?"

Elsie shook her head. "And I can't hear what the attendant said."

The woman's gaze snapped to Elsie's. "Drat."

"You don't have to do this." Elsie tried her best to smile, to reassure this stranger that all was well. "You don't have to stay with me."

"I know." The woman winked. "But don't paint me an angel yet. I've a devious streak, especially when it comes to a certain Parr."

Elsie squirmed. "Lord Armonde is a good man."

She snickered, the sound surprisingly delicate. "That, I'm sure of. It's the sister who's a devil."

Elsie breathed a sigh of relief. "Yes ... but I am no saint."

Her new friend beamed. "Today you are a man."

"The next train leaves when?" the younger man asked, running his hands through his hair.

Both women straightened, exchanging worried glances.

"Ah ..." The man *tsk*ed. "And she could possibly switch cars in Cardiff, eh?"

Elsie's heart sank. Glamorgan proper was halfway between Cardiff and Swansea along the southern coastline. She would be switching cars or hiring a coach from Cardiff. She wondered who had hired the men —it wouldn't be Fitz, he'd be free of her. But Tyndeth—would he have given up so easily? Her brother wouldn't be looking for her, even if he had the means to hire someone.

"Don't fret," the woman whispered.

"I don't suppose you're up for playing the part of fiancé?"

"Not unless you're headed to Cardiff." Elsie shifted next to the woman, praying her new friend would accompany her to Wales.

"I wasn't but I suppose I haven't a choice now." The woman lifted her chin. She was peculiar, that was all Elsie knew of her. "You'll have to lower your voice an octave or two if you're to be my betrothed."

"And grow several inches."

The woman shrugged. "As long as we're sitting no one will notice."

"I think this will be trickier to hide." Elsie pulled on her trouser leg. "I'm—"

Her new friend shook her head. "I've seen you with the Parr's but don't remember your name. And to be fair, I'd rather not know. I do love a good intrigue, but I think you need to keep this secret." The woman nibbled her lip and then in a thick, sing-song accent said, "Call me Lady Goll."

Goll. Elsie blinked, feeling a heavy wave of homesickness at the woman's choice of name. *Goll* was Welsh for lost. "Call me *Direidus.*"

Lady Goll's eyes widened, sharing in their play on words. The glint of mirth disappeared in an instant. She gripped Elsie's hands and with her finger motioned behind Elsie. The men were whispering to themselves, eying the crowd. Both women tucked their heads, Elsie crouching behind the elderly couple. She was a poor excuse of a man, her manner and frame far too feminine.

"Men don't cower." Lady Goll elbowed Elsie. "You should at least try to be masculine."

"A man would ask what they're doing. And why they're staring," Elsie whispered back. "I can't very well do that." She pointed to her face. "One look and they'll know I'm the lady they're looking for."

Lady Goll cocked her head to the side. "Do you really think they're looking for you?"

"I don't know." Elsie fidgeted. "And I have no way of finding out."

The woman nodded solemnly.

"Where were you headed?" Elsie nodded to train car. "Before you found yourself betrothed."

Lady Goll looped her arm through Elsie's. "Do you want the truth or do you want a story?"

"At this point, aren't they one in the same?"

Lady Goll squeezed Elsie's hand. "True enough."

The car attendant called for boarding. Elsie spun to her companion. "You need a ticket."

The woman chuckled, pulling Elsie forward. "I've purchased four tickets this morning. One for Cardiff, one for London, one for Liverpool, and one for Bristol."

Elsie craned her neck to watch for the men. "If they ask about a single woman traveling—"

"They'll have quite the puzzle to solve, won't they?" Lady Goll winked. "Oh my dear, sweet beloved, shall we take our love to Cardiff?"

Elsie held out her arm. "Lead on, love."

They boarded the train and silently agreed to sit in the back corner. With minimal talking they ordered a light meal, Lady Goll eating nothing, only sipping on tea.

"May I ask why you're lost?" There was relief knowing Elsie wasn't the only woman running away.

"Only if you tell me why you're mischievous."

Elsie's heart quickened, realizing one moment of truth could unravel her escape. If Lady Goll—or whatever her real name was—knew Tyndeth, Elsie was done for. The earl had shown just what power he could wield. Her family was in his clutches, never to be released. Except Elsie. She was free. At least, for now.

"Keep your secrets, darling." Lady Goll placed a hand on Elsie's. "I love the thrill of independence. There are few joys left in my life and even fewer family members. Let me cherish our little game."

"Thank you, but I shouldn't have asked what I wasn't ready to divulge."

The woman shrugged. "It's simple, really. There are few reasons why a woman flees."

Elsie could think of a dozen reasons—a different motivation for each person affected. Her goal in leaving Fitz was completely different than fleeing Tyndeth.

Lady Goll stared into her teacup, a frown appearing on her delicate lips. "Why did you dress as a man?"

"I'd hoped it be easier to travel as one." Elsie crossed her ankles and then uncrossed them, worried that she appeared more lady than gentleman.

"You don't think it strange that we cannot travel in the open?"

"You purchased four tickets this morning." Elsie folded her arms and tried to scowl, remembering how Fitz sat next to her just a day before.

"For the same reason you're wearing trousers." Lady Goll sighed and gave a delicate shake of her head. "Maybe one day we can stop running." She smirked, her eyes flicking to Elsie's trousers. "Or hiding."

"I feel as if most of my life I've been hiding." Elsie hadn't realized the two years in Wales would give her such hope, a false sense of independence. She'd never been free. The train's attendant gathered the tickets and their train lurched forward, pulling Elsie's attention to the window of the car.

Outside at the station's deck, the two men were back at the attendant's counter, a third man joining them, his hat pulled low. He didn't wear a coat. The confident walk and the serious frown reminded Elsie of Fitz. Her pulse raced. He wouldn't be here. He'd still be in Liverpool with his parents. They would have convinced him by now that her leaving was a good thing. That's what Lord Armonde's family would be saying, now that Tyndeth had called Matthew's loans.

Fitz had begun to care, that was obvious and one of the reasons Elsie needed to leave. She hurt those around her, even when she tried to help. His voice echoed in her mind. *You are not unwanted.* He would have provided for her, viewing her as a desperate woman in need of saving. She wanted to be cherished in her own right, not because she was weak or in need of protection. Her father had made one thing clear before leaving for war, that Elsie was loved not despite her temper and quirks but rather *because* of her failings. She'd not realized how rare true affection was. But one look at her family underlined the truth. Tyndeth cared more about Elsie's failings than anything else, as well as Lady Bevue and Matthew. Even Lord Armonde acknowledged his family couldn't embrace Elsie.

She placed a hand on the window, wishing Fitz was next to her on the seat instead of Lady Goll. Elsie stared at the three men speaking to the attendant at the station's counter. Fitz had burst into her life just months before, silently giving her a mare. He'd etched his name on her heart. He'd been the foundation in a whirlwind of family and emotions. But she wanted more than pity.

The train started gathering momentum. Lady Goll sighed. "And we're off."

Elsie froze. The man without a coat turned—Fitz stood, a hand rubbing his jaw. She blinked but when the train began pulling away, his image blurred. Closing her eyes, Elsie's heart broke, shattering in pieces. Fitz had come. He was looking for her.

"What will you do?" Lady Goll asked. "When you get to wherever you're headed?"

Elsie opened her eyes. "He was there. He'd come."

Lady Goll raised her eyebrows. "Are you sure?"

"I saw him." Elsie buried her head in her hands. "Just as we were leaving."

The woman wrapped an arm around her shoulders. "Oh, pay it no heed. It's a trick of the mind."

Elsie's head snapped up.

"I've seen a man every time the train pulled away. And when I look back, he's not there."

"It was him." Elsie wrapped Fitz's coat tighter around her, taking solace in his scent. "He didn't have his coat."

"Truly, I don't think he, whoever *he* is, was there." Lady Goll pulled her arm back. "If he was, would that really change what you're doing?"

"No. I suppose not." Leaning into the window, Elsie shook her head. "It doesn't make me feel any better though."

"Then think on the next step." Lady Goll clasped her hands together and gave Elsie a conspiratorial smile. "You've made it this far, what else can you do?"

"You give me more credit than I deserve." Elsie shrugged, her heart too heavy to think of tomorrow.

"Surely you've thought of what you're going to do next."

Elsie fiddled with the hem of the coat. "I was going to ask my old stableman for a recommendation."

"For what?" Lady Goll had far too much excitement for Elsie.

"To help with the horses."

"A woman helping with horses." Lady Goll grabbed Elsie's hand. "How is that not intriguing? I think I've given you exactly the credit you deserve."

"And you?" Guilt crept into Elsie mind. She was being polite, asking about her friend's future. All Elsie wanted to do was cry—and sleep.

"I plan to return on the next train back toward England."

"You what?" Elsie sat up straight. "You're leaving England now."

"True." Lady Goll's smile was hesitant. "But I have quite a few people still looking for me."

"Are you in danger?"

"No more than you, *Direidus*." The woman laughed and squeezed Elsie's hand. "I've found Christmas is less lonely when not surrounded by ghosts."

❧ 34 ❧

FITZBURGH SMITH

Waiting outside the station on the outskirts of Cardiff, Fitz rubbed his tired eyes, sleep threatening to come. The building was one long rectangle, housing both the coach and train station—along with the waiting benches for the renting stables. This was Wales, efficient and economic, and one of the many reasons Fitz felt more at home in this country than any other. He hadn't stopped in days and neither had his nerves. He'd hired separate teams to search every coach and train station. He'd narrowly missed Elsie at Birmingham, according to the men hired and the telegraph from his solicitor who'd notified the train company. He prayed his solicitor was as discreet as promised. That last thing Fitz—or Elsie— needed was Tyndeth finding her first. Part of him wanted to throttle her for taking off by herself. The woman was mad. Then the shame would take hold of Fitz, reminding him of why Elsie ran. She'd not been able to trust anyone.

He'd not heard from his parents yet. They'd gone to London to sniff out the gossip, specifically about Tyndeth and Lady Bevue than actual broadsheets.

Fitz flexed and relaxed his hands on his knees, an effort to stay awake. Elsie was somewhere near here. Her train had arrived not an hour before him. His solicitor had given strict instructions to local coach and train companies: lower your price for a single woman traveling alone and matching Elsie's description. Fitz would pay double once he arrived. He needed to make sure she wouldn't run out of money. He was grateful Elsie had enough forethought to take his coat and hoped she was hidden from opportunists and con artists.

A woman donning a green dress caught his eye, but a quick glance told Fitz she wasn't Elsie. Fitz had seen the woman in London. He recognized her as one of the many debutantes in competition with Lady Alice. He felt a measure of relief. She would not be in league with the Parr family. The woman's gaze flicked to him, then she loudly told the attendant in a Welsh accent, "I'll need two tickets, one for London and one for Swansea."

The attendant mumbled the price while the woman kept looking over her shoulder. "And when does the coach leave?"

Fitz perked up. The woman bought two tickets going in opposite directions and yet asked for the stagecoach schedule. He was waiting for his rented horse to be saddled and was heading toward the Bevue's estate in Glamorgan where he believed Elsie was going. Fitz could only protect her if he knew where she was going. All signs pointed toward her late father's estate.

A groomsman holding the reins of a spirited gelding announced, "Mr. Smith."

Hurrying to the horse, Fitz tossed a coin to the groomsman and turned back to the train's ticket counter. The woman was gone. He caught the green color from the corner of his eye and craned his neck. The woman was marching toward the benches near the stagecoach. Fitz mounted the horse and took the back way around the building.

Finding a bored young boy kicking at rocks, Fitz ordered, "Five pence if I come back and this horse looks exactly as it does now."

"Ay." The boy nodded, a serious look in his eye.

Fitz rushed toward the waiting benches, keeping his head down. He saw several benches in the back. Stealing a discarded newspaper, he placed it in front of his face.

"Are you sure?" Elsie's voice carried. Fitz's pulse pounded in his chest, the newspaper shaking in his hands. "No coat?"

"He was waiting for a horse," the woman in green answered. "But he looked so very tired. And cross. I do believe you were right."

Fitz fought the urge to correct the woman. He wasn't cross. He paused—Fitz wasn't entirely sure the *he* the woman spoke of was him. He glanced down. He wasn't wearing a coat. He frowned—then realized he was frowning. "Blast it all."

An elderly couple *tsk*ed as they walked passed him. Fitz rolled his eyes and leaned forward. He waited but heard nothing. He peered above the newspaper, catching Elsie climbing into the coach in his coat, the collar turned up. His pulse raced—she was here. Dressed as a man without a lick of style, but she was here. And safe for the moment.

He forced himself to wait, his head screaming at him to move. If he showed himself, she'd run. He needed her safe, not running. Elsie returning to Wales—if that's truly where she was headed—made it easier for Fitz to protect her.

The woman in green glanced around, then disappeared back toward the train counter. Fitz jumped to a stand and raced to the coach's station. Before the attendant spoke, Fitz blurted, "The coach that just left. Where was it heading?"

The attendant pursed his lips and blandly answered, "Two coaches just left, one for Glamorgan and one for Barry."

Fitz shoved a couple pounds on the counter. Glamorgan. Elsie was headed back to Glamorgan. There was nothing for her in Barry. Relief flooded him. "I need to send a telegraph."

The attendant sighed. "Like I just told the other lady, we're down. You'll have to send a telegraph from town."

"What lady?"

The man stopped and braced himself against the counter, an argument forming in his eye.

Fitz shook his head. "Never mind."

He ran back to the boy obediently waiting with Fitz's rented horse. He tossed the coins to the boy. "Good job, sir."

The boy puffed out his chest with pride, saluting Fitz. "Anytime."

Pivoting the horse, Fitz picked through the growing crowd at an infuriatingly slow pace. He needed to arrive before the stagecoach. His solicitor had already told him Matthew was refusing to sign the paperwork. Scowling, Fitz spurred the horse to a trot, the crowd dwindling to a few people. Matthew was a bloody fool. Fitz worried the idiot would force Elsie to return to London—and to Tyndeth. Fitz could either wrestle with both Matthew and Tyndeth in London or he could chase Elsie, ensuring her safety. There hadn't been a true choice, she mattered more than anything. Than anyone.

Each mile passed, Fitz's legs taking a beating until the road began to rise, curving into the city. He passed the town and kept urging the horse toward his home. A quick exchange of horses and Fitz was back on the road toward town, this time much slower. He purchased a lamb pastry from the bakery and hid behind the post house, across the street from the coach's station and waited. Sleep pulled at his eyes, willing them to close. The sound of his horse pawing the ground startled him awake. He didn't know how long he'd been asleep, but the coach slowed to a stop. Rubbing his eyes, Fitz watched as Elsie descended the coach, her hands peeking out from the folded sleeves of his coat. She was too far away to tell her expression. She had to be exhausted. Fitz wanted nothing more than to beg her to see reason, to climb on top of his horse while he took care of her. But he couldn't. She'd left. She'd made her choice, even if it was out of fear like Fitz's mother had assumed. He promised he would protect her regardless of a marriage—he would not break that promise. Fitz would show her he cared, that he was unwavering in his affection. More than anything, that Elsie had a choice. She was not trapped.

He kept vigil, not content to remove his careful watch until she'd entered the bakery for food and began walking toward the Bevue estate.

With his horse tied, Fitz entered the post house, a list of telegraphs waiting to be sent. There was a mountain of work to be done on her behalf—now that Fitz knew she was home.

🦋 35 🦋

ELISHEBA BEVUE

The cool morning air whipped through the Welsh countryside, toying with Elsie's hair like a kitten's paw as she walked. She'd slept too late again. The last week had seemed but a day. She'd arrived last weekend only to see her father's childhood home boarded up, not a servant in sight. Before she'd arrived a few years before, the house sat empty every year until summer. Elsie was too scared of Matthew and Tyndeth to risk breaking into the house. She'd made a temporary room in the barn's loft. The empty building pulled at her heart.

Elsie forced her feet to continue. Tomorrow was Christmas—she'd chosen the worst time to look for employment. When she did find work, she would need the stamina. Months before, she would walk the same route on horseback to get to the ridge. Her situation was dire but she refused to despair. She was still drowning in her problems—but she was home.

Elsie had hoped to have secured a position by now, but her inquiries in town hadn't proved successful. Her stomach growled. Last night's dinner was gone but she didn't dare purchase breakfast. The bakery seemed to take pity on her, charging her only a fraction of the posted price. She'd been in Glamorgan for five days but still had not seen the stableman or the housekeeper. She'd kept to the shadows of the Bevue estate, unsure of her next move. If she couldn't find work near Bevue, she'd have to move on. With luck, she could work in the stables somewhere close by. The idea was precarious. She didn't have anyone to recommend her but hoped Griffiths could help.

The clouds darkened, pregnant with rain. She pulled the borrowed hood over her head and ran toward the barn, entering through the side door.

"Who's there?" a man barked.

Elsie froze, her eyes adjusting to the dim light of the barn. "Just seeking shelter from the rain, sir."

"Elsie?" Griffiths's gravelly voice wrapped around her like an old blanket. He lit a lamp, his face glowing in the flickering light. "What happened to you?"

Her hand absently touched her hair. She'd not seen a brush or a mirror in days. She wore the trousers she'd stolen from Fitz along with the hooded robe he'd given her the night they'd boarded the train for Liverpool.

"Oh, child." Griffiths pulled her into an embrace. She braced herself; she would not fall apart. He whispered, "Tell me you're not the vagabond in the attic?"

"I've no place to go."

"You're among family now." He clucked his tongue. "And here I was hoping I'd see you. Not like this but oh, dear. Pantry politics was right for once."

Griffiths hated *pantry politics,* the gossip amongst household servants. His sing-song accent settled her nerves. Elsie smiled despite herself. "I've a favor to ask. But don't feel obliged."

"Done." He placed a sweep against the wall and folded his arms. "What is it?"

"I need a recommendation—" A horse neighed, cutting her off.

Griffiths nodded his head toward the stall. "First horse was delivered a few minutes ago. A carriage is set to arrive any minute."

"Oh." Elsie covered her mouth. She needed to leave. Her family must be coming for Christmas—the London home finally sold. She needed to move on before they found her.

"By the look on your face, you didn't know." Griffiths grunted. "Guess the rumors are true."

"If it's about me, I'm sure they are."

He shook his head. "Word is the house is sold. New owners. I was hoping you'd return. Maybe come and take a few things of your father's."

House is sold. Elsie felt the weight on her chest. Matthew's debts were called in. Tyndeth had kept his word. Her mother would have no one and nowhere to turn. She had chosen Tyndeth over Elsie. Guilt settled on her shoulders. Elsie had chosen her freedom over her family. Elsie deserved her loneliness. "Have you heard from my mother?"

"No, milady."

"Matthew?" She had to ask. Her brother had stitched himself together with lies and liquor. He'd also made a choice, one that he'd finally have to accept responsibility for.

"Sorry, love." Griffiths folded his arms across his chest, sighing with more heaviness than a stableman should bear. "I've a feeling if you're wanting to take anything from the house, now is your chance."

"I don't think I have a right to." The house had belonged to her father's family for generations. And now, the Bevue estate would have new owners. A new legacy. She'd not grown up here, spending only summers in the Welsh countryside, but Glamorgan was home all the same. Her heart heaved. This was where Fitz had claimed her trust. He'd been steady and sure, the only person who seemed to encourage her flaws. But now she was both home and homeless.

"Come now, Elsie." Griffiths guided her out of the barn. "I'm feeling awfully guilty. I just cleaned out the attic. Thought we had a squatter."

"You weren't wrong."

He adjusted the cap on his head and opened the gate between the garden and the barn. "You'll not be staying in the barn tonight."

"I know." Her cheeks warmed. Griffiths would lose his position over a runaway lady.

"You'll be staying with me and the missus."

Elsie stared at him. He tipped his hat and kept his gaze on his feet. She wasn't alone. The stableman had welcomed her years before.

Gentle and quiet, Griffiths had helped Elsie modify her saddle. He'd never lost his patience nor had he turned a critical eye toward her. Griffiths owed her nothing and yet was offering kindness to her. More than her family ever would. She threw her arms around him.

He stiffened, then gave her a rough pat on the back. "We'll sort this out, Elsie."

Thunder clapped overhead. Rain trickled down. Elsie stepped back from the embrace, peering up at the clouds.

"Did you ever learn to dance in the rain?" Griffiths asked with a smirk.

"I guess now's as good a time as any." She followed him to the house, hope filling her chest.

"Best stay here while I get Doris." Griffiths motioned to the sofa, leaving Elsie with a reassuring smile.

She didn't dare move. Fitz's trousers were rolled twice at the waist but the hem still covered her boots, the trousers saturated with dew and mud from Elsie's morning walk. She'd washed her hands in the brook meandering between the Bevue and Fitz's property line, but try as she might, her fingernails were beyond help. She patted her hair, combing her fingers through the tangles. Doris wouldn't recognize her.

Elsie breathed a sigh of relief. The walls seemed to hug her, welcoming her home—if only for a moment. Wales had given her respite instead of a reprimand. And Fitz. Wales had given her a friend. Elsie had hurt him—and if she hadn't left, she'd still be inflicting pain. But his memory gave her hope. At least one person thought her worth saving. Maybe one day she would be worth loving.

The opening and closing of the front door echoed to where Elsie stood. Her heart leapt to her throat. Doris and Griffiths would have entered through the side or servant doors. Not the front. The new owners must have arrived.

Elsie spun around, fleeing outside. Her boots echoed on the stone deck. She just needed to reach the garden; the grounds would muffle her escape. The rain had stopped for a moment. Down the steps, she sighed in relief.

"Stop where you are." A voice, firm and feminine, pinned Elsie where she stood. "You will return whatever you stole this instant."

Elsie recognized the voice. *Lady Alice.* Her heart sank. Holding her head high, Elsie turned around. Anger faded from Lady Alice's face, replaced with haughty confidence. "Why, Miss Bevue, this has turned out deliciously." She clasped her hands together, an enormous emerald displayed on her ring finger. "Have you heard the news?"

Elsie pasted a smile, her stomach twisting. The owners weren't new —Matthew must have proposed. Lady Alice's dowry had solved his problems. Matthew's plan had worked. Of course it had. The world hated Elsie, not her brother. A devoted sister would be happy for her brother. But Elsie couldn't. There wasn't enough benevolence in her. She wondered if Tyndeth had proposed to her mother—and whether that should warrant congratulations or condolences.

"Lady Alice." Elsie curtseyed in her dirty, borrowed trousers. Her face grew hot, her embarrassment obvious. Her clothes were muddy but she would not cower. Not to Lady Alice.

The side door opened. Matthew waltzed to the outer deck, his gait unsteady and his eyes glazed over. He nodded to Lady Alice, his eyes widening at Elsie who fought the urge to run. Her cheeks grew hotter still. She would die of humiliation where she once felt loved.

"This is unexpected." Matthew drew a line in the air with his finger from Elsie's head to toe.

"Congratulations, Matthew." Elsie lifted her chin. Thunder clapped above her. Wales would once again be her salvation. Lady Alice and Matthew would run for cover with the threat of rain.

"For what?" Her brother scowled, turning his back to a glowing Lady Alice.

Alice held out her hand and beamed at the winking jewel on her hand. "It's beautiful."

"I wish you all the happiness." Elsie didn't want to be the first to leave. Stubborn to a fault, she'd hold her ground. She'd run from Fitz and from Tyndeth. She would not run from her brother.

Lady Alice's gaze flicked from her hand to Matthew, then back to Elsie. "You don't know, do you?"

Elsie paused. Matthew held contempt instead of arrogance. Elsie watched them, not understanding the turn of events. Her brother should be gloating, not glowering.

"Let's get this over with," Matthew snapped. "You called us here. Gloat and get it over with."

"Gloat?" Elsie shot a confused look to her brother. He carried the heavy look of captured prey, his shoulders hunched and eyes flitting nervously about. Tyndeth could still be holding Matthew by his purse strings.

Lady Alice smiled. "Oh, dear Matthew. You can pretend all you want, but it wasn't me who invited you here. You're beholden to someone else."

The sky darkened with clouds pregnant with rain. Elsie willed the storm to hurry. She had escaped to Wales to be rid of them, not entertain their game of chess.

"Don't lie to me, Alice." Matthew rubbed his jaw. "Are you capable of that, telling the truth? Is that something you Parrs can do?"

Elsie stifled a grin. They deserved each other in whatever confusing capacity it was. Elsie might be homeless but at least she was free.

"You." Matthew pointed an accusing finger toward his sister. "This is your fault."

"I quite agree." Lady Alice snickered. "Thanks to you."

Elsie gave a curt nod. "I'll leave you to your games. And happiness."

"What happiness?" Matthew snapped his fingers. "I get nothing. Nothing!"

"Oh, come now, Matthew." Lady Alice gave a wicked laugh. "This house was obscenely overpaid. You're one step further from debtor's prison."

Debtor's prison. Elsie swallowed hard. Fitz had said Matthew owed over thirty thousand pounds, an obscene amount of debt.

"You're right." Matthew straightened, his face sobering. "I'm shackled to no one."

Elsie straightened. Matthew was free?

Lady Alice grinned. "I'll be a countess in less than a month."

Matthew took a swaggered step. "If he's still alive."

A quiver of panic crossed Lady Alice. Her face smoothed. The pieces fell into place. Elsie covered her mouth. "You're engaged to Tyndeth?"

"That I am." Lady Alice glanced at her hand once more. "You're welcome, my dear Matthew, for saving you from debtor's prison."

"You didn't save me. You saved yourself from a life of spinster-hood." Matthew spat. "Let's see how long you last catering to that spineless cripple."

Lady Alice arched an eyebrow. "This spinster managed to snare the earl's good opinion and extend your deadline in a month. Something your mother couldn't accomplish in years."

Elsie could take no more. Lady Bevue had sacrificed for nothing. She'd been discarded just as Elsie had. She turned from them. Elsie wasn't close to her mother, but she'd not wished her ill will—a failed engagement to Tyndeth was punishment enough.

"Elsie." A familiar man's voice pierced her, rooting her feet to where she stood.

She closed her eyes, humiliation and embarrassment coming once more, each wave crashing over her. Her name on Fitz's lips echoed in her mind.

"Elsie." Fitz came closer. "Open your eyes, love."

Hesitantly, Elsie obeyed, her heart breaking. Whatever punishment he delivered, Elsie would take. She deserved all of it. He stood between Lady Alice and Matthew, his clothes infinitely finer than Alice's but also more crumpled than Matthew's. Dark circles underlined Fitz's eyes, his face pale. Her mouth fell open. "Are you ill, Fitz?"

Amusement tugged at his lips. "Have you seen a mirror?"

"Or a brush." Lady Alice covered her dainty mouth with clean, slender hands. She was all that was dignified.

Fitz straightened his posture and in a booming voice said, "The Bevue estate was sold to pay a portion of your brother's debts."

"I gathered that." Elsie's stomach growled. She hugged herself, hoping to muffle the sound.

"It's yours." Fitz stepped even closer, concern in his eyes. "Happy Christmas, Elsie."

Happy Christmas. Elsie's mind whirled. Her family had forgotten her, abandoned her for two years—Fitz had taken the sorrow and turned it to joy. He'd done the same with her father's estate.

"What?" Matthew snapped. "You've given *her* the house?"

Fitz tossed a scowl over his shoulder. Returning to Elsie, he soft-ened his gaze. "You belong here."

"What does that mean?" Elsie swallowed hard, waiting for the price. Nothing was free, her family had taught her that. Happiness came at a cost. Or a cage.

"You do not have to cater to anyone. Not me. Not Tyndeth. Not even your wretched family." Fitz waved his hand in the air, cutting off Matthew's scoff. Suspicion filled Elsie. There was another motive at play. There had to be. Fitz took another step closer. "I'm not a roman-tic. Never thought I'd want the marriage life, but you've torn me up inside."

Elsie winced. "Fitz, I'm—"

He took her hand.

She tried pulling it back, all too aware of her dirty fingernails. "Don't look at my—"

"Do you really think I'd be put off by a little dirt?" Squeezing her hand, Fitz shook his head. "You need freedom. And happiness. You shouldn't be kept in a cage. I only wish you'd trusted me enough. Truly trusted me."

Elsie couldn't admit, not even to herself, but she did trust him. She blinked. In truth, she didn't just trust him. She loved him. But her tongue wouldn't move. It was a secret she would take to her grave. Elsie was selfish. And hurtful. She couldn't trap him. Fitz's love was a dream. She wouldn't give into the fantasy. Elsie didn't get happy endings.

"This house is yours, Elsie." Fitz smiled sadly. "Do with it what you will."

He kissed her hand and turned to the shocked Lady Alice and Matthew. "Lady Alice, you were invited for the sole purpose to tell Tyndeth of Elsie's happy fortune. Be prepared, he might die of an unfortunate stroke. Matthew, I invited you to remind you of your legal obligation."

Matthew rolled his eyes. "It's rubbish."

"This will be the last time you have any influence on Elsie, or the remaining debts will be called."

Lady Alice's mouth opened to an O. "*You're* the one who paid off the earl?"

Elsie's longtime butler appeared and began ushering both Matthew and Lady Alice into the house. Elsie watched them go, still unable to speak. Fitz tossed one more glance in her direction before disappearing toward his home.

❧ 36 ❧

FITZBURGH SMITH

The afternoon rain pounded the window of Fitz's study, the weather as dreary as the man watching. Fitz swirled the amber liquid in his glass. He'd yet to take a sip. His parents were to arrive any day. He didn't have the heart to tell them he'd broken his promise. He'd not told Elsie his feelings in person. He'd come close but *I love you* never crossed his lips. He'd done everything but be brave.

Fitz had purchased the Bevue estate for triple its worth—gone was the business acumen Fitz had spent years honing. He'd left Elsie's journal in her study, the last page an entry from him. He'd done the unthinkable and confessed his feelings. He would be leaving next week for Australia and had taken the coward's way instead of confessing his love in front of Matthew and Lady Alice. His brain and heart had played him a fool. The last line, he'd asked her to meet him. She never did.

Fitz set the glass on his knee, unable to turn from the window. The ridge separating his lands from Elsie's was empty, not a horse or girl in sight. Perhaps he was still the fool. He'd invited Lady Alice and Matthew to the Bevue estate. Fitz had thought it clever, but in hindsight, he was no better than the earl. He'd wanted them both to see her twist of fortune, to see Elsie set free. He loved the blasted woman.

Alone, he could admit that he'd always loved her. As a boy, he'd watched from a window—from *every* window of this dratted house. A decade later and he was still on the fringe of the *ton* looking in, wishing for something—some*one* he wanted.

Fitz smirked at the glass, remembering the look on Elsie's face. Her chin was lifted and her back was straight. She'd not given in to her brother or the haughty Alice Parr. Dirt was smudged on her cheek and in her fingernails. Fitz held up his hands, wishing he could hold Elsie's.

He'd reached out to William Johnson, itching to leave Wales once more. And yet here he sat, facing the window like he had as a boy. Fitz had paid a small fortune to find her every move from the Liverpool hotel. Watching her creep into the barn at night had nearly undone him. She deserved so much more. Purchasing the estate took a bit longer, but he'd put her journals in the very center of her father's desk. He'd hoped the reason she'd not come was because she'd never entered the house. And yet she had. Her stableman, Griffiths, confirmed as much when Fitz asked yesterday.

With a sigh, Fitz placed the glass on the desk next to the solicitor's paperwork. Elsie couldn't legally own the estate yet, and the solicitor was in the process of redrawing Fitz's will to ensure Elsie would be provided for should Fitz die before her. He wasn't sure how safe Australia was and needed to make sure nothing—*no one*—could harm her while he was gone.

A knock on the study's door pulled his attention. He gathered his paperwork from off the desk—or rather, his father's desk—and braced for his family's arrival.

"Mr. Smith." The new butler looked positively panicked, his eyes and mouth wide. "There's a—"

The door swung open. Elsie walked in, her faded and threadbare riding habit hugging her frame. She could've worn a sackcloth as far as Fitz cared. Yesterday she wore his stolen trousers and robe. She stole his heart in dirty, ragged clothes just as she did now. She lifted her head, revealing swollen eyes brimming with tears.

"Elsie, are you alright?" He was on his feet in an instant.

Her lip trembled. "Why? Why did you do it?" Clutching her father's journal, she stared straight at Fitz, oblivious to the butler discreetly leaving the room.

"I've done a lot of things, Elsie." Slowly, he set the glass on the table. He was walking a rather tightrope, unsure if he was the cause of the tears. "You'll have to be more specific."

"Why did you give me the mare? Why did you pay off Matthew's debts? Why give me—" She hiccupped. "What are you wanting in return?" He opened his mouth to speak, but she plowed ahead—and inched closer. "You've been kind. And steady. I don't know why." She wiped a tear off her face with the back of her hand, not like the graceful ladies of the *ton*.

Elsie was honest. And raw—and *here*. She'd come. Fitz took a hesitant step toward her, hoping the approach was welcome.

"When you're near, I feel safe. I feel loved but ..." She shook her head, hair falling from the loose plait.

He took another step, noticing the green of the grass on her hem and boots. "I was trying to help." *I love you,* he almost said.

"I'm not a damsel in distress." Her lip trembled.

"Noted." Her tears confused him. Fitz didn't know if he should hope. Even William agreed that Fitz would never understand a woman.

Elsie inhaled sharply. "You don't believe me."

"Did you not cross the country by yourself? Did you not live on your own for two years in a country you hardly knew?" He gave a curt shake of his head. Another step forward. "You are independent. I'd never fault you for it."

Elsie pursed her lips. "You can't say things like that."

Fitz stood, his heart hurting at the sight of her—she was close and yet too far in more ways than one. "You'll not be caged by me, Elsie. But I won't stop trying to help."

"I was trying to help *you*." Her voice caught.

"Help me how?"

"Set you free." Fidgeting, she clutched the journal tighter against her chest. "Save you from an obligation."

"What you call an obligation, my father calls an obsession." Fitz frowned, wanting to comfort her without scaring her off. She stood too far from him, despair in her eyes. "And what my mother calls love."

"Love?" Elsie whimpered and held out her father's journal, flipping to the back. Spinning the book for Fitz to see, she pointed. "When did you write this?"

"The day you returned." Fitz didn't bother looking. He knew the very hour he'd written it. "I was right behind you every step of the way."

"How did you know?" Her voice cracked. Blinking, she tucked her chin, her lip quivering. She traced the words, the simple lines. Whispering, she read, "'I cannot promise titles or privilege. I can't ever get the words to come out right, but I can promise horses and tempers for eternity. I can promise freedom and arguments. I can promise my love —today and forever. Meet me on the ridge.'" She laughed nervously. "Those words are terrible. And wonderful."

"And true."

"But I'm a pain."

"And I swear like a sailor." Fitz grinned, his heart lifting at the hope in her eyes.

Elsie took a deep breath, questions in her eyes. "I promise not to behave."

Slowly, Fitz pulled the journal from her hands, setting it on the desk behind him. "I promise love."

"What you did ..." She broke their gaze, looking down at her shoes. She took a shuddering breath. "How did you—how could you have—"

"Elsie." He reached her, stepping dangerously close. Slowly, he wrapped an arm around her waist, bringing her within inches of him. "I thought Tyndeth had found you. Had taken you."

She ducked her chin and wiped tears from her cheek.

"I sent out a search party. Albeit a discreet one." With a finger, he gently lifted her chin and pulled her closer. She inhaled sharply. He whispered, "I needed to know you were safe."

Hesitantly, she looked up. "Fitz—"

"No, you need to hear this." He brushed his hand against her tear-stained cheek. She leaned into his touch. "I need you to believe me."

"Fitz." Her hand gripped his shirt, her eyes searching his face.

He tightened his arm around her waist. Fitz would be her strength. He would carry her—without caging. He leaned in, their lips nearly touching. "You are not unwanted."

"I've cost you a great deal." Her lip trembled.

"I did it for you." He rubbed a thumb across her lip. "And I'd do it again."

"But you're a bachelor. A determined one. You can't—"

"I am determined, but not to be a bachelor." Cradling her jaw, he brushed his lips against hers. She didn't kiss back. "But I'll not force you."

Her grip tightened. "I ... I just can't believe ..."

"Believe what?" He caressed her cheek with his thumb.

"Why?" Her voice cracked. "Why would anyone do all of this? Have you spoken to your parents—"

"My parents are very aware of my feelings." He pulled her against his chest. "It's you and me, love. My parents would be tickled pink to have me settled. If you'll have me."

She clung to him. "This can't be real."

"I love you, Elsie. I've always loved you." He cradled her face in his hands.

She closed her eyes and leaned in. "Promise me this is real."

"It's as real as I am." He tucked a strand of dark hair behind her ear. He lifted her chin and kissed her nose. She softened in his arms. He kissed her cheek, traveling to her jaw. He whispered in her ear, "But this time, no Scotland."

She sank into him. "No running away together?"

Fitz kissed her neck, forehead. And then her nose. She leaned up on her toes. He kissed her softly. She matched his urgency. He smiled against her lips. With a hand in her hair, he broke their kiss and said, "You've done enough running for the both of us."

Her smile faltered. "I'm sorry—"

He leaned in, touching his forehead with hers. "I'm not."

"Fitzburgh," his father bellowed.

Elsie stiffened in Fitz's arms. He cradled her head against his chest, shielding her view.

James clapped his hands once. "It's about blasted time."

"James Smith," his mother warned. "No wonder your son has your wicked tongue."

"Let's let him utilize that mouth of his." James gave his son a wink and escorted his blushing wife from the study.

"Maybe Scotland would have been better," Elsie said, her cheeks crimson. She turned to the window and smiled wide. Fitz followed her gaze. Griffiths was holding the reins of a hackney mare, a modified saddle on its back. As if on cue, a storm erupted. Both the horse and stableman eyed the clouds.

"It's finally arrived." Fitz had ordered the animal back in London.

The mare neighed, fidgeting in place. Griffiths rubbed its neck. A faraway look crossed Elsie's face. "She's beautiful."

Fitz pulled her hand to his lips. "Your horse is dancing."

Elsie's gaze flicked to Fitz. "I love you."

He led her outside to dance in the rain.

EPILOGUE

The gentle warmth of the Australian morning sun wrapped around Elsie like an embrace. Closing her eyes, she tipped her head and relished the embrace. Even the cursing of the surrounding sailors and the busy harbor didn't distract from Elsie's longing. She wasn't ready to leave her home of the last five years. New South Wales had been as welcoming to her as her late father's Welsh estate. But Fitz was needed in Glamorgan, his father's health taking a sudden turn for the worse. Fitz had offered to leave without her but Elsie couldn't. Home was where Fitz was, not where Elsie lived. She glanced to her mother, standing stiffly beside her. Fitz had generously offered her mother a pension with the stipulation Lady Bevue join them in Australia. Her pride succumbed when her poverty was broadcasted, compliments of Tyndeth and Lady Alice.

Little hands clasped Elsie's, pulling her attention to the dark eyes of her daughter, Victoria. With gentle hands, the four year old delicately took her hat from off her head and pointed to the growing crowd of passengers leaving one of Fitz's commercial ships, aptly named *Direidus*. "Is that our ship?"

"Ay, that's my girl." Fitz's low voice carried from behind Elsie. His arm wrapped around Elsie's belly, his other arm carrying their sleeping son, William.

Lady Bevue cleared her throat and grabbed Victoria's other hand. Grandchildren had softened Lady Bevue in a most unexpected way. "Any moment, dear."

The woman had struggled with the blurry lines of class distinctions in New South Wales. The lack of social decorum—in her mind—was a recipe for lawlessness. She'd railed against the country as a whole until Fitz parceled land to her, in her own name. The estate wasn't on par with the London townhome Matthew had lost years before, but it was twice the size of Elsie's Glamorgan home. More importantly, Lady Bevue's land neighbored Elsie and Fitz's. A fragile repair to the mother-daughter relationship had begun. Far slower than Elsie would have liked.

Lady Bevue eyed Fitz's hand on Elsie's belly and lifted her chin. She might have embraced a woman's right to own land, but still abhorred her son-in-law's dismissal of social rules.

Elsie side-stepped the contact, not because of her mother but rather because of how round she still felt. She'd not had the energy after William's birth like she'd had with Victoria. Her daily walks outside in the sun had been her savior, a gift from a country she'd loved the moment she'd stepped off the boat. She blinked, remembering the awe of everything the day she'd come to Australia—her newlywed life and the vibrant pulse of the country. All of it had given her a sense of peace and freedom.

Fitz squeezed her tightly, whispering in her ear, "You're beautiful, Elsie. Always have been and always will be."

She relaxed in his arm, covering his hand with hers. This wasn't farewell, she promised herself. They would return to the untamed country soon.

The passengers from Fitz's ship had dwindled and were replaced with the cotton from his fields. The American Civil War had allowed Australia to dive into the industry. Fitz had been the first to start harvesting cotton but now, with the industry becoming cramped, he would be switching from harvesting to shipping. He was just a few months from solidifying the sale of his fields, keeping the house and surrounding land that Elsie loved deeply.

The ship's captain approached, hat in hand. "We're ready for you to board, sir." He greeted Lady Bevue who gave only the barest of smiles. She'd slowly thawed toward the lowly captain, but never in front of Elsie.

Fitz kissed his son's forehead and handed him over to Elsie. He waited a moment, a sly smile creeping across his face. "I know it's hard saying good bye for a time. But ..." He winked. "I cannot wait to dance in the rain with you."

His words warmed Elsie. She was a tempest of emotions, while he was a storm of restless ventures. Their love, steady and true, bound them together. He bent down to gather Victoria, her dark hair falling from its plait. She laid her head on Fitz's shoulder, his face beaming at the gentleness. By some miracle, Victoria had entered this world as a quiet, calm child—her eyes watchful and her mind a sponge, soaking up the world around her. Very unlike her parents—and her brother. On cue, William squawked and stretched awake. He would demand food and freedom in a moment.

"Let me hold him a moment." Lady Bevue reached for William, her eyes bursting with farewell.

Elsie handed him over, his lip quivering—a warning of an impending tantrum. Rocking in place, Lady Bevue softly smiled. "Oh, you are a beautiful child." Her smiled grew, shaving decades from her face. "You are so much like your mother."

Elsie froze—her heart suspended. She swallowed the rising disappointment.

"So beautiful," Lady Bevue cooed. She traced his nose and kissed his head. "Stay like her, William. Don't ever lose your spark."

Elsie stared, her mind blank. Fitz placed a hand at the small of her back, whispering, "I made you promise not to behave, but blast it all, I won't be promising my son the same."

Her heart lifted. Without thinking, she stepped forward and wrapped her arms around her mother and baby. "Thank you."

Lady Bevue stiffened. Elsie released her but stopped when her mother patted her arm. They stood, both women blinking back tears. Hope blossomed between them.

Her mother pursed her lips, gathering the rigid pride. "Tell Matthew hello for me."

Elsie nodded. "The invitation is still open. You can—"

Her mother shook her head. "No." She stepped back and took in the harbor, her gaze flicking to the captain. "This is where I am supposed to be."

"We'll return as soon as we're able." There was a promise in Elsie's words. She would return to Australia but also to her mother. Slowly— excruciatingly slowly—the relationship would heal.

Lady Bevue wiped a tear from her cheek. "Please do."

* * *

ALSO BY CLARISSA KAE

Pieces To Mend

Of Ink And Sea

Once And Future Wife Series

Once And Future Wife

Disorder In The Veins (Summer 2021)

Victorian Fairytales

A Dark Beauty, Beauty & the Beast

Cinders Like Glass (Fall 2021)

ABOUT THE AUTHOR

Clarissa Kae is a preeminent voice whose professional career began as a freelance editor in 2007.

She's the former president of her local California Writers Club after spending several years as the Critique Director.

Since her first novel, she's explored different writing genres and created a loyal group of fans who eagerly await her upcoming release. With numerous awards to her name, Clarissa continues to honor the role of storyteller.

Aside from the writing community, she and her daughters founded Kind Girls Make Strong Women to help undervalued nonprofit organizations—from reuniting children with families to giving Junior Olympic athletes their shot at success.

She lives in the agricultural belly of California with her family of horses, chickens, dogs and kittens a plenty.

www.clarissakae.com

Made in the USA
Monee, IL
11 January 2021